VIRGINIA SMITH was born ⸻
Southampton in 2004, at the ag⸻
in Liverpool and, at the time of ⸻ ⸻ ⸻ ⸻ ⸻ ⸻ ⸻ ⸻ ⸻
librarian and living in Southampton with her family and a lurcher
called Ruby. Her poetry and short stories appeared in various
magazines and journals and her first novel, *The Ropemaker's Daughter*,
was published in 2002.

Praise for *The Ropemaker's Daughter*:

*"The Ropemaker's Daughter is truly a novel for the new millennium: passionate,
compassionate, intelligent, insightful, full of unexpected twists and written with the innate
understanding that sexuality exists on a continuum and doesn't need to be pigeon-holed. Smith
manages to sustain an aura of constant threat while exploring the complex interplay between
truth and deception. I loved it. I read it in one setting. I defy you to do otherwise"* – Manda Scott

*"A psychological tense thriller, reminiscent of Helen Dunmore and Daphne du Maurier.
Threesomes, incest, lesbian love and the lies lovers tell – it's all in there... an unnerving debut"*
– The Pink Paper

"An intelligent thriller which has you questioning and guessing right up until the end"
– GCN magazine

*"An amazing first novel... Lovers of Barbara Vine will adore Smith's plotting. The story propels
itself along, with no twist ever feeling forced or unnatural... The Ropemaker's Daughter takes
you on a fantastic ride"* – Gay.com

*"A must-read... Full of unexpected twists, [Smith's novel] explores the themes of truth and deception
through her character Rebecca, themes that will keep you gripped to the last page"* – Reading Evening Post

*"This is a book where the various aspects of living a lie are explored on many levels... This novel is
totally engrossing... I for one am eagerly awaiting her next"* – Lesbian Worlds

"A compelling suspense novel, which asks the question 'Who can you trust?' and comes up with some frightening answers" – Libertas! Dykelife magazine

"The message of the novel seems to be that there is no integrity without honesty. I am sure Virginia Smith intends that to apply as much to her own writing as to the fictional love affair she portrays with the professionalism of an experienced novelist" – Kenric magazine

"Movingly written... the book is also packed with juicy red herrings and slick plot twists... An exciting development in thriller-writing that avoids the tired clichés of dyke detective novels, brings in wider questions and ideas, and keeps you guessing until the end" – Rainbow Network

"This is [Smith's] first published novel and I hope that there will be more to come, because her writing is light, interesting – and, as a reader, you are intrigued by the world she creates... An enjoyable read" – G3 magazine

"An intense thriller/mystery... A great story which will keep you amused for ages" – 3 Sixty magazine

"Well-crafted... The contrast between the reassuring rhythm of the writing and the tragic effects of Rebeccas's lies creates a paradox which, for the most part, works well... A page-turner" – What's On

"A cracking read... I couldn't put it down. Well structured, well paced" – Out in Greater Manchester

"This one hooked me completely... It's a hell of a story. Buy it or order it and you'll have a great curl-up evening ahead of you" – Liberty Press

The Carradine Diary

VIRGINIA SMITH

DIVA

The excerpt from *After Two Years* by Graham Greene has been reproduced
by permission of David Higham Associates.

First published 2004 by Diva Books,
an imprint of Millivres Prowler Limited, part of the Millivres Prowler Group,
Spectrum House, Unit M, 32-34 Gordon House Road, London NW5 1LP
www.divamag.co.uk

A catalogue record for this book is available from the British Library

ISBN 1-873741-93-6

Printed and bound in Finland by WS Bookwell

Distributed in the UK and Europe by Airlift Book Company,
8 The Arena, Mollison Avenue,
Enfield, Middlesex EN3 7NJ
Telephone: 020 8804 0400

Distributed in North America by Consortium,
1045 Westgate Drive, St Paul, MN 55114-1065
Telephone: 1 800 283 3572

Distributed in Australia by Bulldog Books,
PO Box 300, Beaconsfield, NSW 2014

for Lisa:
True love, true north

A mattress was spread on cottage floor
And a door closed on a world, but another door
Opened, and I was far
From the old world sadly known
Where the fruitless seeds were sown,
And they called that virtue and this sin.
Did I ever love God before I knew the place
I rest in now, now with my hand
Set in stone, never to move?
For this is love, and this I love,
And even my God is here.

Graham Greene
From *After Two Years*

INTRODUCTION

Virginia Smith was a lovely writer and a lovely person, in every sense. She died too young this summer in a car accident, at the age of only 35. Anyone who has read her first novel, *The Ropemaker's Daughter*, will know that her main character Rebecca crammed a lot of different lives into her own, stealing other people's stories and passing them off as her own experiences. Although I am unsure whether Virginia would agree – I got the impression that she felt other people viewed her as conventional, when she was anything but – she too lived many lives in a short time and, although 35 years is painfully brief by any measure, she filled those 35 years well with joy and pain. She went to university; she had a book of poetry published; she touched her many friends and family members with a thousand kindnesses; she married; she was a librarian; she lost a parent; she had a novel published; she was divorced; she dived head-first into her first relationship with a woman (her beloved partner Lisa Wing); she became a second mother and step-parent to Lisa's three teenagers. Pretty full life, any way you look at it, though admittedly a lot of these major events I have cited occurred in the last three years when *I* have known her, and there is a danger of my over-emphasizing those events to which I was privy. I have no doubt that Virginia had manifold adventures and significant events and important friends and relationships far prior to this new century.

I had the lucky experience of being the reader who plucked Virginia's *Ropemaker* proposal (then entitled *Clouded Apollo*) from the slush pile and passed it on to Helen Sandler, who was commissioning editor and publisher of Diva Books at the time. Perhaps because of this, I always felt a bond with Virginia, and within a year we had become friends as opposed to having an editor/author relationship, (which also can be quite an intense link). Even at this first reading,

I remember hanging on Virginia's phrasing and storytelling – it's the type of slush-pile moment you wait for, the "Hey, this is really good" moment. I thought her writing was moving and gripping and poetic, and Helen thought so too, and so did all the reviewers once the book was published.

It is heartbreaking that we will never get a chance to know how Virginia's writing would have developed. Aside from the two novels she had published with Diva Books, there was also the aforementioned poetry book, at least one earlier, unpublished "first" novel and an unfinished new book that she felt to be her finest yet. Manda Scott called *The Ropemaker's Daughter* "a novel for the new millennium". Helen Sandler said, "There is no doubt that her work would have continued to grip readers for decades to come." But we will never get the chance to know how and what Virginia would have written at 45, or 55, or 65, 75, 85. I do know that they would have been great stories, because Virginia wrote great stories right from the beginning.

The Carradine Diary ticks many of Virginia's personality boxes: an infatuation with words and word-play, sensitivity, wicked humour, kindness, modesty, humility, a great love of nature and the environment, romance, the capacity and courage to change one's life completely, the belief in love, the belief in a higher power. Many people will feel that it deals, like *The Ropemaker's Daughter*, with truth and lies and consequences – and this is true – but, for me, one of its greatest themes is freedom. Anyone who knew Virginia knew that she believed in personal freedom, free-wheeling freedom, wind-blowing-in-your-hair freedom, and that she bestowed this belief on others and was always open-minded and willing to consider new thoughts, ideas, opinions. What more important thing is there in this world than to be a free animal? Virginia was free, and she was whimsical, and she was playful. Virginia enjoyed her life and we enjoyed our lives with her. Her death is not only a literary loss but, as her girlfriend said, "A world in which there is less goodness".

Virginia was also a good sport – once, assigned to the "erotic writing" panel at the Libertas! Festival in 2002, despite only having written a few lines of actual sex in *The Ropemaker's Daughter*, Virginia gave it her amused best amongst a panel consisting of far raunchier authors. I think readers will be pleasantly surprised that *The Carradine Diary* is equally romantic but less coy, something that is probably the result of her growing more comfortable writing about women together.

She and I had many positive conversations about sexual fluidity and our irritation with society's need to box people in. She was bemused by, and yet open to, the lesbian culture she found when she embarked in her early 30s on a new relationship with a woman. There is a great, underrated sense of entitlement and pride that women coming from a "straight" culture bring into a "lesbian" culture – a conviction that their new same-sex relationship is worth "just as much", and should be acknowledged as "just as good". This sense of happy entitlement comes across clearly in *The Carradine Diary*. It certainly was also the case in Virginia's private life as well.

Virginia and I met monthly for Thai food in Soho to discuss our writing and our lives, after which we'd go to Borders and buy books on their 3-for-2 offer. Because she was a librarian, she'd read absolutely everything, and she introduced me to many novels and authors, and bought me my Borders books once when I was broke. She was brave and good and loved the wilderness and language, and especially poetry (she once paid for both our Thai meals when she'd won a cash poetry contest, generosity which was typical of her). As Helen Sandler put it, "Virginia was a lively, warm and involved person and a thoughtful friend, sending cards and gifts and keeping up email correspondences." She was so giving and so talented, and took a large interest in other people's lives (she commissioned a painting off me in 2003, and asked whether it could be used as the cover for this edition – sadly, she never got to see it). I always felt greatly optimistic after seeing Virginia, and I'm sure many others did too. It's such a tragedy and I really miss her. I thought it would be very difficult to read and edit this novel after she died, and of course it was, but with her life-force and humour infusing the story, I was surprised that I still felt truly hopeful while reading and once I had finished reading as well. I can feel her here now, happy over the imminent publication, celebrating and being free, sharing her optimism with all her present and future readers.

Kathleen Bryson, August 2004
Publisher and Commissioning Editor, Diva Books

One

She's standing in the arrivals lounge, holding a little square of cardboard high in the air. It has written on it "ABBY MARTIN, AIR CANADA", except that the cardboard is upside down, so the words just look like a set of hieroglyphics. I've never met her before, but her face is familiar from magazine articles and from the flyleaf photos of her books. She was even on television a month ago, talking about her new biography, and she seems to be wearing the same clothes now as she was wearing then. In fact, it looks as if she may actually have been wearing them *since* then. She has an attractively rumpled air about her: dark grey hair sticking out a little all over her head, as if someone has plugged her into the mains and flicked the switch.

I begin to steer my luggage trolley towards her, but she looks past me, and a little smudge of concern settles on her forehead.

I speed up a little, smiling, but my trolley starts to get away from me on the downward slope, so that I have to pull back on it hard. I end up skidding to a halt in front of her. She raises an eyebrow.

"Mo Laker?" My voice is all breath.

"Yes?" Her face bunches itself together for a moment, but then she opens her mouth into a perfect O. "Oh Lord!" she says, placing her fingers on my arm. "Are you Abby? Sorry. I was looking for someone smaller. Gayle said you were small, and blonde."

I lift one of my feet off the ground and point at my heeled boot. "The wonders of elevating footwear."

She laughs, a smoker's laugh. There's broken glass at the back of it, and a bed of ash. She taps my shoulder with the cardboard.

"And what about the blonde part?"

"God. She *always* says I'm blonde. I think she just likes telling people she has a blonde girlfriend. It makes her feel like she's shacked up with Claudia Schiffer." I touch my hair with the tips of my fingers. "Mousy, I think, wouldn't you say?"

Mo Laker is smiling. "Did you have a good flight?"

"Yes, thanks. It was long, though." We start to walk across the airport concourse towards signs for the car park. The air feels sharp in my lungs, icy after the saccharine heat of the plane. "*And* I ended up sitting next to a farmer from Saskatoon who wanted to tell me all about the ingredients of sheep dip."

Mo Laker laughs her smoky laugh again, a sudden scatter of stones, and turns to look at me.

"And how was Gayle when you left her?" She steps ahead a little and pushes open the huge glass doors. The afternoon sky outside is bright blue, scarfed with feathery clouds. "Is she going to miss you?"

"I doubt it. She's got her final exams coming up, loads of work to do. And besides..." I follow her down a concrete walkway, careful not to ram my trolley into her ankles. "The rugby World Cup is on TV. I'll be surprised if she even notices I'm gone."

Mo throws me a smile over her shoulder. "Now I'm *sure* that's not true."

We turn a sharp corner and I stop dead in my tracks, because, instead of blue sky, there are indigo mountains suddenly, ragged fists punching at the skyline, and beyond them, in all directions at once, stretches a sea made of glass.

Mo is threading her way ahead of me across the half-empty car park, but she must sense that I'm no longer at her heels, because she spins round and shields her eyes against the sun.

"You okay?"

I start moving again, nodding, watching as a sudden breeze lifts her hair and blows it across her face. She pushes it back with her fingers, then digs into the pocket of her leather jacket and pulls out a huge bunch of keys.

"Admiring the view, madam?" she asks, when I reach her.

"I'd heard it was pretty, but, God – it's gorgeous."

"Some places have magic in them, you know. Some of the places I've visited, written about, but *this* place…" She takes a breath and closes her eyes, and when she opens them again, I'm startled to see what look like tears clouding across the blue of her irises. Her pupils are very black. She blinks hard. "The First Nation Indians called it Esquaveigt: *Land Cradled on the Waves*." She takes a few more steps, stops alongside a big green dusty car. "A shitload more romantic than plain old Prince William Island, but there you go, that's the creativity of the colonising English for you." Grinning, she unlocks the car door and leans down inside. "It's a bit of a dustbin on wheels, my car, I'm afraid." Her voice is muffled. I watch through the window as she flings things about on the rear seat, making space for my rucksack. "Hope you don't mind." Her cheeks are a peachy pink when she reappears.

"God, no. Of course not, and look, I want to say straight off how much I appreciate all this, you giving me this job and…"

"Hey!" She puts a finger to her lips. "I've seen your work, remember? It should be me thanking *you*."

I whistle a doubtful breath into the air. "I don't know about that."

"Well, I *do*. This is my biggest project yet. Lucy Pritchard is like a bloody goddess over here, and nobody's managed a good critical biography of her. All the biographies so far have been written for children. Mine's going to be aimed at an adult readership, and I want it to be… *orgasmically* successful. Do you really think I'd have paid for you to come all the way out here, if I didn't *know* you were the best I could get?" I shrug. "Do you think I've asked you out here as a favour to Gayle or something?" She doesn't wait for an answer, but starts hauling my rucksack off the trolley and into the car. "Because I haven't, you know. She's an old friend, yeah. She used to be a good friend at Uni, but not *that* good, Abby."

I tilt the rucksack from underneath and, between us, we manage to settle it onto the rear seat, where it sits hunched up like a plump child.

Mo pushes the driver's seat back into position and smiles at me.

"I'd looked at such a lot of bad art work, pretty much given up on finding someone who could do what I wanted, and then Gayle sent me your portfolio." She lifts her palms into the air, lets them fall. "And that was it."

"Really?"

She sighs. "Really."

"I've never done anything this... professional. You know that?"

She clicks her tongue against the roof of her mouth.

"That's not an issue. Christ Almighty, you should have seen some of the shite the so-called *professionals* submitted." She breaks her voice into pieces. "I fairly *cried*, I can tell you." And then she jerks her head towards the car. "Now, come on and get in. We'll head back to my house and you can freshen up, and then I want to show you the proofs of the book. I can't *wait* to see what you're gonna come up with."

I once had sex in the crypt of Winchester Cathedral, with a lady stonemason called Michaela. She was restoring Jane Austen's gravestone, which meant that she had special privileges inside the building. I doubt that fornication behind the font was one of them, but I didn't care. She had muscles like cords of steel between her shoulder blades, and the dust of a literary diva ghosting her fingertips.

I only knew her for a day, a winter's day – the air raw and white, and the streets sleepless with Christmas. At 10 a.m., she'd come stalking into the college library where I worked and had asked for information on the history of bras, and it wasn't until I'd spent a good ten minutes guiding her through books bursting at the seams with foundation garments down through the ages that she finally shook her head, smiling, and said gently, "No, no. The history of *brass*."

Maybe that's what did it, that moment of surprise, like standing on a cliff edge, looking down at the white sea crashing below. I'd only ever backed sharply away before. This time, I let myself fall.

She took me out after work, to a Spanish café on the Square – barrels of wine stacked black behind the bar, bunches of onions, and sausages as long as broom handles hanging from the ceiling. I drank a whole bottle of Rioja to myself, and listened to her talk about her work, naming the tools she used, dipping her head towards me as if with a set of secrets: *bullnoses, scribers, broad boasters, dreadnought files, Long Portland punches*. I liked the sound of them, the way her mouth shaped them, and by the time we stumbled out into the dark, I just knew I was going to have to sleep with her, and I did.

This was a while ago now. I'd only just finished at art school. I was shiny and new, and certain of nothing but my own talent, my own fingers holding a brush or a pencil. I thought I was going to reshape the world by reinventing it in paint, in ink, in sparkling innovation. That night with Michaela was supposed to be the start of it all, an apotheosis, a point of change, but it got forgotten somehow, in the cold light of day, and besides, a month later I met Gayle and a month after that, we moved in together, and I stayed working at the college library because we needed the money, and somehow the world didn't seem to need reshaping anymore. It looked solid – square and solid, and as if it could manage perfectly well without any tampering from me.

But now, riding along a wide highway, with bright green trees ablaze in the sunshine, and Mo Laker sitting by my side, smoking, of all things, a *clay pipe*, I'm beginning to think that maybe there *is* something unique that I can fashion out of all of this. It's a long time since I thought that. I was furious with Gayle when I found out she'd sent my portfolio to a stranger. I hadn't shown my work to anyone for years, but now I can't help feeling a lilt of expectation singing through my blood, and each time I glance across at Mo, she's smiling and telling me about her book, and I'm all the while looking past her at the trees and the road signs and the sky and the big black birds that are flying alongside the car. I'm thinking how I will draw them. All at once, the world is raw again, holding itself in waiting for me. I am attentive to every sign suddenly, every whisper, and somewhere, at the back of it all, there's a cliff edge, a white sea crashing far below, and myself, falling.

Two

Mo Laker lives in a ramshackle, whitewashed house overlooking the beach, at a place called St. Catherine's Point. She tells me that the house is called "The Old Sea Box" and that it used to be owned by a Scottish sea captain who was famous for playing the bagpipes.

"When the wind's in the right direction," she says, as we climb a few wooden steps onto the veranda, "you can still hear the sound of the pipes, wafting mournfully through the house."

"Really?"

She nods, her face solemn as a sheet of marble.

I try to recall the first few bars of "Scotland the Brave", or the haunting cadence of "Amazing Grace".

"What are they playing exactly?"

Mo crinkles her nose at me a little and grins. "'Donald, Where's Yer Trewsers?'"

"No *way*! Seriously?"

She takes a breath, leans towards me, says quietly, "Nah. Not seriously." And then she swings her keys around on her finger, like a gunfighter with a Colt 45, and flicks her door key clear of the rest. She points it at me. "But that's what this job's about, you know? Sorting out what's real from what's bullshit. I've been writing biographies for nearly six years now, and you always get some degree of invention when you're doing research. You interview loads of people, to get a balanced picture, and it works, mostly, but then there's always some old duffer who spins you a yarn, who thinks they hold the key to the mystery. Being in the limelight makes them bold, resourceful, but *this* time..." She rolls her eyes. "You wouldn't *believe* some of the stuff I've heard. Every man and his dog have something to add to the pot." She

7

slips her key into the lock and eases the door open, steps inside. I can smell cedarwood suddenly, and the keen tang of the sea. "They're all either Lucy Pritchard's long-lost second cousin twice removed, or their great-grandfather once helped her onto a tram in the rain, or the man who lived next door to them in 1978 was the nephew of the son of Pritchard's illegitimate daughter, Esmerelda..."

"I didn't know she had an illegitimate daughter Esmerelda."

"She didn't, but that's what I mean. It's all a load of old cobblers, and you'll have to contend with it too."

I shuffle my rucksack off onto the floor. "Why will I?"

"Because as soon as you tell people you're illustrating a biography of Lucy Pritchard, they'll want to open their hearts to you, offer you their own sordid little piece of the jigsaw." She wags her head at me. "And you mustn't let them."

"Okay."

"Okay." She exhales the word and smiles at me. "Right, then. Let me give you a quick tour of the house and then I'll fix us something to eat, yes?"

I nod hard. Gayle had warned me that Mo was "a strident personality". At least, she'd said that "a strident personality" was a polite way to describe what Mo was. She'd talked about when they were at college together in London, how Mo had claimed Gayle for her friend; sat down next to her on the first day of lectures, struck up a conversation and never let go. "Like being sucked up into the eye of a tornado", that's how Gayle described the experience of their friendship, but when I asked her why she hadn't tried to shake Mo off, wrestle herself free, she'd just shrugged and said that, once you got used to the tornado thing, it was really quite pleasant. Mo's energy was contagious, that's what she'd said, and she had a good heart.

I think about this as I follow her through the house. First of all, I try to drag my rucksack with me, but, without interrupting the flow of her speech, Mo quietly reaches down and unclasps my fingers from the straps, shaking her head.

The room we are in seems to be all wood, like the cabin of a ship, with blond panelled walls and huge, coloured rugs set at jaunty angles over the floorboards. A long sofa, covered with a blue calico throw, is set against one wall, and a glass dresser full of rustic-looking pottery is set against the other. There are books and papers everywhere, and a row of empty wine bottles sitting sentinel-like in the open hearth.

Mo leads me along a low-ceilinged corridor to the kitchen, where what I assume to be her writing desk sits under a cluster of spotlights. If she writes there after dark, she must feel like she's on the stage, with all that focused light beating down on her brow, sparking bright off the white squares scattered beneath her wrists. I touch the edge of the desk as we pass and it is cool as water. My fingertips feel wet when I take them away.

She shows me how to coax the temperamental water-heater into action by banging it three times with a spanner, and then she opens each of the kitchen cupboards in turn and tells me to help myself to anything that tickles my fancy. She pats the little wood-burning stove in the corner as if it were her favourite child and advises me not to try to light it on my own.

"First time I tried it, no one had warned me about the residual oxygen deposit. I stuck a lit match up the flue and *bo-um...*" She makes an explosive gesture with her hands. "Took my eyebrows clean off!"

I'm not sure whether I should laugh or not, but Mo doesn't give me time to decide. She turns away and opens the kitchen door wide so that a gust of breeze shoulders into the room and presses its little fists against my chest.

I take a breath. "The sea here smells different to the sea at home."

She turns back to me, nodding. "Yes, it does. Sharper, right?"

"And warmer, somehow."

I think of chilly Southampton Water, and the thick brown Solent swirling patches of ice.

"That's because of the Gulf Stream. The water between the islands holds the heat of the sun longer." She cups her palms. "It gets kind of enclosed, carried back and forth between the bays. Even in winter, you can swim if you want."

"I'm going to like it here." I say it quietly, but something loud and agitated is burning hot behind my breastbone. I close my hands over my chest to keep it in, and then I stare out at the green tide, trying not to blink, trying to swallow this new place whole.

"I'll be wanting you to capture this if you can." Mo gestures out to sea. "Well, not *this* exactly, but Pritchard's stretch of coast; her family owned a house up on the north shore, about forty miles from here, looks a lot like this, same feel to it. She had a spot down on the beach where she used to go to write.

"But look..." She moves past me, back into the living room, nodding for me to follow. "I'm going to try really hard *not* to dictate to you the specifics of what I want done. You read the proofs in your own time, look at a map of the island, and then just..." She starts to climb the stairs, but halts ahead of me and turns. The light is behind her, filling her hair with tiny filaments of gold, like sparks from a furnace. She sighs, opens her eyes wide. "I *guess*, just... drive off into the sunset and come back with your own version of the story. That way" – she takes the last few stairs in two big strides – "this book will be a collaboration. I will have given Pritchard back her life in words, and you'll have given it back to her in paint."

"Actually, I only work in pencil, and charcoal, really. Is that okay?"

Mo grins at me. "What*ever* does it for you, sweetie." She opens a wooden door ahead of us and steps back against it so that I can enter. "Now, this'll be your harmonious feng shui space at luscious chez Laker. What d'you think? I half-decorated for you specially, see?"

The room is narrow, with a bed set against the wall to the left and a long wooden bookcase, filled with paperbacks, running the entire length of the opposite wall. Mo has given half the room a coat of lime paint, but her brush strokes stop abruptly under the window ledge, and from that point onward the walls are covered with what looks like very old grey and yellow wallpaper. When I peer more closely, however, I realise that it isn't wallpaper at all. It's some kind of elaborate stencilling.

I crouch down and run my breath over the pattern.

"I thought that might catch your eye." Mo has her arms folded. "Intriguing, isn't it?"

"Who did it, do you know?"

"The guy I bought the house from says it's original, dates back to the first people who lived here, which means it's over a hundred and fifty years old. I was planning to paint over it. It's a bit too dingy for my liking, really, but..." She places her hand on my shoulder. "I thought it might appeal to your art-equals-immortality way of thinking, get you in the mood a tad."

For a moment, I can picture a woman in long skirts, high-buttoned boots, her hair clasped in two long braids down her back, like interlocking fingers. She is down on her knees on the bare boards, a long silver pen in her right hand and a small round terracotta pot of India ink in her left. Her face is filled with a baffled kind of light as she works. Her dark eyes are heavy-lidded, drunk on concentration, but her mouth is a straight line, absolute. I can smell the ink, an intimation of iron, like new blood. When she touches the nib to her tongue, I can taste the thick dark shine of it. It fills my mouth like tears.

Mo squeezes my shoulder. "Abby?"

I look up into her face, blinking. "I'm so pleased you asked me to come out here. I just feel really strongly that this is going to be..." I stand up fast and take a breath. "Well, I don't exactly *know* what it's going to be yet, but it's going to be *something*. You know when you feel so excited about something, so fired up by the thought of something, that you can't find words for it, or a shape for it, and you just have to ride it out and wait, and... God..."

Mo is smiling with what looks like all of her teeth.

"Easy, tiger," she says, laughing. "I can't cope with all this

11

unbridled verve on an empty stomach." She claps her hands together. "What would you say to a mushroom risotto, or paella maybe? The shellfish here are amazing – scallops the size of tennis balls."

"Lovely."

"Would you like to take a bath first, freshen up, or maybe you fancy a lie down?"

As soon as Mo mentions sleep, my limbs begin to melt into the carpet. I am suddenly, unexpectedly, *irretrievably* weary. I try to stand up straight against the wave of it, but my mouth opens helplessly in a yawn. The hum of the plane is loud inside my head again, and my stomach feels hot, vaguely nauseous. Something damp and heavy is welling up inside me.

"Actually, that might be a good idea. If I try to get an hour's sleep in now, I might avoid jet lag later."

Mo nods and looks at her watch. "I'll come wake you about seven then. You can chop some shallots while I shell those tennis balls. Slippy little suckers and no mistakin'!"

She winks at me and turns away, easing the door closed behind her, and as soon as she is gone, I sit down on the bed and kick off my boots. I know I should have asked Mo if I could call Gayle, or send her a quick e-mail. I'd promised her I'd be in touch as soon as I arrived, but I feel so sleepy, and so wonderfully far from home suddenly, so caught up in the celestial shine of this island adventure. I don't want to talk to Gayle, hear her voice crackling sharp towards me across the miles, telling me the rugby scores, counting down the line how many pages of her business accounting textbook she's managed today.

I climb out of my jeans and pull my T-shirt top off over my head, and then I lie down on the bed in my underwear and pull the white sheet up under my chin. The air is warm. I close my eyes and listen to the sound of the sea, waves breaking over shingle and sand, like someone saying, *shhh... shhh*, very softly, over and over again.

Three

I wake to the sound of a door closing – a sudden click that pulls me up straight in the bed, my ribcage held in tight, the sheets tangled around my ankles. For a moment, I can't remember where I am, or how I got here, and the narrow room, with its sharp, unfamiliar images, seems to swim in and out of focus. I blink hard and take a breath, letting Mo's face and the memory of her husky laugh filter back into the frame. A column of pale ochre light is moving intermittently across the walls – a couple of seconds' darkness between each sweep. Clambering out of bed, I peer out of the window into a velvety grey: the sea like a ripple of silk stretching away to the horizon. Out on the ragged headland is a lighthouse, a shaft of yellow dropping in an arc across the water, tumbling my room into shadow, falling onto my face like sunshine.

My rucksack is leaning against the bookcase. Mo must have brought it up while I was sleeping. I pull my watch out of one of the side pockets, but realise that I haven't yet altered it to local time. I've never been very good at working out time differences, which frustrates Gayle beyond measure.

"It's just basic subtraction and addition," she says with a sigh whenever we travel abroad. But it's always been more than that to me. I've always been fascinated by the fact that if you get on a plane in London at 10 p.m. on a Saturday, you can arrive in Sydney at 10 a.m. on the Sunday, but you'll really have spent *twenty-four* hours in the air. How can that be? How is it you've managed to reclaim twelve hours you've already lived through? All that extra time, spiralling toward you like a miracle. You feel like you should do something memorable with it: save a life, solve an impossible equation, fulfil a fantasy. Last time we flew, I *did* suggest to Gayle that we could make that gifted time unforgettable by joining the mile-high club, but she declined. I understood her reticence, I suppose. We *were*, after all, on a flight to Rome, with a gaggle of elderly, black-clad nuns on their way to meet the Pope. They stared at us, the hairy moles on their chins like extra eyes, just watching for us to put our mortal souls in danger by shagging in the tiny toilet. I'd have done it, though, if Gayle had been willing, just to catch the hum of their disapproval, receive it like a musical accompaniment to our sin.

Mo is calling. I struggle back into my top and poke my head around the door. She's halfway up the stairs with a wooden spoon in her hand. She's wearing a pair of tartan pyjamas. She smiles when she sees me.

"What's the time, Mo?" My voice is full of cotton wool. "I was going give you a hand with supper, wasn't I?"

"You still can, love, but why don't you run yourself a bath first? There's plenty of time."

"Thanks. That'd be great."

"There are fresh towels on the stool in the bathroom, and feel free to use whatever bath stuff you find." She waves her spoon at me, holds her breath for a second. "Gayle called, by the way."

"Did she?"

"I told her you were sleeping."

"Thanks."

"I told her you'd call her later."

"Right."

She inclines her head. "You okay?"

"Fine. I'm fine, just a bit... disoriented, you know?"

"I'll open us some wine, shall I?"

"Wonderful."

She dips her chin towards me, then turns and trots away down the stairs. I can hear her singing, in a sultry Nina Simoney voice, "My Baby Just Cares For Me". I join in softly with the chorus, lifting my hair and scrunching it into a fist, tying it up, and then I pad across the landing and into the bathroom. The walls are rough brown wood, cool to the touch, but the air inside the room is moist and warm, smelling of shampoo, and vaguely too of tobacco. Mo must have had a bath already. Her clay pipe sits like an exclamation mark on the window ledge.

I turn on the taps and rub a circle clear on the steamed-up mirror, and suddenly my face swims up as if from the bottom of a pool. I blink hard, pull my top off over my head, discard my underwear, and then I lean forward with my hands either side of the sink and think about Gayle. Her name feels somehow barbed when I say it inside my head, and I don't know why. Maybe it's just displacement, because I'm here, so far from home, so far from her. Or maybe it's just plain old guilt, because I'm so happy to be here – far from home, far from *her*. I think about having to return her call later, and my temples begin to ache.

Pouring a little of Mo's ylang-ylang and patchouli oil into the water, I swirl it around with fingertips, and then I step in and lower myself very gently, take a breath and sink right down beneath the surface, feel the water pressing its palms tight against my body. When at last I come up for air, I can hear the sound of the telephone ringing.

Mo has cooked paella, with saffron rice. She's sautéed scallops in garlic and coriander and prepared a huge green salad. We eat looking out over the bay, where the air is lilac-coloured, and the dark line of the sea opens and closes like a mouth. We finish one bottle of white Rioja and then Mo opens another, and the world begins to sway to its own tune, and my heart throbs like a bruise inside my chest.

We talk about Mo's writing, and she fetches the proofs of her book and slides them into my lap.

"Bedtime reading." She refills my glass. "Take your time with them, though. I'm out of town for the next few days. I told you about that?"

I nod. "Yep. You're visiting your editor in Vancouver, and then

15

you're going to see some friends."

She puckers her lips a little. "Well, *one* friend actually, in Vancouver – one particular friend." She rolls the word particular around on her tongue as if she likes the taste of it.

"Ahh! I see."

"This is a try-out. We've been seeing each other for a few months now, but this will be our first vacation together."

"Crunch time?"

She shrugs, opens a cupboard door behind her and takes down a small porcelain jar.

"I dunno. She's nice and everything, but I'm not gonna get myself all bent out of shape about it. If it works, it works, if it doesn't..." She slaps a hand to her chest and looks to the ceiling. "We'll always have Paris!"

"Paris?"

"Well, no, not Paris exactly, but some okay times, you know?" She opens the little jar and slips her fingers inside. "I'm a great believer in holding onto the good stuff, enjoying it, however fleeting it might turn out to be. It's all a gift, right?"

"I guess."

"What about you and Gayle?"

I lift my shoulders a little, let them fall. "We're okay. Getting on and getting by, you know, but we're okay, really."

"Last I heard, you'd had a proper old commitment ceremony and everything: wife and wife."

"That was Gayle's idea."

She tilts her head. "You weren't up for it?"

"I was, kinda. I just didn't really see the need for it. We were fine as we were."

"But, you're okay, still, the two of you? You're happy?"

"I'm not *un*happy." I hesitate. "Why? Has she said something to you, about us?"

"Christ, no. Why would she? She and I aren't exactly confidantes these days. It's a lifetime since I knew anything about her really."

"You *were* close though, back in college?"

She thinks for a moment. "We were mates, sure, but... Close?" She shakes her head, just the once. "I don't know. I was a fair bit older than her, remember, which kept us... separate. She wasn't always very tolerant of my lifestyle choices, either. I was a bit of a one back then, exploring my sexuality right, left and centre, though not so much centre." She winks at me. "Your Gayle was a bit... prudish."

"That'd be about right."

"I liked her, though, ever such a lot, really. She was sweet. A moody old bint at times" – she grins – "but sweet, and I loved how easily shockable she was, too. One time, she was out with me and my friends, at a club, and there was this live strip show going on." She rolls her eyes. "Poor old Gayle, she just didn't know where to look. We were all elbowing our way toward the stage, to get a better look, make sure the girls were doing it right, you know? But Gayle, she stayed all upright and resolute at the bar." She shakes her head. "One of life's innocents, our Gayle, no?"

"I guess."

"She always held the world at bay back then, kept herself at arm's length." She pulls a little silver package from the jar and sits down at the table. "Does she still?"

"Pretty much, these days."

"That must get *irksome*."

I can't help smiling. There are many words I've used to describe Gayle over the years, but irksome has never been one of them.

"It's okay. I'm used to it. She's an accountant, after all. They're not exactly Olympic standard when it comes to communication skills, are they?"

She pushes her tongue into her cheek, nodding, slipping open the sliver package with her fingernails. She lifts her eyebrows, holds them still.

"Some hash, madam?"

A little oblong of resin sits in her open palm – a doll's house chocolate bar.

"Thanks, but I don't smoke any more." I pull myself up in my chair, my limbs already slick inside and slow with drink. "You could break a tiny piece off for me, though."

She nods, uses her knife. "It's better if you don't touch it with your fingers. Takes the edge off." She lifts her hands towards me. "Open your mouth."

I do, and she slips a tiny sliver of resin straight from the knife onto my tongue. I feel the cold tang of steel for a moment, and then a grainy warmth, fragrant and bitter, like cardamom.

"Just let it dissolve," she says, smiling at me, splashing more wine into my glass. "Nothing like a bit of sneaky peak to get the party going, eh?" She opens her eyes very wide. "You're a lot less uptight than Gayle, aren't you, unless *she's* a lot less uptight than she used to be?"

I take a sip of wine, hold it in my mouth for a moment, swallow hard. "She's not."

"How d'you manage, then? Don't you want to take a sledge hammer to her, rough her up a bit?"

I watch Mo's fingers preparing a joint. They are long and slender, dexterous. She is smiling at me, her face pale against a square of dark sky.

"Sometimes I do." I say it quietly. "Sometimes I look at her and I love her so much I want to cry. Other times, I look at her, and I think *ohmygod!* I can't possibly do this for the rest of my life."

Mo laughs. "The age-old dichotomy, my dear. Can't live with 'em; can't live without 'em."

"*You* do, though, live without them. At least, I thought you did. I was a bit surprised to hear about your girlfriend in Vancouver. Gayle said you were celibate."

"I was, kinda, but it turned out to be boring as fuck, mate." She lifts the joint to her lips and lights it, inhales, holds the smoke in her lungs. She mouths at me, "I got myself back into the game" – and then she exhales, gently – "started over with men, just in case I'd missed something first time round." She narrows her eyes. "I hadn't, of course, so I circled back to laydeeez, but they're no bloody easier. What they lack in the penis department, they make up for in attitude. Don't you find?"

I nod slowly, feeling the hash burning in my throat, liquid sunlight. I keep sipping at my wine – the muscles in my cheeks beginning to thaw. My whole face seems to be smiling now.

"Gayle had a crush on you back in college, you know?"

The one thing I wasn't supposed to say to Mo, and out it tumbles, ringing its bell, tangoing up and down the table.

She raises her eyebrows. "I know."

"She said you didn't. She said she kept it secret from you."

"Secret!" Her voice is a shriek. "If you call her getting drunk and telling me she wanted to make mad, passionate love to me and push me to the very edge of sensation, *keeping it secret*, well then yes, she did."

I can't help myself. I start to laugh. "'The very edge of sensation'?"

Mo draws deep on her joint, grinning. "To be honest," she whispers, breathing a stripe of smoke down her nose, "I think the edge of sensation was just a *tad* ambitious. I doubt she'd have got me as far as the corner shop."

I don't know what time we go to bed, Mo and I. I can remember lying on the sofa listening to Ella Fitzgerald CDs and drinking brandy. I can remember Mo dancing round the room in her tartan pyjamas. I can remember her having to help me up the stairs because somehow my legs had turned to elastic, but the rest is a blank, with something feathery at the edges.

I wake to the sound of a car pulling up outside the house and to Mo's voice raised in greeting. Rolling myself softly out of bed, onto the floor, I peer out of the window. A cab is parked outside, and a small man with a bald head is loading Mo's bags into the boot. She is standing by the open passenger door in a pair of dark glasses. I tap gently on the window and she looks up, slips her glasses down her nose.

"I've left you a note," she calls, lifting her hand to wave. "I'll see you at the end of the week, yes?"

I nod, call, "Have a good time," through the glass.

She blows me a flamboyant kiss, mouths, "And you," and then she pushes her glasses back up again and slips into the car.

I wait until the cab is moving away down the driveway and onto the road before I try to stand, and then I steer myself, like an unruly shopping trolley, towards the bathroom, and start to run a bath. The steam feels good in my lungs, cleansing, and when I eventually step into the warm water and lower myself under the surface, my body seems to give itself up to the heat and the lilt, until gravity dissolves and I'm free-floating, silver bubbles star-bursting against my skin. I stay in the bath until the water turns cold, and then I climb out and wrap myself in a towel, go downstairs like that and look for a tumbler so that I can drink some water. I know Mo showed me where everything was yesterday, but I can't remember where the glasses are. There are so many cupboards to look in, and I'm so thirsty that, in the end, I just stick my mouth under the tap and drink. I drink for a long time, until my tongue hurts and the water becomes a flare of ice against my gums, and then I wander through into the living room to find Mo's note.

It's propped up against a bottle of wine on the coffee table, alongside a map of the island and the proofs of her book. Little yellow Post-It notes are sticking up among the pages.

Dear Abby,

My car is parked at the side of the house. Please feel free to use it. Keys are hanging on the hook above the door. If you need to get hold of me, my mobile number is stuck on the refrigerator. Make yourself at home, and have a good week. See you Friday.

Love, Mo

I fold the note and take it with me to Mo's computer, which is switched on – little toasters and slices of buttered toast flying fast across the screen. I sit down, the wood of the chair cool against the bare skin of my thighs, and I log into my e-mail account and send a quick mail to Gayle, light and breezy, telling her about the flight, asking her about the rugby. When I click on SEND, I feel relieved, and suddenly, haphazardly cheerful. The air in the room is bright white and thick with the smell of the sea. I breathe it in, hold it in my lungs for as long as I can, and then I take Mo's proofs back upstairs with me, climb into bed and start to read.

Four

I can remember reading books by Lucy Pritchard when I was small. They all featured a mischievous farmer's son called Hector Price, one of those turn-of-the-century, ragamuffin characters who slipped inside your heart with their brown curls and their candour, and set up camp there, forever. Except, I didn't much like him. He got on my nerves. All my little friends read the books avidly and fell in love with them, but Hector was just too saccharine-sweet for me, too good to be true. No matter what trouble he got himself into, he'd always come up smelling of roses in the end, and real life wasn't like that, as far as I could tell. The books made me cross, and restless for something I couldn't have. I quite liked the world they conjured up – an island idyll, amiable and soft, seductively genteel, politely rural, utterly unlike the Greater London suburb where I was trampling out my childhood – but Hector himself, he just didn't do it for me. Looking back now, I guess he was a bit like Huckleberry Finn, minus the paddle steamers, though, and nowhere near as interesting.

As I sit in bed with Mo's book, the day lifts and falls around me, and Lucy Pritchard begins to take shape – a spirited child from a strict Baptist family, an outspoken young woman at college, a respected schoolmistress, loving wife, successful author... Nothing *precisely* extraordinary about her – a mild and sensible life when it came down to it – and yet I find myself absorbed by the unravelling of it, by the energy of Mo's writing, the vivacity of her style. I look for her brush strokes, the angles of meaning, the gradual way that Pritchard begins to lean into the light towards me. In fact, I am so absorbed that I fail to notice a thin darkness smoothing itself at the glass. It isn't until my stomach begins to feel tight and empty and my eyes start to hurt that

I finally glance at my watch, and am startled to find that it's nearly six o'clock in the evening.

Climbing out of bed, I switch on the lamps and get dressed in a halo of yellow, and then I hurry downstairs with Mo's proofs tucked under my arm. The house seems to be holding its breath, the cool air parting as I move through it, closing behind me without a sound. I open a few cupboards in the kitchen to see what there is to eat, but I feel furtive and conspicuous. I know I'm *allowed* to look inside Mo's cupboards, but nosing among her groceries suddenly feels as brazen as leafing through her diary. Maybe it's because I'm here, in her house, without her. I've never been in a situation like this one before, and its potential for bad behaviour is going to my head a little. I could rifle through her personal papers if I wanted to, or maybe look up all sorts of illegal porn sites on her computer and then let *her* get the blame. Instead, I scoop up the map of the island that she has left for me, pull on my jacket and take down her car keys from the hook above the door. They are attached to a pink and blue key-ring that has the words "Girls Who Do Girls Do It Best" emblazoned on it. It makes me smile.

The nearest town is called Port Hove and it's less than fifteen minutes away. We stopped off there briefly on our way back from the airport yesterday, so that Mo could post some letters. It's actually the capital city of the island, but it didn't look like any capital city I'd ever seen: just one long street full of antiquated-looking stores, and pubs and restaurants, and people walking their dogs or riding their bikes. I liked the feel of it. I liked the look of the sky falling everywhere at once, and a rust-coloured sun splashing down soft into the water.

Before I leave the house, I run back upstairs and unpack the smaller of my two sketchpads and a box of pencils and then, taking Mo's book with me, I lock the front door, twice, just to make sure I've done it right. The windows are creaking gently in their frames and would take nothing more than a gentle nudge to shatter and fall, but I do my best to secure the house anyway, even running round to the back door to make sure that's locked too.

For a while, I can't help but just stand and look out at the ocean, sweeping towards me and away – the creamy surf breaking into shallow waters, spilling onto the pink and white sands below. All along the curving line of the bay, little lights are flickering, and I wonder if the people inside those houses are looking out at the ocean as I am now. How could they *not* be looking at it? I've often wondered what it would be like to live with a view like this one, to open your curtains every morning and feel your breath sucked clean away by so much beauty, right there on your doorstep. Would you grow complacent after a while? Would you eventually look and see only a tangle of shapes, a blur of colour? I know I wouldn't. I could stand here forever and not grow tired of what's before me, and I know, from Mo's book, that that's how Pritchard felt about the sea too, how she gave herself up to it, time and again, lived all her life with the whisper and the roar of it in her blood. She couldn't help writing about it. Every one of the Hector books is full of the sea. I read the books when I was eight, maybe nine, years old, and the only sea I knew then was a curve of caramel-coloured English Channel. Pritchard's Atlantic – thick with fish, charged with space and circling air – was a dream to me then. I can't believe I'm standing here now, on its shores. Swallowing hard against the wind, I push my hair away from my face, and find that my cheeks are wet with spray. I don't wipe them dry. I like the feel of the salt on my skin.

I drive into town with the map open on my lap, back along the coast road and then inland for a while, past a hospital and a school, and then along a wide avenue banked by huge old colonial houses and tall poplars. When I reach a church, I turn left and park the car, because I know I'm on the outskirts of town now. There are more people around suddenly and the air feels warm, and crowded with gathering sound. I walk in the same direction as everyone else and soon turn onto the main street, but it looks different in the twilight. A handful of harbour-front blocks are silhouetted against the sky, and yellow gas lamps illuminate the brick walkways that snake around them. A street sign reads WELCOME TO OLDE PORT HOVE. I walk the entire length of the street, from the old end of town to a swatch of newer buildings and a little shopping mall made of glass, and then I walk all the way back and stop outside a row of cosy-looking restaurants and cafés, with streetside patios. On the steps of one of them, a small jazz band is playing. A huddle of men in stripey waistcoats and bowler hats, and a woman who looks like Cleo Laine, but isn't, all look up from their instruments and smile at me as I move past them.

Inside, the café is decked out like a Western saloon bar, which makes me laugh, because the sign outside said that this was a seafood restaurant, and I don't remember there *being* any sea in the Wild West. Regardless, I choose a table in a corner, beneath a cluster of candles, like a lit bouquet. The light here is gentle, making shadows out of everything, but clear enough for me to be able to draw, and that's what I want to do. For the first time in a long time, that's *exactly* what I want to do. I open my sketchpad and then I open the box of pencils, choosing one at random, and, for a while, I just hold it in my fingers, move my fingertips over it, soft as I can, and then I run my tongue over the tip. It is gunmetal grey when I taste it, and that's the colour I want, the shade and the hue that are lilting towards me like good karma.

When the waiter comes to take my order, I ask him what he recommends, and he suggests the steamed island blue mussels, and then he leans towards me a little, looking at the pad in my lap.

"Are you an artist?" His accent is full of vowels.

"Kind of."

"What are you drawing?"

"Nothing yet."

He smiles at me, shows me the tips of his white teeth. "What kinds of things are you *planning* to draw?"

"Not sure."

"You could draw me."

"I could."

"On second thoughts…" He straightens up. "You *couldn't* draw me, because I move too fast, you see. Quick like a cat, that's me."

"Really?"

"I'd just be a blur." He smiles, takes a breath. "Anything to drink?"

"Just water, thanks."

He dips his head towards me and then moves off towards the kitchen, and as soon as he's gone, I start to draw.

At first, the pencil feels strange in my fingers, rigid and alien. It scratches across the paper, making shapes that I don't want to make, tracing angles that I haven't asked it to trace. When a pitcher of water arrives at my table, I pour myself a huge glass and drink it down in one go, and then I just sit for a while, looking around the restaurant, surmising, taking it in.

This time when I press the pencil to the surface of the paper, I breathe deep from my stomach, feeling the air sliding into my lungs, a rush of red, and as I breathe out – slowly, very slowly – I let the pencil move with the length of my breath. I concentrate my gaze on one exact point: a bottle of wine on the opposite table, half empty, backlit with a dusty aura from a single candle burning behind it – a simple thing. A child's choice of subject, surely, and yet, as I draw, I feel the old power settling inside me like a fall of snow, and when the waiter arrives with my steamed island blue mussels, I leave my sketchpad open on the table while I eat, glancing intermittently at the bottle and at my drawing of the bottle, and I feel gratified. I can still do it. I can still draw, and draw well, which means Mo hasn't brought me all the way out here just to disappoint her. I order a glass of wine to celebrate, and then I flick my sketchpad to the next clean page and begin drawing again and, as I draw, the strangest thing happens. Inexplicably, and without any warning, I start to miss Gayle. I try to swallow past it, focus all my thinking, all my *feeling*, on the man at the opposite table, his fingers absent-mindedly circling the neck of the bottle of wine, his pale head lowered over the pages of a book. I try to trace the little space of dark beneath his cheekbone, the looping curve of his chin, but it's no good. I have to put the pencil down, because, infuriatingly, there are tears in my eyes. I blink them away, take a few sips of wine in quick succession, and it is then that I remember it, although, of course, I have never really forgotten it – the first time Gayle and I met.

I wasn't long out of art school. I'd taken a job at the library to pay the rent. I was waiting for something heart-stopping and transforming to happen to me, but, in the meantime, I used to go, on my day off, into London, to visit the galleries. I liked the smell of them – lilacs and water, furniture polish. I liked moving through rooms heavy with light and silence. I liked to sit in front of my favourite paintings and make copies of them, and that was what I was doing the day I met Gayle. I was at the National Gallery, sitting with my legs folded beneath me, my sketchpad open in my lap, my leather jacket and my basketball boots on the floor beside me, and I was making a copy of Caravaggio's *The Supper at Emmaus*: the risen Christ, looking a little like Andrew Lloyd Webber, sitting at a table with the disciples he'd met on the road, revealing himself to them in the breaking of bread. I was making a good job of it, although I was having trouble with the shadows, and I'd given the servant in the background ears commandeered from the planet Vulcan; but, even so, I was becoming pleased. I was focused and absorbed. I was startled when someone spoke to me.

"That's good."

I glanced up to see a tall woman with sandy hair and small glasses peering down at my sketchpad. She leaned forward from the waist to get a better view, and the little rucksack on her shoulder slipped forward and bumped me in the back of the head, gently, and then she bounced down onto her haunches so that her head was level with mine.

"Must have been quite a moment." She looked into my face, her eyes very blue and inquisitive. "Don't you think?"

I shook my head, chewed the end of my pencil for a second,

realised I was doing it, stopped. "*What* must have been quite a moment?"

"That one." She pointed to the painting on the wall. "The moment of revelation. I mean, you think about it... There they are, right" – and she opened her palm, lifted it toward the painting – "these disciples. They've just watched the man they thought was their *Messiah* crucified and buried. They meet some random bloke on the road, do the polite thing and ask him in for a pan o' scouse, and who does he turn out to be? Fucking JC himself, come back from the dark side to tell them all is not lost." She shook her head, made a little clicking sound out of the corner of her mouth. "Quite a moment."

I took a breath, looking at her, looking at her throat and the angle of her jaw ribboned with bars of light and dark refracted through the windows above.

"I guess so." I said it quietly, but she glanced at me quickly, like I'd surprised her, like she'd forgotten I was there, and then she smiled.

"Makes you think, doesn't it?" Her eyebrows were raised.

"About what?"

"About how these moments of revelation can be concealed inside something ordinary."

"I guess." I nodded slowly, looking her straight in the eye, as brazen as I could manage. "I mean, you're right. Yes. You *could* just be walking along the road, or eating a meal, visiting a gallery, and suddenly something... transforming might happen to you." I held her gaze. "And maybe nothing will ever be the same again because of it."

I could feel something digging like a fist into my stomach. I couldn't say anything else, but that was okay, because she started to climb to her feet then and held out her hands to me, said flatly, like it was already decided, "A drink."

It wasn't a question, but it sounded, at the time, very much like an answer.

Five

Next morning, I get up early, while the light is still white, and I start to drive. I stop in Port Hove and buy some savoury bagels from a bakery, and I eat them in the car, flicking through the proofs of Mo's book. The little yellow Post-It notes sticking up intermittently among the pages mark the different sites that she wants me to draw. This seems simple enough, especially as one of the sites is right here in Port Hove: the home of Pritchard's maternal grandmother, Eva May MacLeod. Pritchard lived here while she was studying for her teacher's certificate at the local college. I locate the house on the map, and then I locate it on foot, and I sit on a wooden bench, with my back to the water, and start to draw. I've always been all right with houses: their solidity appeals to me – the sheer and sharp edges and angles that make them what they are – so I draw quickly, and last night's uncertainty evaporates like water spilled in the desert. I breathe easy, and something comes out of my fingers, soft as smoke, vaguely sullen. I spend less than thirty minutes drawing, and then I pack my equipment away and walk back to the car with the sun in my throat. This is how I'm going to do it; I know that now: head down, hard-hearted. I'm not going to give myself space to feel insecure. I'm going to be unswervingly professional and disciplined. Back in the car, I eat the last bagel, even though I'd promised myself I'd save it for later, and then I drive out onto highway three, and head for the north shore.

The landscape changes: mountains and sea giving way to sloping fields and little hamlets bordered by cherry trees and stillness. Everywhere, there are birds: some brightly coloured, some deep black, swooping into the path of my car – a rainbow of feathers. The day is growing warm, so I wind down the window, letting the gentle lowing of cows and the rumble of tractors drift toward me and away, and gradually the sea begins to flash by again, at blue intervals, glimpsed like a promise beyond the hills.

I drive for less than hour, before I start to see signs saying WELCOME TO THE HOME OF HECTOR PRICE. Mo had warned me about Lucy Pritchard's celebrity status, but I didn't expect this – Hector's freckled face grinning down from every billboard, his chubby fingers pointing the way to Hector's Motel, Brasserie and Grill. The tiny town of Burntwood Creek, where Pritchard lived until she married, and where all her books are set, drips with the syrup of little Hector. Everywhere you look, he is.

I park my car outside Pritchard's family home, now a museum, and I wander down into town with my sketchpad clutched to my chest like a shield. The air here feels thick and cloying, and the shops are choked with Hector memorabilia. The sea is held at bay by a string of shore-front hotels and a theatre which, all year round, stages the musical version of *Little Hector of the Creek*, Pritchard's most popular book. People are already queuing outside for tickets.

I get to work quickly, making a sketch of the overcrowded bay, the lighthouse, the main street, the imposing Baptist church where Pritchard worshipped, and where she met her husband, the Reverend Ethan MacKay, but I don't concentrate on the contemporary detail, the ruinous and touristy look of things. I will rework these pictures later and blend them back into Pritchard's circle of experience, or will try to.

I stop at a little Lebanese restaurant in a quieter part of town, and eat a bowl of spiced vegetables and fish, with wild rice, and a carafe of white wine, very bitter to the taste – and then I return to the car and sit inside it to draw Pritchard's family home, which somehow makes me sad, because it looks nothing like it should, nothing like it would have looked when *she* lived here. The basic structure is still in place, but the gardens, front *and* back, have been given over to miniature golf. A prefabricated gift shop has been stuck unceremoniously onto the side of the house, and a six-foot plaster Hector is standing by the front porch, in his blue dungarees, welcoming visitors. If you shake one of his mechanical hands, he says, in a voice so sickly-sweet it makes you want to vomit: "Be sure not to miss my priceless pony ride, daily at 3 p.m., to visit Lucy Pritchard's grave!" In his other hand, he's holding a placard that reads CHILDREN GO FREE WEEKDAYS!

I try to draw the house without the things that have wrecked it, but I don't have much success, especially as people keep peering into the car to see what I'm doing. One old lady even taps on the glass, and when I wind down the window, she leans right in and says, "Are you from the TV?"

"No." I try to smile at her

"Oh." She looks disappointed. "Only I saw this show on cable last week and it said that there was going to be a big exposé programme about Lucy Pritchard coming up soon – the truth behind the legend!" She licks her lips. "You're not involved with that?" I shake my head. "You wouldn't say if you *were*, though, would you?" And she taps the side of her nose, mouths, "Say no more."

I wind my window closed, fold up my sketchpad and, for a while, I just sit there, staring at the house. Shouldn't I be able to overcome difficulties like these? Shouldn't I be able to take on the look of a professional and move through my assignment as if the truths of it didn't matter to me? I've never been very good at that, though, never perfected the art of not caring. I look at Lucy's home now and all I can think is how bad she'd be feeling if she were sitting alongside me in the passenger seat. She'd be peering through the windscreen – her small face anxious, disbelieving, her pale hands fluttering open in her lap.

"What have they done?" she'd be saying, quietly, her voice wet with tears. "What *have* they done?"

And I wouldn't know how to answer her.

I start to drive again. I leave Burntwood Creek behind and snake a route out onto the north shore road. The sky is darkening above me now and, when I wind the car window down, a stiff breeze sweeps in and whips my hair about my face as if I'm in a Tampax commercial. I lean my head back on the headrest as I drive, and breathe the sea as if it's air and not water. When I run my tongue over my lips, I am thirsty suddenly. That's how salty my skin tastes.

I am heading for Carradine, a tiny seaside hamlet where Pritchard taught before she married. She was here for less than a year – an unremarkable year at that, according to Mo's biography – but the schoolhouse where she taught is still intact: blackboard, chalks, desks – they even have a couple of her actual dresses there, pinned onto headless mannequins. The idea of a headless mannequin gives me the heebie jeebies, but I drive on regardless, and the sky continues to crowd above me, so that, by the time I reach Carradine, a fine rain is falling, and I am cold because I haven't dressed for anything but sunshine. I park outside a Baptist chapel, and reach into the back of the car for my leather jacket.

Carradine is tiny, and deserted, and off the tourist track. There's so much of Lucy Pritchard elsewhere that no one bothers to drive all the way to the empty end of the island just to see a couple of her dresses. I am the only visitor today, and I walk the entire length of the main street, and back again, in less than ten minutes. It seems to be all trees and sky and sea, no people at all: only one dog, even – a thin grey lurcher, its wiry eyebrows raised in puzzlement at the sight of me. It's sitting outside a general store that looks like it's been lifted from the set of *Little House on the Prairie* and, when I step inside, the dog steps inside with me and, at once, a tall, angular woman behind the counter starts to wave her hands in the air.

"Out! *Out!*" she shrieks.

I think for a moment that she might be talking to *me*, but then I realise she's glaring past me, at the lurcher. It glares back at her, defiant, and then it sits down.

"Filthy animal!" The woman scoops up a newspaper from the

display and leans as far as she can across the counter, starts swishing at the air. "Get your hairy butt *out* of my shop." She's out of breath, her face sealed tight with outrage. "Ooh, I'll have you one of these days, Ezekiel, swear to God I will, you miserable old cur…"

But Ezekiel has had his fill of insults for one day. He lifts himself to his feet and walks purposefully towards the door, like he has somewhere much more interesting to get to. Just as he reaches it, however, he pauses and lets out a discreet little fart.

"And don't you come back, you scabby old mutt!"

The woman huffs into her chest for a second, shaking herself straight in her clothes. She slips the newspaper back into its rack, and turns to me with a dazzling smile: all teeth and gums.

"Now, miss," she says, her voice high and bright. "What can I do for you today?"

I buy a local newspaper and a bottle of mineral water that must have been in the cooler for months. It is a baton of ice. I move it from one hand to the other and back again, and then I ask the woman for directions to the old schoolhouse, which turns out to be pretty much opposite where we are standing. She comes to the door with me when I leave, and points across the road to a grove of spruces with a rough path running between them.

"Just head on through the cut. Five minutes' walk."

"Thanks."

"You're on holiday here, are you?"

I nod. "A working holiday."

"Oh?" She folds her arms across her chest.

I remember what Mo said about not telling every stranger I meet that I'm here to illustrate a biography of Lucy Pritchard, but the woman is looking at me expectantly. Her face, up close, is grey and looks like it might be made of putty. If I pressed my finger to her cheek, I'd leave a dent.

"At least the rain's stopped." I squint up into the sky.

"For now it has."

"Oh, well. Thanks for your help."

"You're welcome."

I wave my newspaper at her jauntily. "Bye, then."

She nods, goes back into her shop and shuts the door but, as I head off to the car for my sketchpad, I can feel her eyes on me and, when I glance back over my shoulder, I can see the shape of her, gaunt and white and curious behind the glass.

I stay in the car for a while, sipping at the water, even though my teeth ache with the cold of it, and then I start flicking through the pages of the *Carradine Chronicle*. It makes me smile. This week's central headline reads, SMALL HYBRID PIG ESCAPES FROM MARKET – and it's accompanied by a picture of what looks like a pink beach ball, with legs, racing across a field. A string of men in Wellington boots are lolloping after it. If this is the most exciting and newsworthy event that happens in Carradine, then no wonder poor old Lucy had such a shit time of it while she was here. In her biography, Mo describes Lucy's year in the village as "the least stimulating and the least creative period of her life", which makes me picture her sitting on a stool, marking schoolbooks, her little round spectacles slipping down her nose, her body slouched and soggy with boredom.

When I walk back past the general store, the woman behind the glass is gone, but Ezekiel is sitting outside again, waiting for another customer to open the door so that he can slip inside and cause havoc. He is a dog who delights in pissing people off, I suspect. I like him.

I cross over the road and onto the path between the trees, following its curving route through a huddle of birches and thick brown maples. The ground beneath my feet is an ochre-red and surprisingly soft. When I glance down, I see that my boots look like they've been smeared with blood.

The schoolhouse is exactly where the woman in the shop said it would be, and it's as well-preserved as Mo's biography promised. There's a blue sign pitched outside which says, simply, "THE WRITER LUCY PRITCHARD TAUGHT AT CARRADINE SCHOOL FROM SEPTEMBER 1898 TO JUNE 1899." The door is open, so I wipe my feet on a ravelled mat in the entrance porch, and step inside. It turns out to be just one long room – rows of desks either side, and a narrow aisle down the middle. In the centre, there's a shiny black stove with a thick pipe running up into the ceiling, and at the front, there's a dark green blackboard that stretches the entire length of the wall. Either end of the blackboard, are the headless mannequins wearing Lucy's dresses.

My boots squelch softly on the floorboards. I can smell the mud I've carried in with me, and I can smell the sea leaking in through the old windows too, but there's another smell prickling sharp towards me, and I can't quite place it. I run my hands over the blackboard and feel its century of chalk dust, grainy against my fingertips, and then I pick up a nub of chalk and bring it to my lips. It is pale and lilacy when I taste it, and it drawls a whisper across the blackboard when I write my name there.

The headless mannequins would be looking at me disapprovingly, if they had heads, I'm sure, but, as it is, they just stand with their stiff backs and their ridiculously tiny waistlines, and let me touch the clothes they are wearing as if I were on intimate terms with them. I test the fabric, lift the black and green cuffs of lace onto my palm and hold them there, rustling like a handful of old leaves. These are sensible dresses, practical dresses, with high puritan necklines and long, fitted sleeves, and I realise after a moment that the sharp, animal smell in the room is coming from them, from the dresses. The fabric has turned sour with the years, with decades of damp, and tongues of salt forever licking at threads and stitching. They are unravelling, slow as the universe, but ever so gradually breaking apart, breaking down. I think of Lucy wearing these dresses, her body warm and fluid and alive inside them, her white wrist, with its heartbeat of a bird, circled by the ring of lace in my hand, and suddenly I feel intrusive and shamed.

I look away, out of the window, but there are only trees, thick with leaves set to fall, and a sky as grey as dust.

"Good afternoon."

I know that there are tears in my eyes when I spin around to the door, but I don't have time to blink them away, because a tall young woman is walking quite fast towards me, her shoes thumping like fists on the floorboards, her mouth open and smiling.

"I'm sorry I wasn't here to welcome you." She has a hammer in her hand. "I was mending one of the fences out back." And she slips the hammer onto one of the desks and wipes her palms clean on the pale thighs of her jeans. "Did you just want to have a look round on your own, or would you like the whole tour?"

"Er..." I take a breath into my lungs, hold it there, gathering myself in. "I guess the whole tour, if that's what you *do*. I mean, I didn't know there was anybody here to do that, a tour."

"Well, if you'd come this time next week, there wouldn't have been. We close up for the winter."

"Just under the wire, then."

She nods. "Is there anything particular you'd like to know, or shall I just do you the standard package?"

"Standard package'll be fine."

"Okay. Well, now." And she closes her hands together for a moment, thinking herself into it. "Lucy May Pritchard," she begins, "taught here at Carradine School from September 1898 to June 1899. While in the village, she boarded with a French Acadian family, named Robichaud, who owned a farm on the Delmont road. The two youngest Robichaud children were numbered among the fourteen pupils whom Lucy taught here. She was an efficient and well-respected schoolteacher, and an active member of the local community, particularly of the Baptist Union, where she played the organ at Sunday services..."

She sounds like a textbook, but her eyes stay bright with the shape of Lucy's days here, and she draws me into them, so that all at once I can see Lucy's little feet, in their black-buttoned boots, treading the organ pedals, her slender fingers pressing the keys... God knows how many times this woman must have said these words, watched faces like mine filling up with detail, but she doesn't look jaded, and her mouth goes on, moving over Lucy's name as if the shape of it fits snug.

"If you'd like to follow me..." – and she walks to one of the mannequins, and places her palm over the curve of its shoulder. "This is one of Lucy Pritchard's own dresses, bequeathed to Carradine School by Lucy's eldest daughter, Dr Rosalie MacKay, after her mother's death. In the only photograph taken of Lucy Pritchard and her pupils while she was here in Carradine, she can be seen wearing this very dress."

I find myself nodding. "Do you have that photograph here?"

"No. It's kept at the birthplace museum, in Burntwood Creek."

I wince slightly, remembering the six-foot plaster Hector standing guard outside Lucy's front door. "Oh."

"You've visited Burntwood Creek?"

"Unfortunately."

She grins. "Not to your liking?"

"Well, it *would* be, I suppose, if my liking was for inconceivable tackiness."

She laughs then, a nice laugh, deep and engaging.

"Well, maybe this'll be more your kind of thing then..." And she moves towards a little wooden display case set against the far wall. I stand alongside her to look down into it, but for a moment all I can see are our faces reflected in the glass – hers and mine, looking into our own eyes and into each other's. Her eyes are topaz blue, nearly translucent, and there's a line from a poem circling inside my head suddenly, as I'm looking into her eyes, looking into mine: *the voice of your eyes is deeper than all roses*. I can't remember where it comes from, but I'm thinking it – can't *stop* myself thinking it – for a moment, and she is looking at me hard now, her eyelashes long, and as black as her hair. If she fluttered her eyelashes, she could seduce a continent, I'm certain, but she doesn't flutter them. Instead, she points with her finger.

"These are the only effects that Lucy left behind her in Carradine when her year here was over. The Robichauds wrote to her to ask if she wanted the items forwarded to her, but she said no, to keep them." She moves her finger to the edge of the glass and presses it there so that it leaves a tiny print, like a breath. "The lace handkerchief has survived well, as you can see, but the gloves have disintegrated quite badly. They were very delicate to begin with, of course, and then the spectacles got broken when a tree came through the window in a storm one night and smashed the display case."

I peer through the glass – a sheen of water with green underneath – and I can make out the shape of the lace handkerchief, desiccated, creamy at the edges, *and* the small gloves, waxy-looking and frayed, black in places where the seams are open mouths. But when my eyes settle on the twisted spectacles, their arms awkwardly folded, like someone had taken them off in a hurry and were coming back for them any minute now, the breath catches in my throat and I have to look away. They look so naked, so heartbreakingly frail, and private.

I remember one time, at art school, my friend Angie decided to model for one of the life-drawing classes that I attended. She needed the money and had no fears about standing starkers in front of thirty strangers, but when she came into the room and took off her robe, I couldn't look at her. I just couldn't look. I wanted to run over to her and cover her up, tell her to go and put her clothes back on *this instant*. I couldn't concentrate on drawing her at all, because she just seemed so exposed, so unutterably vulnerable, and I knew I shouldn't be looking.

That's how I feel now, in front of the display case. I want to cover it with my body so that nobody can see in or, better still, I want to unlock it and take the fragile, intimate things inside it out, bury them somewhere, let them die.

The tour guide is looking at me. "Are you all right? You've gone really pale."

"I'm okay."

"Are you sure? Here, why don't you sit for a minute?" And she slips her fingers under my elbow and leads me to one of the desks. The chair, when I sit in it, is built for a child, so that my hipbones ache against the wood, but I'm glad, because the pain gives me something to think about and I steady myself against it.

"You could carry on with what you were saying, if you like." My voice is softer than I want it to be. I clear my throat, try again. "The rest of the tour?"

"That's about it."

"No scandal?"

She shakes her head, just the once, slips her fingers into the pockets of her jeans. "Listen. I've got a thermos of coffee out back with my tools. Shall I go and get it? It's pretty cold in here."

"No, really, I'm fine. I ought to be getting back to my car, getting back home."

"Are you driving far?"

"Port Hove, more or less."

She nods. "Shall I walk back to your car with you then?"

"No. I'm only parked out on the road. I'll be all right."

I pick up my sketchpad and the wallet of pencils, realising as I do that I haven't drawn anything here in Carradine. In fact, I've barely drawn anything all day. The blood seems to be snaking slowly through my veins, but I say, as brightly as I can, "Thanks for the standard package."

"Well, you're welcome, Abby."

"How d'you know my name?"

She gestures to the blackboard. "You're the only visitor we've had all day."

"Ah yes. Sorry about that."

"No problem. I was planning to ask you your name, if you hadn't already written it down for me."

I feel a warm, bristling sensation at the base of my spine. "Were you?"

She nods. "And you were planning to ask me mine?"

"No, I wasn't."

"But you are *now*?"

"*Am* I?"

"Yep. Because I've been very kind to you, you see, giving you the tour without charging you the ten-dollar entrance fee, offering you coffee – which I don't usually do for tourists – not reporting you to the authorities for defacing government property..." She takes a step towards me, looking into my eyes. "It would be very..." – she thinks for a moment – "... uncivil of you, to leave here without asking me my *name* at least, don't you think, Abby?"

"But I would have paid the fee if I'd known, and I didn't want any coffee, and I wasn't defacing government property. I was practising my art." I lift my sketchpad into the air as explanation. "I'm an artist."

She holds out her hand to me, smiling, fluttering her eyelashes ever so slightly. "And I'm Elise Robichaud."

Six

The air around us is very still suddenly, but the sea moves inside it like someone breathing.

"Robichaud?" I close my fingers around hers and she squeezes, keeps hold of my hand.

"Yes. My great-grandfather, Henri, was one of the Robichaud children." She lets go of my hand, but it stays where she left it, cupping the air. "And my grandma, Marie, she still lives in the farmhouse out on the Delmont Road, the house where Lucy lived while she was here." But she lowers her eyebrows at that. "It's a family home, though, the farm – not open to tourists."

"Oh, but I'm not a tourist. I mean, I'm not here to invade anybody's privacy or anything."

"You're English though, right, and on holiday here?" I nod. "And you're... an artist?" I nod again.

She lifts her chin a little, waiting for me to fill in the gaps.

"I'm..." I clear my throat, trying to think my way around it and out the other side, but... I look into her face. "I'm here to illustrate a biography of Lucy Pritchard, actually. There's a woman called Mo Laker and she's written a book about Lucy and she's paid for me to come out and illustrate it for her." I shuffle my sketchpad onto my hip like a child. "I'm supposed to draw the school. That's why I'm here, in Carradine. Not a tourist exactly, you see." I think for a moment. "More of a pseudo-tourist."

"Well, we don't get many of them in these here parts." She picks up her hammer from the desk and pushes it into the back pocket of her jeans. "I'll walk you back to your car."

This time, I don't argue, because I want her to say she'll show me the farmhouse on Delmont Road. I want her to tell me I can even draw it if I like, and if she walks me back to my car, well then, that gives me a few more minutes to prove to her that I'm genuine, and not out simply to clamber up the ivy of her ancestral home and gawp through the windows.

I follow her to the door, and she closes it behind us with a heavy click, like a full stop.

Outside, it has begun to rain quite hard, so we move fast through the trees, and twice my boots slip sideways into the mud, so that she has to reach to steady me. Each time she does, she says, "Easy there…"

The dark is coming on, and her face is pale against it, like paper – all angles and edges – stark as a shaft of sunlight.

It strikes me suddenly that I'm tramping through a dense patch of woodland, in an unfamiliar area, with a complete stranger who has a hammer in her back pocket. Nobody knows I'm here. She could turn out to be a madwoman. She could do anything she liked to me, and then roll my body into the ocean like a sack of stones, and nobody would *ever* know. She doesn't, though. Instead, she leads me safe out onto the road, and we are opposite the general store again, with Ezekiel trotting towards us on his pipe-cleaner legs.

"Hey, Zeke. Have you been causing trouble again?"

The dog knocks his head against Elise's legs, pushing through between her knees, and Elise laughs her nice laugh again, her eyes squeezing closed.

"He upset the woman in the store before," I tell her. "She went for him with a newspaper and everything."

"You'd think the two of them would've called a truce by now. They've been at it long enough."

"What d'you mean?"

"Well, he's hers. Zeke's *her* dog."

"*Hers?*" I squint towards the store, lowering my voice. "But she hated him. She called him a scabby old mutt."

"She always calls him that. Water off a duck's back, isn't it, Zeke?"

44

And she scratches at the dog's ears, slips a finger under his collar and keeps it there. "Let's get you gone, boy, eh?"

We start to walk, Ezekiel between us, his tail slicing at my calves. I can see the car up ahead, so I fumble in my pocket for the keys. They jangle like loose change, and when I take them out, Mo's "Girls Who Do Girls Do It Best" key-ring catches the light and makes Ezekiel lift his head in interest, sniffing at something sparkly. I close my fist around the keys before the dog can snap them away from me, and then I ask Elise, lightly, "Won't that old cowbag in the store mind you stealing her dog?"

She glances at me out of the corner of her eye. "That old cowbag in the store? You mean my mother?"

"Oh, Christ! She's not, is she?" I feel the blood shoot straight up into my cheeks. "Oh, shit. I'm really sorry."

But Elise is grinning at me, waving her hand. "Don't be. You're not far off the mark, to be honest."

We have walked straight past the car, so that I have to skid to a halt and rock back on my heels, turning, pointing. "This one's mine."

Elise eyes it with curiosity. "It's a beast. It's huge." She cups her hand over her eyes against the window and peers inside. The back seat is just as Mo left it: unbridled chaos. She straightens. "It's very... lived-in."

"It's my employer's car, really, Mo's car. She suffers from the *opposite* of obsessive compulsive disorder?"

"Yeah? What's that, then?"

"Couldn't-give-a-flying-fuck disorder, I think they call it."

Elise dips her head towards me. "I think I suffer from that."

"Me too."

"Well..." She clears her throat. "You drive safely then, Abby."

"Thanks." I tap around the lock with my car key, but the air is grainy now and thick-blue with twilight, and I can't find the hole. I feel stupid, tap-tapping at the metal like an old lady without her glasses, with Elise watching me, and Ezekiel's tail still patting at my

45

calves as if to hurry me along.

"Shit!" I say it very quietly, but Elise huffs a laugh into the air and takes a step toward me, gestures for the keys. I give them to her, and she drops down onto her haunches, moves her fingers over the lock for a second and then slides the key straight in without even looking, turns it, opens the door with a flourish, like a footman.

"How d'you manage that?"

She clears her throat and stands up, Mo's key-ring dangling gaudily from her thumb.

"Natural talent, I guess. Either that, or I'm just good with my fingers."

I swallow hard as she hands the keys to me and I open the door and drop my sketchpad onto the passenger seat. It falls open at the bottle of wine I drew last night, in the café. I think how I could oh *so* do with a drink right now, and I wonder about asking Elise if there's somewhere we could go, she and I, to drink and talk. But I bite back the words. She wouldn't be interested. She's a tour guide. She's just being polite, walking me back to my car after I came over all pale and ridiculous at the schoolhouse. That's all she's being – polite.

I slide myself into the driver's seat, my heart knocking tight against my ribs.

"Thanks for the tour."

"No problem." She leans down into the car, her arm curving onto the roof, and I catch how she smells: woodsmoke and oil, but something sweet, too – like fern rubbed into your fingertips.

"You'll be coming back, will you, to do your drawings?"

I nod. "Guess I'll have to."

"Maybe we'll meet again, then?"

"May*be*." I prod my key into the ignition hard and turn it. The car grumbles into life. "Thanks again." I reach out and pat Ezekiel's head and he butts against my hand, very soft, noses further forward into my lap.

"Hey, mister." I ease him away. "We barely know each other."

Elise stands up straight and tugs on the dog's collar, just the once. "Zeke." She sounds cross. "Come away." She looks into my face. "Sorry. Dogs are a bit short on social graces."

"So are people, sometimes." I catch it back. "I mean, *some* people. I didn't mean... God, I wasn't talking about you."

She leans back down into the car again and, for one stunned and confused moment, I think she might actually be about to kiss me. She doesn't, though. She just smiles and says, "You need to get something done about your starter motor. It's screwed."

"Okay."

"Nice key-ring, by the way."

And, with that, she winks at me, steps back and swings the car door closed. Mo's windows are mottled and grey, but I can see Elise through the haze as I drive away, Elise holding onto Ezekiel with one hand, lifting the other hand to wave me goodbye, and I keep sight of her in my rear-view mirror as I go, getting smaller and smaller – just a speck in the end, with an even smaller speck by her side. I keep thinking she will turn and start walking away, but she doesn't.

Back at Mo's, I make some strong black coffee and sit in front of the computer, trying to compose an e-mail to Gayle. The wind is throwing tiny pebbles against the windows, slicing through the wooden bones of the house, making them creak. I cover my ears with my hands and stare at the screen. It was only last night that I was missing Gayle so much I couldn't contain it. My heart was molten lead inside my chest with longing for her, with reaching my way back to our beginning and savouring the shine of it, but now... I shut my eyes, looking for her, watching for her face, but there's nothing there.

I stand up and walk around the room for a while, sipping distractedly at my coffee, trying to think about something else, deciding whether or not I'll go back to Carradine in the morning. I already know that I will.

I sit down in Mo's black swivelly chair and start spinning myself round in gentle circles, making the room veer in a coloured arc – towards me and away. It's on the fifth spin that my eyes skim over the titles of the books on Mo's desk, and one of them stops me spinning and makes me slide the chair forward on its little castors and switch on the cluster of spotlights above me. It's a book called *My Dear Mr. Evans,* and it's a published collection of letters from Lucy Pritchard to her lifelong Welsh penfriend, Thomas Evans. Mo quotes quite extensively from these letters in her biography, because Lucy was surprisingly candid in them, choosing to share with her penfriend details of her life that she shared with no one else. The two never met, and Mo asserts that this is why Lucy felt able to break the codes of her own privacy and spill her beans to Mr Evans without reserve. I've only ever read the excerpts that Mo uses in her book, but, when I start flicking through the pages now, I find that she has actually left *out* as much as she has put *in*. There are two long letters from Carradine for instance, and Mo makes no mention of them at all in the biography. I open the book flat on the desk and start to read.

Carradine,
Prince William Island,
Canada.

December 10th, 1898.

My Dear Mr. Evans,

I had no idea it was going to be this long before I should get around to answering your letter. You will think me a very poor penfriend indeed. All these years we have been corresponding, and I still find myself striving to match the regularity of your letters. Please excuse this most recent silence. As you will note from the unfamiliar address at the top of this page, I have been busy settling my life into the routines of a new district.

I have taken a temporary position as teacher to a rural community in the north-west corner of the Island. I am so far not over-burdened with work, as there are only fourteen pupils in the entire district. Imagine the contrast with some of the large schools I have had! But a couple of advanced pupils give me comfortably enough to do, and I simply love teaching here. The children are all so nice and intelligent. The schoolhouse is about three hundred yards from the house where I board, and is a very pleasant one in a grove of spruces. I feel as if I have lived in Carradine all of my life. It is a friendly place with lots of young people, and I am having a lively time.

The teacher here before me was Alain Robichaud. He wished to get a substitute for six months during his absence at college and my application was accepted. I board at his father's – Mr. Charles Robichaud. They are a nice family. Both Mr. and Mrs. Robichaud are as kind as can be. Emilie Robichaud, a girl of my own age, is very jolly. We share a room, get along splendidly and have no end of fun. There are two other little girls – Marguerite, aged thirteen, and Pensie, ten, both of whom I teach, and two boys. The youngest, Edouard, is about fifteen and is an enchanting little chap. He has a talent for the piano, and he and I are excellent friends.

The eldest boy, Henri, is about twenty-seven, slight, rather dark, with brown eyes. He is quite a handsome young man, although, in truth, he does not impress one as handsome at first.

The whole family and I drove across the bay to Delmont this last weekend, in order that we might attend a local wedding, and it was a fine occasion indeed, with music and dancing and a winter clam-bake down by the shore. We lingered with the wedding party late into the night and were forced to drive the buggies back across the ice in the dark. We had no end of fun and jolly chatter, there and back, to say nothing of a pleasant drive. It has not taken me too long a time to become acquainted with the Robichaud children, and I have made up my mind concerning Emilie, since I know her best of all. She has no trace of intellect or culture – no interest in anything beyond the farm where she lives and the circle of young people who compose the society she frequents, but we talk and jest and tease each other continually, and keep the house ringing with mirth and laughter.

It gratifies me to say that, all in all, I am very happily situated here in Carradine. The lines of my professional career have been cast in pleasant places this time at least.

I hope that you will write soon and share with me all your news, good and ill. I shall endeavour to be more prompt in my reply.

With all good wishes,
Lucy Pritchard

I sit back and slip the book into my lap and, for a couple of minutes, I just stare into the spotlights above me, like their glare might make things clearer, but it doesn't. Why didn't Mo quote from this letter in her book? She said that Lucy's year in Carradine was the least creative and enjoyable year of her life, but this letter to Evans sounds like Lucy was having a riot. A "lively time", she calls it. Nothing like Mo describes. The Robichaud family had welcomed her into their home, she liked the school where she was teaching, she had lots of friends, and I wouldn't mind betting she had her eye on "handsome" young Henri too. Why didn't Mo mention any of this in the biography?

I reach for my mug and take a sip of coffee, but it is luke-warm now and thin brown on my tongue, so I take it into the kitchen, empty it down the sink and pull a bottle of red wine out of the cupboard instead. I don't bother with a glass, just swig it straight from the bottle, like an old lush. There's no one here to see me, no one to stand with their hands on their hips and make me feel like white trash for not sipping gently, for not knowing which vineyard, which grape. I can see Gayle suddenly, swirling a teaspoonful of wine around in her glass, peering at it, sucking it sharp onto her teeth – barely a taste. I used to try to joke her into knocking it back in one hit, a whole glassful. I don't bother any more. I blink the image away, lift the bottle to my lips and keep it there as I walk back to the chair and pick up the book again. Lucy's second letter from Carradine is even longer than her first.

Carradine,
Prince William Island,
Canada.

March 10th, 1899.

My Dear Mr. Evans,

Thank you for your letter of December 20th, and for the generous Christmas gift which accompanied it. You have long been acquainted with my love of Mr. Tennyson's verse, so you will know that the book was received with much pleasure, and a deep gratitude. I hope that you enjoyed a restful Christmas with your family in Penclawdd, and that your mother's leg is much improved.

Christmas here in Carradine was delightful. I have never in all my life seen such a tree as the one Mr. Charles and Henri brought home. Mr. Evans, It fairly filled the parlour! Though Christmas Day was gloomy and rainy, we gave no thought to the weather, but sat down to a succulent roast-goose dinner with sweet potatoes and green beans, and a fine red wine that Mr. Charles had procured during his last trip to Vancouver. After dinner, we repaired to the sitting room and reclined on cushions around the fire, sipping at our drinks, while Pensie played the piano and sang, and the younger children gave recitations of their favourite poems. Marguerite Robichaud recited the whole of Alfred Noyes' "The Highwayman", without a word out of place, and succeeded in reducing all the ladies present to tears.

In due course, I was challenged to a game of chess and, I must confess, I rose to that challenge with all the seriousness of battle in my blood. You know how I hate to be beaten in any activity requiring the application of intellect, and chess is a game at which I have enjoyed some success in the past. I tried hard therefore to concentrate all my efforts, but the noise of the festivities eventually drove my opponent and me upstairs, and we completed our game by candlelight in the semi-gloom of my gable room.

On Boxing Day, Henri drove me over to Celleron, on the north shore road, where I spent three days with my Grandmother, who was in those parts visiting her sister. It was indeed a quiet time, after the noise and bustle of the Robichaud household, but the stillness was broken on the second day, by the welcome arrival of the Reverend Ethan MacKay. He is our minister in Burntwood Creek, and the leader of the Baptist Union there. I believe I may have mentioned to you that he and I had become good friends before I left for Carradine, and this friendship has since then deepened through a lively correspondence. He is a fine, educated man of some standing in the local community, and although there are those who accuse him of a degree of stuffiness, I do not myself see it. The Reverend Mackay spent a day with us, during the course of which he and I walked along the cliffs above Celleron in bright winter sunshine. I could have walked on into infinity. You know, Mr. Evans, how I do so love to walk, but the Reverend MacKay's hips are bad owing to an accident with a large farm animal when he was a child, so we were obliged to turn for home.

On the third day, Henri arrived in the buggy to carry me back to Carradine, and I must confess to being somewhat relieved at the prospect of departure. I love my Grandmother dearly, and my Great-Aunt, but they are both so appallingly deaf and irascible, that my nerves were fairly in ribbons by the end of my stay.

Back in Carradine, life continues most pleasantly. Today, Emilie and I are fixing up the tea grounds for a christening party, and tonight she and I and the rest of the family have been invited to the Dougray Hotel in Delmont, where a young cousin of the Robichauds,

Stella, is celebrating her engagement to a gentleman farmer from New Brunswick. It promises to be a grand affair indeed. We are to spend the night at the hotel, which is something I have never done in all my life before. I am quite nearly dead with the anticipation of it, although what I am to wear to the event, the Good Lord himself only knows. All my dresses are so very proper. *Oh, the limitations of a country schoolmarm's wage!*

I trust that this letter finds you well, Mr. Evans, and may I take this opportunity to wish you a happy and healthy New Year, the last year, as it is to be, of the old century. I wonder what the new century will hold for us.

With all good wishes,
Lucy Pritchard

That was Lucy's last word from Carradine. Her next letter to Evans is dated September 1899, and she's living in the village of Summerskill, at the eastern tip of the island, and she's married to the Reverend Ethan MacKay. I flick to the back of the book and scan the index for any more references to Carradine, but there are none. I look under Robichaud, because surely she must have kept in contact with the family, but there's no further mention of them, either.

I sit back in Mo's chair and start spinning again, very slowly. There's a picture of Lucy pinned to the wall above the desk and, each time I spin past it, her eyes meet mine and hold my gaze. If she was having such a wonderful time in Carradine, as the two letters to Evans suggest, then why did she never write to him *again* from there? Maybe she was simply too busy with her parties and her buggy rides and all her new friends, but if that's the case, then why does Mo say that Carradine was a dead loss for Lucy – socially barren, mind-numbingly dull?

I stop spinning and look hard into Lucy's face. She has her head inclined, and her chin lifted, like she might be listening for something, and her lips are parted, just a little. She isn't smiling. Her eyes are black as onyx in this picture, heavy-lidded, and she's wearing an expensive-looking dress with puffed sleeves to the elbow and a narrow 'V' of dark silk dipping at the waist. On her head is a hat, like a small, black satellite dish, with a single peacock's feather poking out of it. I know, from Mo's book, that this is one of a set of photographs that Lucy had taken at a studio in Vancouver, the day after she accepted the Reverend MacKay's proposal of marriage. She looks defiant in this picture, resolute. Her eyes keep hold of mine, not letting go, not giving anything away.

I decide to ring Mo. I need to ask her about getting the car fixed, assuming Elise is right about the starter motor being up the Swanee of course – and, also, it will give me a chance to tell her what I've done so far, such as it is, and maybe to ask her about Carradine too, but when I dial her mobile number it's a man's voice that answers, very loud.

"Yes?"

"Oh, hello." I hesitate. "Actually, I think I might have the wrong number."

"Who d'you want?"

"Mo Laker."

"Yep. She's here. Hang on." His voice veers away, muffles. "Mo. Some girl for you." And then his voice veers back, bumps against my ear. "She's just coming."

"Thanks."

He sniffs. "You her girlfriend?"

"No, just a friend."

"That's a shame. You could have come down and joined us. We could have made a night of it, the three of us." He sniffs again. "I'm always telling Mo she doesn't know what she's missing. She could do with a good seeing-to if you ask me. You all could. The way I look at it..."

"Give me the phone, Ryan!" It's Mo, sounding breathless and annoyed. There's some scuffling, then, "Hello?"

"Hey, Mo. It's me, Abby."

"Oh, hi." She brightens. "How's it going, love?"

"Fine. Who the hell was *that*?"

"My editor, I'm afraid."

"Blimey O'Reilly."

"Hmm. I *know*. Was he giving you a hard time?"

"I think he was up for giving us *both* a hard time."

She chuckles. "Ignore him. He's drunk. You okay then?"

"Yep. Getting on, you know how it is..." I clear my throat. "But I think we might have a problem with the car."

"What problem?"

"Well, this woman I met, while I was in Carradine, she said she thinks the starter motor needs looking at."

Mo is quiet for a moment. I can hear the clatter of crockery in the background, a hum of voices.

"Carradine?"

"Yes. I was there, drawing the school, and, well... anyway. Shall I take it to a garage for you?"

"What woman in Carradine?"

"She was the tour guide."

She doesn't say anything for a moment. The air hisses lightly between us. Someone is calling her name.

"Don't worry about the car," she says at last, very quickly. "I'll sort it out when I get back. It'll be okay until then, I'm sure." Then she hesitates, adds carefully, "Did you draw the school?"

"No, actually. I need to go back tomorrow and do it."

"Don't bother. Looks like we're going to be pushed for time on the book after all. They've brought the publication date forward, for various reasons, so you just concentrate on drawing the main sights, the ones at the top of the list I left for you. Okay?"

"Okay, if you think so, but..."

"I *do* think so." And her voice slams shut. "Look, I must go, Abby. See you Friday."

"For sure, yeah."

She hangs up, leaves me standing with the receiver cupped my against my neck – slick as a bone, as grey as dismay.

Seven

They say that nearly all of a writer's work takes place in his unconscious. It's *there* that the last word is written before the first word ever appears on paper. He doesn't invent the details of his story. He remembers them. Well, that's what it's been like for me today, driving across the island, drawing all the places on Mo's list: houses, churches, rocky stretches of coast, small slate villages huddled in the blue. They were already there somehow, in my fingers, in the shades my pencils chose, the lines they traced, and the more I drew, the simpler it all became – as if I wasn't making anything new at all, just reaffirming something old. I've been working hard. I left the house at seven this morning and I've been on the move ever since. Mo would be proud of me, and that's the plan, of course. If she gets back on Friday to find that I've drawn all the places on her list, just as she asked, then she can't really tell me off for going back to Carradine.

I leave it until last. I don't hurry any of my work. I let the day melt slowly on my tongue, but the thought of Carradine sits at the back of everything, showing through, like a watermark, and by the time I start to drive the last stretch of highway towards the village, the afternoon has already begun to fold itself down into dark. I doubt I'll be able to draw the schoolhouse today, with the sea-light fading so fast, but then it strikes me, of course, that I haven't actually come to draw the schoolhouse. I've come to ask Elise about Lucy's letters.

I park outside the general store, its little lights blinking at me earnestly, and then I make my way quickly through the trees. If Elise was working here this time yesterday, then hopefully she'll be *out back* with her hammer again today but, when I reach the school, its doors are locked shut and Elise is nowhere to be seen. I walk all the way around the building and around the perimeter fence, too. I even walk a little way into the woods that scramble dark-green down towards the sea, but the light there is thin as water, so I double back and stand, slightly breathless, with my hands on my hips.

It is then that I hear a sound – a rustling sound, rhythmical, getting closer. I peer hard into the darkness, thinking there might be a fox or a badger out there, snuffling its harmless way home. Then I remember that there *are* no foxes or badgers on Prince William Island. Maybe it's a bear then and, if it is, well, that's okay, because I know exactly what to do. I read it in a book. You have to roll about in the foliage for a minute of two, so you smell like the forest, and then you have to prostrate yourself on the ground and pretend to be dead. I could do that. Although, in that same book, there was a story about a woman who'd encountered a bear while she was trekking through Sumatra, and he'd carried her off to his den in the hills and kept her there. She'd had a whale of a time, apparently – eating coconut buds, green leaves, sweet papaya; sleeping all summer long in a bear's embrace, his coat as black as molasses, sleek as sin. When the forest rangers came to rescue her, she didn't want to go. She said she'd fallen in love, with the bear. I could do that, if it *is* a bear out there in the trees, but what if it's a homicidal maniac instead? I'm not so sure I could fall in love with a homicidal maniac. Fortunately for me, it's neither. It's Ezekiel.

"I *thought* that was you, Abby."

For one mentally deficient moment, I think it's actually Ezekiel who's spoken, as he shambles his way towards me, with his ears falling in a heap about his head, but then I see that there's someone following and, when I see who it *is*, my heart splashes light inside my chest, and I start to smile.

"I didn't think you were coming back today."

Elise's face, up close, is broken into pieces by the dark.

"I said I would, though, didn't I, to draw the school?"

"But it's too dark."

I hesitate, looking around me as if I've only just noticed. "Yes, it is."

"So, then?" She lifts her hands, palms upward – pale starfish swimming through the air. "How were you going to draw the school if you couldn't see it?"

Ezekiel has settled himself across my feet, rooting me to the spot. I clear my throat, ready to tell Elise the *real* reason I'm here but, just as the real reason is about to come out of my mouth, it starts to look a bit ridiculous. I mean, what does it matter, really, if Mo didn't go into detail about Lucy's time in Carradine? The biography is supposed to be a critical one, concentrating on Lucy's writing, not on her buggy rides about town. And, if Lucy doesn't mention Carradine or the Robichauds after she leaves them, well, that's her prerogative, isn't it? She was entitled to move on. We all are. I look into Elise's face, feeling stupidly like Nancy Drew, minus the sensible shoes and the plaits, but ready to accept that there's probably nothing nasty in this woodshed after all.

"I just timed it wrong," I say at last, shyly. "I thought there'd still be enough light."

"The dark comes on quick here." She sounds like a character out of a Thomas Hardy novel. "We best be getting out of the woods."

"Why? Are there bears?"

"No." She loops her arm around my shoulder and switches on the torch in her hand. It throws a cone of minty-coloured light onto the path ahead. "Weasels."

"Weasels?"

"Yep."

"But they're not dangerous."

"One on his own, maybe not, but these woods are *full* of weasels, and when they're in a big old pack like that, they can get pretty vicious. They're the Mafia of the small mammal world you know, weasels."

"Really?"

Elise nods, and I can feel the pressure of her arm across my shoulder blades suddenly – the weight of it, like approval. Behind us, in the trees, I catch the murmur of the Mafia weasels – demanding money with menaces, drinking hard liquor, leaving squirrels' heads in people's beds.

I feign a coughing fit, to cover my laughter and, when Elise asks me if I'm okay, I tell her I'm just cold. She snuggles me into her body, all the way back to the road – her hair moving against mine:

black as molasses, sleek as sin.

*

The lights in the general store are out by the time we get back to Mo's car. I fumble for my keys.

"*Déjà vu.*" Elise's voice has a smile inside it. "Us in the dark. Big car. Tasteful lesbian key-ring…"

"It's not mine."

"So you said."

Ezekiel is walking in circles around us, between us.

"I was thinking." Elise takes a breath, looks away from me towards the trees, but they are black against black now: nothing to see. "Would you like to get a drink, before you go? There's a bar." She points down the road, towards the ocean. "You said you were cold."

"Something to warm my cockles, you mean?"

Why I choose now to use *that* phrase for the first time, God only knows. I try to bite it back, but Elise is laughing light, like breathing.

"That's one way of putting it."

"I don't think so." I've said the words before I realised I was thinking them. "I ought to be getting back, that's all."

"Someone waiting for you?"

Gayle's face ripples across my vision, her features going astray, like sunlight under water. I blink my eyes closed.

"Not exactly."

"Just one drink. I'll walk you back after."

I slip Mo's key-ring into my pocket, very slowly. "Okay, then."

She doesn't put her arm around me this time. We walk with Ezekiel between us, and we don't say very much. I watch my feet stepping into the torchlight, looking surprisingly delicate, like a dancer's feet, the toes of my boots lifting light and then dark, over and over.

After a few minutes, the black air changes to grey, then to ochre, and suddenly we are standing outside the diminutive Merchantman's Pub. It's set apart from the houses, nothing behind it but the water. Its fluted windows are full of stars and sky. It reminds me of one of those old-fashioned seaside cafés at home, selling ice cream and kiss-me-quick hats and little spinning windmills on sticks, but this establishment doesn't sell any of those things. It sells liquor and pork scratchings, and that's about it.

Inside, Elise orders two large brandies from a landlord with a red beard, who winks at me, and keeps winking at me whenever I catch his eye, and then we sit by the fire to drink them. The lights are low, and the bar is empty, except for us and Ezekiel, who stretches himself out like a rug across our feet.

I sip my brandy quickly and it bronzes my throat, sets my stomach softly ablaze. I can feel my eyes narrowing.

"So, this is Carradine nightlife, then?" I look pointedly around the room.

"It's early yet. It'll pick up later. There's fiddle music here most nights."

"Woo *hoo!*" I don't mean it to sound disparaging, but it does.

"Can you play any instruments, Abby?"

"No. You?"

She shakes her head, unsmiling. "That's why I have such a lot of respect for people who *can*."

I take a big sip of my brandy, feeling crass and stupid, but my voice, when it comes, is spiked with drink, and defensive.

"I guess I just don't have the discipline it takes to learn an instrument."

"Drawing's disciplined, though, isn't it?"

"Different kind of discipline."

She slides her elbows onto the table and lifts her glass to her lips, holds the brandy in her mouth for a moment before she swallows. She keeps her eyes on me, very dark.

"What d'you mean?"

"Well, it's not something you learn, exactly. I mean, you learn to be better at it; you discipline your skills. But you don't learn *it* itself, really. It's already there when you start out."

"It's a gift, then, you mean, natural talent?"

"That always sounds so self-righteous, though."

"It shouldn't. If you're good at something, you should be proud of being good at it."

"I dunno. I'm not sure about pride. I'm not even sure I'm any good and, anyway, people say that drawing's like writing or composing music. It's merely the refuge of the miserable. Happy people don't write or draw or anything for its *own* sake, because they're fully employed in living instead…" I fall over the cliff edge of what I'm saying and drain my glass as fast as I can. "Like you, maybe, Elise." Her name smoothes itself over my tongue. "*You're* fully employed in living."

She smirks. "What makes you think that?"

"Well, you're *out* there, in the world, aren't you? The natural world, I mean? You work outdoors, with your tools, and you know about fences and cars, and weasels…" I swallow really hard, hoping the winking landlord will come swooping in to clear our glasses, but he doesn't. "You're at one with nature, aren't you?"

Elise sits back in her chair, grinning at me. "I'm a history teacher."

"Pardon me?"

"I'm a history teacher. I work in Vancouver. I've only come back to the island for the summer. I don't usually come at all, but my sister's in Europe, travelling, and I'm covering for her, doing the school tours and helping out with Grandma."

I drop my elbows onto the table.

"God, I feel stupid."

"Don't." She touches my arm with the tips of her fingers. "I'm flattered, really. Suddenly, I'm the Henry Thoreau of the dyke world. I like it." She stands and scoops both our glasses up in one hand. "Another drink?"

I look into her face, the light behind her, little sparks of yellow bouncing into the corners of my eyes, and I nod.

"Just a small one."

"Are you hungry? Would you like some pork scratchings?"

But I lift my hands, waving the prospect away. "I can't eat anything that has hair on it."

"Wise woman."

She lingers a moment longer, standing there looking at me, smiling down at me. I think I should maybe say "Ta-da!" in a bright little voice, giving her permission to go, but she goes on her own in the end, and I watch her at the bar, my eyes stalking her. I can't help it. I'm not even *trying* to help it. But, when she turns towards me with our drinks, I pretend I'm not looking, start to make a fuss of Ezekiel instead. I think he may have been fast asleep, actually, because he jerks his head up sudden when I touch him and bumps it hard on the table leg. He scowls up at me reproachfully.

A few more people have begun to come in now, and Elise nods to them, calls hello. They glance at her and nod, and then they glance at me and raise their eyebrows.

"Friends of yours?" I ask Elise, when she sits down.

"Just neighbours." She lifts her glass. "What shall we drink to?"

"Don't know."

"How about chance encounters? Hey, no. Even better. How about *fate*?"

"Okay."

I should tell her. I should stop flirting, or whatever it is I'm doing here, and I should just come right out and tell her about Gayle, and suggest that maybe we just drink to each other's good health instead. But I don't tell her.

We clink our glasses together, hold them touching for a moment, then we drink, and the brandy is a flash of crimson in my mouth. I feel like a fire-eater. I know, when I speak, my words will come out forked with flame, but suddenly it's Elise's words that are forked with flame.

"You wear a ring on your wedding finger," she says.

"Yes."

I slide my glass onto the table, but it catches on a knot of wood, so that I have to reach to steady it. Elise is looking at my hand. I know she's thinking about touching it. She leans towards me a little, then away. I move both my hands under the table.

"Is it a special ring? Was it a gift?"

"In a manner of speaking, both, really."

"Why d'you wear it on your wedding finger?"

"Well, that would be because…" I look her straight in the eye, try to hold my reflection steady. "That would be because it's *kind of* my wedding… ring, really, I guess."

I know it's not possible that I actually *see* her face darken. I know that faces can't physically darken. Maybe it's the veil of air between us that changes colour, then. The sheen splinters. There was light before, and now there's a kind of grey, like smoke. It hurts my eyes.

"Your wedding ring."

She doesn't say it like it's a surprise, and she's nodding her head, politely interested, but she won't look at me. She reaches under the table and ruffles her fingers hard through Ezekiel's fur.

"So, you're *kind of* married, then?" Her voice goes up on the first syllable of "married".

"I am."

"Who to?"

"Gayle."

"Right." And she looks at me then, holds my gaze. "And you're happy… being *kind of* married, to Gayle?"

I don't know what to say to her. I've opened my mouth to say yes, but the word has turned tail and run for the hills. I pick up my glass instead and drink my brandy, and Elise does the same, and then she stands up. Ezekiel sidles out from under the table, and they both stand there then, side by side, looking at me. I want to say something wise and helpful and clarifying, but wise, helpful, clarifying things are scarcer than hen's teeth in situations like these.

Elise throws me the dying star of a smile.

"I'll walk you back to your car," she says.

The bearded landlord winks at me flamboyantly as we leave, but I don't feel as if I deserve any winking, flamboyant or otherwise. I deserve a slow death, involving red ants maybe, lots of them, or disembowelment.

Eight

Mo's car won't start. If there's ever been a time I wanted to get away from somewhere with a screech of tyres and a whirl of dust, it's now, but Mo's car just won't start. I turn the key in the ignition, over and over, but the engine just clicks, very soft, like it's clearing its throat.

Elise stands outside the general store with her hands in her pockets, watching me. She's turned the torch off. I can't see her face. She's indistinct now, a set of shapes, but the night air falls cold and sullen around her, and it's started to rain, so she's getting wet. I just wish she'd turn and go. Eventually though, she comes over to the car and taps on the window. I wind it down very slowly.

"You didn't get the starter motor sorted, did you?"

"Mo said she'd do it when she got back on Friday."

She leans into the car so that our faces are close, and then she pulls the keys out of the ignition.

"Friday's too late, Abby."

"What d'you mean?"

"I mean it's dead. You're not gonna get it started tonight. I'll call the garage in Celleron for you in the morning."

"In the morning?" My voice is very high. "Can't we call somebody now, though? A breakdown service?"

"A breakdown service isn't going to have a new starter motor for *this*." And she steps back a little, looking at the Mo's car like it's a taxing maths problem. "The garage in Celleron might have one, but I don't know. They could order you one in, maybe."

"But how am I going to get back to Port Hove tonight?"

"You're not."

I climb out of the car. "I'll get a cab."

"There aren't any."

The rain is streaking between us, white against the black. Elise blinks hard against it.

"You can stay the night with us. Mom won't mind."

"I don't think that's such a good idea." I fold my arms across my chest, little runnels of ice water seeping under my clothes, snaking over my skin. "There must be an alternative."

Elise shrugs. "It's up to you, Abby." She has to raise her voice over the swell of the rain, huge drops bouncing now onto the roof of the car, slow-motion explosions of water. "But it'll be okay," she says. "If you come back with me." She closes her hand around my wrist. "Mom and Gran will be there. You'll be okay."

I want to shout to her that I'm not worried about *that*. I know I'll be okay. I don't doubt her and I don't fear her. Maybe I should, but I don't. It's not *her* intentions that I'm questioning here, and it's not *her* resolve. It's my own.

But I reach into the car for my bag, because what else can I do, and then I close the door and lock it. When I turn to her, she has switched the torch on again. Her face is all dips and hollows, a collage of shadow.

"Is it far, Elise?"

"No."

She turns away from me, calls to Ezekiel, who has been sheltering under the trees, and the dog trots ahead of us home, leading the way, very upright, like it's his job. There's something of the mountain rescue dog about him, it strikes me – blazing us a path through the dark, bristling with doggy zeal. Except that Ezekiel doesn't like puddles. He tiptoes over them, fastidious, and, when another dog starts barking at him from behind a fence, he darts off into the undergrowth and disappears.

Lucy said, in her letter to Evans, that the Robichaud farm was only three hundred yards from the school where she taught, but we seem to run for miles, Elise and I, before she at last slows to walking and then steps off the road onto a gravel driveway. I follow her, very quiet, my breath lifting like a wane of smoke. The rain is beginning to ease now.

"Are you sure they won't mind?"

"Gran'll be asleep."

"What about your mum?"

We walk round to the back of the house – a big house. I can't make out the shape of it very well. I press my hand against the door frame while Elise unlocks the door, and the wood is so cold, it sticks to my fingers.

"Mom won't mind."

But she whispers it as we step inside, as if maybe her mum actually *will*. There's nothing I can do about it now. I follow Elise into the kitchen, and we slip off our wet shoes, pull a couple of chairs up close to the steaming black range, and hang our jackets over the backs of them.

The kitchen is warm and full of light, and I can smell roasting coffee beans and something sweet, like cinnamon. I've never been in a kitchen as big as this one. It would take a good few seconds to walk all the way across it. I think of my tiny kitchen at home. If you stand in the middle of it and stretch out your arms, you can touch both walls at once. I press my fingers to my temples and Elise asks me if I'm all right.

"I feel bad about this."

"Don't. It's no trouble."

"Isn't it?"

She looks away from me sharply. "No. You can have Gen's room."

"Gen?"

"My sister. Genevieve. I told you she was away, in Europe."

She opens a tall cupboard in the corner, pulls out a couple of towels and tosses one of them to me. I ruffle it through my hair to dry. God knows what I must look like, but the words *backwards*, *through* and *hedge* come swiftly to mind.

67

"It's Lucy's room," says Elise. "I mean, it's the room Lucy stayed in while she was here."

I feel a small chill and I'm not sure why.

"Lucy's room."

I don't say it as a question, but Elise inclines her head.

"But I thought you'd like that. Seeing where she lived." Her hair is sticking up where it's wet. She runs her fingers through it, makes it worse. "I can ask Gran if it's okay for you to draw it, if you'd like to, for the book. She's a private person, Gran, but I bet she'd be cool about it, as it's you."

"Me?"

She steps back on her heels, lets her head drop, just a touch.

"You know what I mean," she says.

It is at that point, that her mother comes quick-stepping into the room, her feet swift and soundless in fluffy slippers.

"Elise," she says, when she sees me. "I didn't know you were bringing someone home?" She keeps her eyes on me while she says it, and she's smiling, but something that *isn't* a smile is twitching at the corners of her mouth. "You came into the store yesterday." She points at me, vaguely, holds her face towards me.

"That's right. You gave me directions to the school."

"Abby's car broke down." Elise steps between us. "I said it would be okay for her to stay."

"Of *course.*" She's wearing a long, floral dressing gown, and she pats at her chest for a second, thinking. "Elise can make you up a bed on the sofa."

"I said she could have Gen's room, actually."

She turns towards her daughter then, full tilt. "Gen's room?"

"The sofa will be fine, really." I fold the towel that Elise has given me, neat as I can – a good houseguest. "I'm just sorry to inconvenience you."

"It's no inconvenience." She reaches out and pats my arm, just the once. Her hand is pink, very warm. "Gen won't mind you borrowing her bed for the night, I'm sure, what with her being on the other side of the world and all." She turns to Elise. "Well, I'm away to my bed then, Elise. You'll have to do your best to entertain... Abby." She spins back to me. "It *is* Abby, isn't it?"

"It is."

"Well, it's nice to meet you, *again*."

And she laughs, a sudden, sharp, tinkly laugh, like someone tap-tapping a glass with the tip of a spoon. The tiny bones inside my ear resonate.

"I'm Ruth, by the way." Her laughter stops as abruptly as it began.

I start to lift my hand and extend it, thinking she's angling for a proper introduction. She sees me doing it, watches me reaching my hand towards her, but she doesn't raise hers to meet it. Instead, she slips both her hands into the pockets of her dressing gown, and then she turns and leaves the room.

"She minds," I say to Elise, after she's gone. "She minds a lot. Are you sure I shouldn't just go?"

"Go where?"

"Isn't there a motel or a B&B, or something?"

"No." She opens the door of the refrigerator and pulls out two bottles of beer, hisses them open on the edge of the counter. She hands one to me. "Don't worry about Mom. She's just a bit territorial. She doesn't mean to be rude."

I lift the beer to my lips and taste it, but its bitterness makes my eyes water.

"I'll fix us something to eat." Elise opens the refrigerator again and roots around inside it. "Why don't you go and change out of those wet clothes? Gen should have some stuff in her closet that'll fit you." She turns towards me with a huge bunch of leeks in her hand – a poor man's bouquet. She points it in the direction of the stairs. "Her room's the first on the left."

"Thanks."

I move past her, through the open door, my bare feet aching on the wooden floor, but she calls after me, "Pasta okay, Abby?"

"Lovely." I give her the best smile I can, but I can feel blood pulsing fast into my temples now, and I've started trembling. There's something very cold pushing out from inside me, or pushing *in*. I can't tell which.

"That *would* be lovely, yes," I say again, deliberate, but Elise takes a step towards me.

"Look. About what happened, in the pub?" She still has the leeks in her hand. I look at them, and keep looking at them. Their long, silky leaves are pock-marked and pale as water. "I'm sorry I reacted badly." She takes another step. I can feel her heat, smell the musk of the rain on her clothes. "I shouldn't have assumed anything about you and your life."

"It wasn't your fault. I should have explained earlier."

"You shouldn't have *had* to. It wasn't my business."

"Yes, it was. I knew what I was doing. I mean, I knew what impression I was giving you." I shake my head, lifting my hand, and pressing it lightly to her chest. I can feel the beat of her heart against my palm, complex channels of muscle and sinew twisting in my grasp. "I just wanted…" But I don't have the words for what I wanted, or even the right to have wanted it.

"What? What did you want, Abby?"

She says it quietly, mildly, looking into my eyes, but suddenly her face starts to fragment and the air becomes difficult to breathe. Her hair is deep black, curling back over her ears, sticking damp to the collar of her shirt. I lift my hand, slow, pushing my fingers forward, circling them around the back of her neck, into her hair. It feels like wet feathers in my fingers, barely there at all. And then I kiss her, and I didn't even know I was going to do it. Right until that moment, I thought I was just going to slip away upstairs and come back composed, wearing another woman's clothes, a new skin. But I kiss her, and she kisses me back, pushing her tongue inside my mouth, tasting me like I'm a new thing, and irresistible. I angle my throat towards her and she kisses me deeper, keeps the kiss soft and open, but something starts to seep warm into my belly, so that I have to pull away. I smooth my forehead against her shoulder blade, my hands still moving on her body.

"Adultery in the heart." I whisper it into her clothes. "That's what they used to call it, at church, when I was young. Adultery in the heart."

"Abby."

She tries to make me lift my head, but I won't do it. My voice when it comes again is dust.

"They used to say that if you were committed to one person and you so much as *looked* at someone else with desire, then you were committing adultery, in your heart, and that was just as bad as doing it for real."

"Yes." She's standing very still now, her arms tight around my shoulders. I can feel her taking my weight. "You believe it's true?"

"I do."

I try to straighten up, lean away from her, but her hands catch me back.

"I shouldn't stay here, Elise. I mean, I shouldn't be doing this, with you. This isn't what I *do*. I've never done this."

"It'll be okay."

"No, it won't."

"We'll pretend it didn't happen." She bumps her head soft against mine, running her fingers over my hair. "We'll undo it."

"How?"

"Well, maybe not undo it exactly, but... diffuse it."

"I don't understand."

She looks away from me, her face biting hard into a smile that has no substance.

"It was just a kiss." She curves her hands over my shoulders, presses her thumbs into my skin, fusing us. "We'd both been thinking about it, wondering what it would be like, and now we know. It's

71

done, and the world hasn't ended, and it won't."

"Just a kiss?"

She nods. "A good kiss." And she smiles at me like she means it then. I can almost believe she means it.

"And tomorrow," she says, "we'll get your car fixed and you'll head off into the sunset, and that'll be it."

"Forgotten."

The word is barbed when I say it, but Elise nods, and takes her hands away from my shoulders, very slow.

"Go and get changed, Abby. You're cold. You're shaking."

I turn away from her, but I can feel her watching me. All the way up the stairs, I can feel her watching me. I don't turn back to look. I keep my eyes on the carpet beneath my feet – cornflower blue, with tiny red speckles. It's as spongy as new grass, and so warm after the cold wood of the kitchen. I focus on the warmth. I sink into my body and let the tide of physicality take me. My bones ache deep with the damp, and my head hurts. I think about the brandy I drank in the pub, and a swell of nausea lifts into my throat and settles there.

Once I'm safe inside Gen's room, I just sit down heavily on the bed and lean forward as far as I can, trying to steady my breathing, but I can't do it.

Gayle. Her face has been eluding me for days, but now of course, it's all I can see: her eyes, almond-shaped and sleepy; the way the corners of her mouth turn up even when she isn't smiling; the shape her hair makes when it dovetails down pale against her neck... I close my eyes, close my hands tight in my lap, but they are filled with wet feathers still, and I don't know how to empty them.

Just a kiss. Just a kiss. I say it over and over inside my head, like a mantra, and I keep saying it while I climb out of my wet clothes and choose some fresh ones from Gen's closet. I find a pair of soft khaki jeans that just about fit me, and a black fleece top. They feel good against my skin – comforting, like touch. I use a brush on the dresser to tidy my hair and then I bunch it up into a fist and secure it with one of Gen's slides – which is the colour of mahogany, shaped like a Star of David.

Looking round the room, I take in what Gen must be like, and I warm to her. This room is all about comfort. The walls are painted in rich, Mediterranean colours, and there are big exotic cushions everywhere, and books everywhere, and swathes of silky material netting the room, turning the ceiling into a sky. There are a few drawings pinned to the wall, nudes mostly, good ones. I wonder if Gen has done them herself. She seems to like pictures. Her nightstand is crowded with photographs in frames. I pick one up at random: a slim girl on a horse, looking back over her shoulder. She's wearing a white shirt, and jodhpurs and long, tan riding boots. She has a riot of dark hair, and eyes that are indigo, blazing black with laughter. She's unmistakable, the spitting image of her sister.

On the wall above her bed is a large sepia photograph, a studio portrait that catches my eye. I kneel up to get a closer look.

"The Robichauds in their Sunday best, no less."

Elise is leaning in the doorway. She hands me the bottle of beer that I left downstairs and then she moves behind me, so that she's looking at the portrait too. It's a family photograph, and nobody in it is smiling.

"It was taken in 1899," she says.

"While Lucy was here?"

"On the day she left, actually. She paid for it, as a leaving present, a gesture of thanks."

"And this is all of them, the whole family?"

"Yep." Elise points to the two people in the centre of the picture: a sturdily middle-aged couple, seated. "My great-*great*-grandparents, Charles and Frederica."

I look closely. Charles Robichaud is a long, thin, angular man, with a face like a wet flannel hung too long on a doorknob, and his wife looks exactly like Whistler's mother: a lacy handkerchief balanced airily on her head, her pointed chin jutting towards the camera like she might be wanting to take the photographer's eye out with it.

"And then there's Henri of course, my great-grandfather, and next is Emilie..."

"She looks like you." I turn slightly, so that I can see Elise out of the corner of my eye. "Emilie. She looks a bit like you."

"Funny you should say that. It's usually the similarity between Emilie and Gen that people comment on."

I look back to the picture. Henri and his sister are standing close together, behind their parents, leaning into each other a little. Henri isn't quite looking at the camera, but Emilie is, her face tilted slightly upward, hair falling loose about her shoulders. Her hands are folded across the front of her dress, and she's holding something in them. A flower, a single flower. A rose, maybe, but it's difficult to tell for sure.

To the left of Henri, there's a younger man, in an ill-fitting suit and a high collar.

"Edouard?" I ask Elise, pointing.

"Yes." She hesitates. "You know their names, then?"

"I read Lucy's letters from Carradine. The ones she sent to her pen friend, Thomas Evans. She talks about the family."

Elise doesn't say anything, but I feel her shift a little behind me.

"And the two girls?" I point again, sparking my voice with interest, trying to break the ache of tension.

"Marguerite and Pensie. But then, you already knew that."

"I didn't know what they looked like."

"Well, now you do."

Her voice is brittle and, when I turn to look at her, there's something webbed behind her eyes.

"I've made some coffee," she says, "and now I'm gonna cook. I thought you'd maybe like to watch some TV, or something."

"Sure."

I follow her down the stairs and into the living room. It's huge, and all wood – very sleek and brown, and functional. There are bookcases all around the walls, packed with antique volumes. When I look at them closely, I see that not only are all the fiction books arranged in alphabetical order, by author, but the non-fiction books are shelved according to the Dewey Decimal System: precisely numbered by subject.

"Are there any librarians in your family, Elise?" I call to the kitchen.

"Not as far as I know." Her voice clatters among the cutlery. "There are a couple of vicars, though."

"Anally retentive vicars?" I say it very quietly, but Elise pops her head around the door all of a sudden, makes me jump.

"Sorry?" She has a long, thin packet of spaghetti in her hand. "Did you say something?"

"I was just wondering about all these books."

"Ah, yes. They're Mom's pride and joy. Her *libra-rerry*, as she calls it."

"She has a passion for literature?"

"She likes the way they look."

"Oh."

She disappears, and I switch on the TV and settle myself into an exceptionally squashy armchair. I seem to disappear into it, until just my head is showing, or so it feels, and then I use the remote control to flick through the channels, settling at last on an old episode of *Buffy the Vampire Slayer*. It's the one where Buffy's nice friend, Willow, has a super-evil vampire alter ego who is running amock in a black leather catsuit. I can remember watching this episode with Gayle. I can remember her talking at length about how vampires didn't exist and had never existed, and how network television shouldn't be perpetuating the myth that they *did*. Me? I just liked the funky costumes in that episode, and the fact that the actress who played Willow got to be bold and bad for once, and sassy, and sexually up for pretty much anything.

By the time Elise comes into the room with two bowls of pasta on two trays, I have almost forgotten where I am, which was the plan all along, of course. She has to say my name twice before I look up.

"Thanks."

"You okay?"

"Sure." I nod toward the screen. "Sidetracked by Buffy, that's all."

"Easily done."

She sits down in the squashy chair to my left, sinks deep.

"You know," she says, "they say that everyone, sooner or later, falls in love with Buffy. You won't be able to mark the *exact* moment it happens, the precise episode, but suddenly, you'll be sucked in – no pun intended – and there'll be no going back."

"Is that so?"

"Yep. She's irresistible, eventually, for everyone."

"Why's that?"

"Dunno." Elise starts to eat. "Something about the irony, maybe. I mean, in every other movie or book or TV show, if some tiny little blonde woman wandered into a dark alley, late at night, then that would be *it* for her. Curtains. But Buffy." She looks delighted. "She kicks ass."

"So it's her fighting skills that you admire? It isn't the fact that she's a foxy babe sex kitten" – I glance at the screen – "in kinky boots?"

"That too."

I start to eat the food that Elise has prepared, and it's lovely: spaghetti with chopped leeks and artichokes and pine nuts, in a creamy sauce. She has sprinkled a few tarragon leaves over the top, just like they do in Tuscany. I can remember going there with Gayle, years ago, and thinking that the tarragon leaves looked like dandelion stems, tiny green tongues. I wouldn't eat them then. I do now.

"This is great," I tell her, meaning it. "Where did you learn to cook like this?"

"Grandma."

"Is she Italian?"

"Nah. She's French Acadian, like the rest of us."

"I don't really know what that means? Sorry. I know that Canada has a big French population, but, *Arcadian*?" I lift the bottle of beer to my lips. It fizzes metallic on my tongue – thin and sharp after the pearly sweetness of the pasta. "What *is* that, exactly?"

Elise smiles. "Not *Arc*adian. *Ac*adian."

"I still don't know what that means."

"It comes from the Greek originally. Means *rural contentment*, but we're not very rurally contented, these days. Our ancestors were. They came to Canada early on in the seventeenth century, from France, settled here as farmers."

"So the Robichauds are direct descendants of the first settlers?"

"Pretty much."

"Blimey."

Elise regards me from beneath her eyebrows.

"It doesn't count for anything," she says, and her voice has a gritty edge to it. "It's not considered a mark of distinction. French families have always had to struggle for acceptance. Carradine's no exception. This community is a sealed knot, you know? Impenetrable. We've never been accepted here, and never will be, not really."

"I hadn't realised."

"Why would you? You're just a tourist."

I feel stung by that, but I keep my face steady.

"Of course. You're right. Yes."

"We have our own flag now, though."

She says it quickly, and there's a schoolgirl enthusiasm about her that disarms me. I look into her face and she's smiling with a secret.

"It's a lot like the flag of France, but there's a gold star in the blue, which is supposed to symbolise hope – the guiding light of our future." She stands up and lifts the tray from my lap. "Each colour on the Acadian flag has a symbolic meaning: blue, for the sea surrounding us; red, for the blood of our ancestors, and white, for the purity of our line…"

"Groovy."

She nods, hesitates. "But hey, look, I'm talking to you like you're one of my students."

"I don't mind."

"Can I get you anything else?" Her eyes meet mine for a moment, fall away. "Would you like some wine?"

"Brandy, beer and wine." I press my palm to my stomach. "A heady combination."

"Is that a yes?"

"That's a no, but thank you." I glance at my watch. "We probably ought to just go to bed, go… to sleep, I mean…"

I wince at the sound of my own voice, but Elise is still smiling at me. She backs away towards the kitchen, the trays balanced in her hands like she's just about to juggle with them.

"I'll see you in the morning, Abby," she says, and is gone.

That night, I dream that Lucy Pritchard and Buffy the Vampire Slayer are sitting in the old schoolhouse, with their feet up on the desks, smoking clay pipes. Lucy is wearing a dress made out of the Acadian flag, and Buffy is wearing Gen's white shirt, jodhpurs and riding boots. They are arguing about something, their voices raised, but, as soon as I sit down with them, they stop arguing and both turn to look at me.

"Why have you come?" Lucy asks me crossly. "You shouldn't be here."

"I've come to draw the school," I tell her. "For Mo's book."

"No, you haven't." Her eyes narrow to slits. "That's not why she's come, is it, Buff?"

And Buffy shakes her head slow. "No," she says, very quiet. "She's come for the sea, and the blood of the ancestors, and the purity of the line."

I feel afraid suddenly, and breathless, like I've been running. "No, I haven't. They're not what I'm looking for."

Lucy stands up, and I notice that her skirts are moth-eaten, hanging ragged around her ankles. She glides towards me, without the look of feet, and then she bends low, stares into my eyes. Her pupils are bright and dilated.

"What *are* you looking for, then?" she asks, and her breath is the scent of dried roses. It threads into my throat, catches there.

"I'm looking for the gold star in the blue," I tell her. "I'm looking for the guiding light of my future."

Lucy and Buffy the Vampire Slayer start to laugh, and then Lucy reaches forward and presses her fingers to my lips.

"Not here," she whispers, moving her thumb across my mouth hard, like she's wiping something away. "It's not here, Abby."

And the air fractures then, breaks apart, until it looks like lots of jigsaw pieces, jumbled. I spend the rest of the night, in my dreams, trying to put the picture back together again, but I can't do it.

Nine

I wake late into the morning, to the sound of the sea. The light streaming through the windows is apricot-coloured, rippling into the room like water.

Turning onto my side, I pull the covers up tight under my chin, and look at the crowd of faces on Gen's bedside table. Some are smiling at me. Some are not. I wonder who they all are. I wonder which of them are central to Gen's history and which are secondary characters, just passing through. One of them is a baby, sitting on someone's lap, except you can't see the someone; you can only see the baby. She's wearing a bright pink Babygro, with ducks on it, and a tiny white knitted bonnet, and she's not looking as pleased, or as adorable, as she no doubt should. In fact, she's looking like nothing so much as an irritable bag of sugar. Her indignation makes me smile.

Reaching an arm out of bed, I bring the photo closer to my face, and then turn it over and unclip the back panel of the frame. On the reverse side are written the words *"Elise at six weeks"*. I slip it back onto the bedside table, but shuffle it to the front a little, so that I can look at it while I get dressed, and then I make my way tentatively down the stairs.

The house feels eerily silent around me, numbed and empty, as if nobody's home, but, when I reach the kitchen, I find that actually, someone *is*. An old lady with iron-grey hair tied up tight in a bun, is sitting at the kitchen table. She is hunched slightly forward, her hands clasped around a red china mug, but she looks up and smiles when she sees me.

"You must be Abigail," she says quietly, and there's a French lilt to her accent, the middle syllables of her words lifting sharp. "Can I offer you some tea?"

"That would be lovely. Thank you."

She gestures to the chair next to hers, but I see that Ezekiel has his head resting on it, the remainder of his long body spilling like a puddle across the floor.

The old lady pats him away, and then she pats the chair.

"Come," she says. "Seat yourself. I shall put on the kettle." And she pushes herself up from the table using her hands, and walks slowly to the range.

"I'm Marie," she says, glancing at me over her shoulder, her black eyes twinkling. "Elise may have mentioned me to you?"

"She did. Yes."

"Her *sage femme*, no?"

"Pardon me?"

She turns and folds her arms carefully across her chest, the little bird-bones in her wrists standing out blunt and white against the dark wool of her sweater.

"*Sage femme*," she says again, like I should already know what it means. "Wise old woman."

"Ah, yes."

She looks at me steadily, but doesn't add anything more, and the room begins to fill up with silence. I breathe my way through it, leaning my elbows forward onto the table and resting my chin on my upturned palms, like a child. I really want to say something cordial and interesting, but I don't know what, and disquiet starts to prickle like static under my skin. Marie keeps looking at me and, even when the kettle begins to boil behind her, she doesn't immediately turn away.

"Is Elise home?" I ask her at last.

"She is with your car. A man from the Celleron garage is looking it over for you."

"Oh." I sit up straight. "I should go, then. She doesn't have the keys."

"Yes, she does."

"But... they're upstairs in my bag."

I start to stand, but Marie lifts her hand, pushes at the air.

"Elise *has* the keys," she says, and she turns away then, slides the kettle from the stove. "She took them from your bag early, so that you could sleep on."

"Oh."

I swallow hard at the thought of Elise coming into Gen's room while I was sleeping, at the thought of her looking down at me – my body in disarray, the covers thrown off perhaps – my actual nakedness compounded by the nakedness of sleep.

"She will come back soon," Marie assures, slipping a mug of strong black tea onto the table in front of me. "You can go if you want to, to join her, but I feel that there's really no need." She folds herself down into the chair next to mine. I almost think I catch the sound of her joints creaking. "Perhaps, for a while," she smiles, "you could just stay and talk with me."

"Sure. Of course."

I sip at the tea she has made for me, closing my eyes against a silky waft of steam, and Marie says, "Good. Very good," and then she nods, just the once, like it's a done deal. "Elise tells me," she says, narrowing her eyes, "that you came to Carradine to draw the old schoolhouse?"

"That's right."

"You are illustrating a book?"

"Yes. A biography of Lucy Pritchard."

"Is it a good biography?"

"Yes."

She turns her face to the side, but peers at me out of the corner of her eye, like a jackdaw.

"But is it *accurate*?" she asks, and her voice is sharp suddenly, and exacting.

"I... think so." I taste the tea again, burning my tongue. "I mean, I don't know very much about Lucy Pritchard myself, but the author of the book has done a lot of research, so I'm sure what she's written is accurate."

Marie slips her hand forward and closes it over mine on the table. I look into her face.

"Mo Laker." She breathes the name, and then she seems to suck her breath back in again, like it hurts.

"You've heard of her, then?"

I try to keep my voice bright and airy, but something in Marie's face has given way, imploded.

"She came here," she says.

"She did?"

"Ruth wouldn't let me talk to her, but I followed her back to her car when she left, without Ruth seeing, and I showed it to her. She said she thought it was a fake, but it isn't a fake."

I blink my eyes closed for a second, trying to make sense of what Marie is saying.

"Ruth wouldn't let you speak to Mo?"

She covers my hands with both of hers then, presses down hard.

"No," she whispers. "She doesn't want anyone to find out about it."

"Find out about what?"

Just then, there is the sound of feet crunching on gravel outside. Marie turns her head sharply towards the door, then spins back quickly to me. She leans in close, her mouth against my ear.

"The diary," she says, and then she stands up, just as Elise comes striding in.

"Gran." She looks surprised. "You're supposed to be upstairs, resting, remember?"

Marie wags her head from side to side, like she's heard it all before, and then she moves toward Elise and slips her arm through hers. Elise is wearing pale jeans and a charcoal-coloured top, tight-fitting, her black hair standing out blacker still against the morning light. Marie takes hold of her granddaughter's hand.

"I'm too awake to be resting, *chérie*," and she smiles in my direction then, a big smile, like we're old friends, "and besides, I was looking after your Abigail. *You'd* run out on her." She knocks lightly on Elise's shoulder with her fist. "Did you want her to think that the Robichauds don't know how to tend to their guests?"

Elise looks at me, lifts her eyes to the ceiling, says wearily, "No, Gran."

"No, indeed." She nods to herself, adds sharply, "*Non.*" And then she simply slips away from Elise and slips out of the room without another word, without a backward glance.

"Is she okay?" I ask Elise, after Marie's gone.

"Mostly." She sits down opposite me at the table. "Why? Did she not *seem* okay?"

"Well, she started out fine, but then she got a bit... agitated."

"It's her age." She asserts it, very sure. "She's vague these days, and she's on a lot of meds, for angina, and osteoporosis. They fuck with her head a bit."

"She called herself your *sage femme.*"

Elise grins. "She hasn't said that for ages. It's an old Acadian phrase. The *sage femme* was the wise woman of an Acadian village, a midwife, a soothsayer..."

"Multi-talented."

She nods. "Gran fancies herself as multi-talented, that's for sure."

"Evidently."

Elise slides my mug towards her and lifts it to her lips but, before she's had time to set it back down again, I say gently, "She mentioned that Mo had been here."

She looks at me, holding my gaze.

"Yes," she says.

"You didn't say you'd met her when I told you about the biography." She shrugs. "And, when I spoke to her on the phone the other day, she didn't say she'd met you, either." She shrugs again. "When was she here?"

"A couple of weeks ago. She just wanted to talk to Mom about Lucy." She stands up, wanders over to the refrigerator and opens it, peers inside. "Do you want anything to eat?"

"No, thanks." I shake my head. "And *did* she?"

Elise is still squinting at the frosty shelves. "Did she what?"

"Talk to your mum, about Lucy."

She nods, pulls out a small carton of eggs, and then she turns towards me, smiling.

"Of course," she says. "She was on a research route, across the island. She stopped off here, stayed for about an hour, made some notes, and then she left." She inclines her head. "I'm sorry I didn't mention it to you, Abby, but it didn't seem important, really."

I take a breath, hold it cold in my lungs.

"It's not, I suppose. I'm just surprised she didn't mention having been here, or having met you and your mum."

"We probably weren't worth mentioning." She reaches for a black skillet hanging on a long hook above the range. "I think we disappointed her."

"How so?"

"Well, Lucy didn't exactly set the world on fire while she was in Carradine. Schoolteaching. Organ-playing at the Baptist Union. They're not exactly sexy-for-sale, are they? I think your Ms Laker was hoping for something a bit more salacious."

"I guess." But something is seeping hot into the pocket of my chest, because things aren't right here. *Something's* not right. I want to ask Elise about Lucy's letters to Evans, the letters that paint such a different picture of her time in the village, and I want to ask her why she thinks that her mother wouldn't let Marie talk to Mo. Most of all, I want to ask her about the diary that Marie whispered to me about just now, but I don't ask her any of these things. Instead, I reach for the kite strings of perspective and I hang onto them tight, and I don't let go, because I'm just being melodramatic surely, and intrusive, and, if I let my questions spill, then either Elise will resent me for elbowing my way into her family's business, or else she'll think I'm a brick short of a load and start to pity me, or, worst of all, she'll laugh at me, and I don't think I could bear it if Elise laughed at me.

So, I sit at the kitchen table, drinking my tea, watching Elise cooking her eggs, and then watching her eating her eggs, and I listen to her telling me what's wrong with my car. She was right, apparently, about the starter motor. The mechanic from Celleron has ordered a replacement.

"But it won't be here until Friday, I'm afraid."

"Friday!"

"They're having to get it shipped over from the mainland."

"What am I going to do until then?"

"Well, you came here to draw the schoolhouse. You could *do* that."

"I can't *stay* here, though, Elise."

"Yes, you can."

She is sitting opposite me at the table again, drinking a mug of cinnamon tea, and she reaches across suddenly and presses her fingertips against mine. I ease them away.

"I can't." I look into her face. "Don't you remember what we said last night, about my driving off into the sunset so that this *thing...*" – the word confounds me – "between us, could be forgotten?"

"I remember. Of course I remember, but you can't drive off into the sunset if you don't have a car."

"Can't I borrow one?" She shakes her head. "Steal one?"

She breathes a laugh into the air then, very light, reaches for my hand again. This time, I let her take it.

"It'll be all right, Abby." She dips her head towards me. "Trust me."

I sigh into her words, but there's something else too – an agreeable feeling of powerlessness, of being given up to the elements, a reed in the wind.

"Do you ever get the feeling that God gets off on undermining people's good intentions?"

Elise nods. "Yep."

I lean towards her, until I can see little flecks of indigo and gold in the black of her irises.

"Why d'you think we bother, then?" I can taste her breath in the space between us. "Why don't we just abandon our good intentions, and go with the flow instead? It would make more sense, to do that."

"We can't, though, can we? Because we're *defined* by our good intentions, by the choices we make, and if we make selfish choices, then we become selfish people." She turns my hand over in hers and traces her fingertips across my wrist, into my palm. "And we don't want to be selfish people, you and me. Do we?"

"Don't we?"

"No." She looks at my hand, concentrating hard. "We want to be better people than we are, and the only way to do that is to make *selfless* choices – always to choose someone else's happiness over our own."

"Shit! That's such a hard way to live, though, Elise."

She looks up. "It'll be worth it, in the end."

"But what if we don't want the end? What if we want the *now*?"

She smiles at me, but it's a sad smile, and she looks tired suddenly, almost as if she's ready to close her eyes and fall asleep, right there at the table, with her head pillowed forward onto her arms.

"We always have to struggle to do the right thing," she says, and there's closure in her voice, an end to it.

"'Say not the struggle naught availeth'."

She furrows her eyebrows. "Sorry?"

"It's a line from a poem, by Arthur Hugh Clough, I think. It's about keeping hope alive, forging onward, all that malarkey."

"Uplifting then, no?"

"Allegedly. The last line is something about always looking westward, because that's where the land is bright."

Elise stands up and moves around the table, until she is at my side. She places her hand over the curve of my shoulder and then she moves her fingers under my hair, lets my hair tousle and fall through her fingers, over and over again.

"If *I* look westward," she says, "there isn't any land; there's only the sea."

I nod. "Yes, and when I was at home, in England, if I was looking westward, then I was looking towards Canada. I was looking here. Westward was here."

"And is the land bright, now that you've reached it, now that you're here?"

I nestle my face into the soft skin of her palm, and then I look up so that I can see what's in her eyes.

"Oh yes," I tell her, and I mean it.

I'm sure, if I tried really hard, I could find a way back to Port Hove. I could insist that Elise take me to Celleron, and from there I could probably hire a car and drive away into that sunset we've been talking about, but I don't insist that she take me anywhere, because there's nowhere I'd rather be right now, than here, in Carradine, with her, and the worst thing is, I'm not even feeling bad about Gayle any more. She has receded. The fact of her, the solid and concrete truth of her, has melted away inside me, to a pool of colour, indeterminate. I *want* to feel terrible about it, guilty as hell, but somehow, God knows how, I just don't. My life before, with all its associations, has somehow fallen away, and there is only this kernel of meaning, this place, this time, and Elise.

So, I stay, and I draw the schoolhouse, because Elise is right: that's what I came here to do, and if I can think myself back into my assignment, then maybe I can remember who I'm supposed to be, and who I'm *not* supposed to be turning into. But Elise comes with me when I go to draw the schoolhouse and, while I sit outside the building on the grass with my sketchpad and pencils, she moves about *inside* the building, cleaning, stacking chairs, securing windows. It's that time of year when the school closes up for the winter, and she has chosen today to prepare it for hibernation, so that every time I lift my head to look and to draw, I catch sight of her through the windows – dipping and bending, lifting furniture, turning towards me and away. A couple of times, she lifts her arms high above her head to reach for something, and the top she's wearing rides up. Her stomach is pale brown, like sand, the soft muscles clenching beneath her skin like fists. I want to move my fingers over those muscles, feel them contract beneath my touch. I want to push my palms up under her shirt. I want to…

Suddenly, she's calling my name, and when I look up I see her striding towards me, smiling, wiping her hands clean on a rag. The sky behind her is china blue, speckled with white, and she is very dark against it, growing darker the closer she gets. She's only a few steps away from me, when my heart starts to break into bloom inside my chest. I can feel tendrils of green and red snaking their way through to the surface of my skin, but I keep my face open and plain, shielding my eyes against her.

"Are you nearly done, then?" She drops down onto her haunches by my side and leans forward to look at what I've drawn, but her face falls. "Oh."

I look at what I've drawn too, and it's awful. The dimensions are all wrong, and shadows are falling in mistaken places. It's a child's drawing, ragged, inept. I close my sketchpad.

"Bad day," I tell her, but she looks into my eyes.

"Did I put you off? I mean, did you need the interior clear? I bet I put you off."

"No. Really. It's just a bad day. My creative juices aren't… flowing."

She raises her eyebrows. "That's a shame."

"Yes."

I start to stand up, and she slips her fingers around my forearms, eases me to my feet.

"You can come back tomorrow," she suggests. "Draw it again. I'll keep out of your way."

"I don't need you to keep out of my way."

"Don't you?"

I shift my body forward into hers, not touching, but nearly.

"No."

But we both turn, very sharply, at the sound of a woman's voice jostling toward us through the trees.

Elise frowns.

"I think that's my mom..." And suddenly Ruth appears on the path with her hands on her hips.

"I need you to shift some boxes for me, Elise," she calls, not coming any closer, and not looking at me. "Jamieson's have just been by with the order, and I can't be moving all those boxes about on my own, not with *my* back."

Elise nods. "I'll be there in a sec. Just need to finish here."

Ruth screws her face up, just a little, like she might be about to sneeze, and then she turns away and slips her shadow back among the trees.

"She *really* doesn't like me, does she?"

But Elise shakes her head. "She doesn't like anyone. Since Dad left, she doesn't like anyone."

"I wondered where your dad was. You hadn't mentioned him."

"Well, he left, last summer."

"Where'd he go?"

Elise shrugs. "Don't know."

"*Why'd* he go?"

"Don't know that either, exactly."

I'm not sure whether to press her on the subject or not. Her face is still open and smiling, but her eyes keep slipping past mine without really looking.

She takes hold of my hand. "Listen, I need to finish here and then sort those boxes for Mom, but it's early yet. There's still some good light." She looks up into the sky, and her neck angles toward me. I want to count the soft notches of muscle in her throat with the tips of my fingers, with my lips. "We could take a walk, down to the beach maybe. You could draw, or not, depending on whether your..."

"Creative juices are flowing?" I shake my head. "You know, when you say something, use a phrase and then, like, *really* wish you hadn't?"

She nods. "While I was at college, I led a seminar on the German Reformation, and instead of saying that Martin Luther had nailed his ninety-five theses to the door of Wittenberg Cathedral, I said he'd nailed his ninety five *faeces* to the door of Wittenberg Cathedral, right there in front of the whole history department, all the professors and everything. God, *and*" – she starts to look animated – "I went to New York, for an education conference last year, and got to meet Stephen Hawking, who's always been one of my heroes, but when I was introduced to him, it was like this veil of stupidity dropped, and all I could come up with to ask him, was if his wheelchair had any enhanced features." She shakes her head. "The world's leading authority on astrophysics, for Christ's sake, and I go and ask him if his wheelchair can do wheelies!"

"Hey, at least you've actually *met* someone famous. The closest I ever got to fame was going backstage on *The Sooty Show* when I was small." I hesitate. "D'you even get *The Sooty Show* over here?"

"Oh, yeah." Elise nods enthusiastically. "I used to have the hots for Sue, actually, when I was about six and a half."

"That's really sweet" – I think for a moment – "and *disturbing*."

She grins at me. "Backstage, though? Cool."

"It wasn't. There were all these Sooties hanging upside down on hooks. It was awful. I wanted to cry. My mum had to tell me they were stunt Sooties."

Elise starts to laugh, and I start to laugh too, and it's lovely, this moment of us standing in the woods, laughing into each other's face. I can't remember the last time I laughed like this. I never laugh like this with Gayle, and that's when it stops of course, catches and falters, chokes – when I think of Gayle's name. I look away from Elise, crouch down quickly and start to gather my sketchpad and pencils together.

"I'll go back to the house and dump these," I tell her, not looking up. "Shall I meet you at the store?"

"No." She's watching me closely when I stand up again, but I keep my face smiling. "Best I meet you at the house, really. I won't be long."

"Okay." I turn to go then, nonchalant, but she catches hold of my arm.

"You keep remembering, don't you?" she says, and her voice is very careful, attentive.

"Remembering what?"

"Gayle."

"How do you know that? How do *you* know what I'm feeling, when I barely know what I'm feeling myself?"

"Because I can see her. I can see her behind your eyes."

"Can you? I can't."

"Yes, you can."

She brings my hand up between us, presses our palms together, keeps them there, and we start to lean into each other, swaying against each other, as if the breeze has taken us.

"Selfless choices, Abby, remember?" – and she sighs then, a breath of grey, and lets my hand drop.

This time when I turn to leave, she doesn't call me back.

I let myself into the house by the back door, feeling stealthy and presumptuous, because this isn't my home, and I'm staying here under what feel like false pretences, but Ezekiel hauls himself up off the kitchen floor and sidles towards me as soon as I'm inside. His fur is as coarse as shredded wheat, but when you ruffle it through with your fingers, which he seems to like, you find that his skin is silky-warm and sleek beneath. I sit and stroke him for a while and he gives himself up to me with abandon, lays his head in my lap and looks up into my face as if he might quite like to seduce me.

When I eventually climb the stairs, I find that all the doors on the first-floor landing are closed, and the air feels chilly and very still suddenly. The light up here is murky, strangely opaque. I hurry into Gen's room, slip my sketchpad and pencils onto a bookcase, and then sit down heavily on the bed. The sky outside my window is feathered with cloud now, but Elise was right about the light still being good. I could easily draw in this light. I could draw *her*. I think what a good nude she would make, how the sunlight would splash sharp and crystalline onto her body, and how I would catch it and tame it, letting her limbs, her breasts, her face reassemble themselves as I drew; how my fingers would translate her, fathom her, find her out. She'd let me do it, I'm sure, if I asked. She'd let my fingers find her out.

I swallow hard, closing my eyes, letting myself fall back deadweight onto the bed. My head bounces, missing the pillow, landing askew on something else. When I turn my face to the side, I find that I'm looking at the corner of a book, a small brown leather-bound book, smudged and elderly. Its edges look like they've been nibbled at by tiny mice. I shift over and pull it out from under the pillow, and when I open it, I have to sit up really fast, a tiny pulse sparking sharp in my wrists and in my temples, because the first words I see are, *"Lucy May Pritchard. Carradine Diary. 1898."*.

Ten

I read the first entry twice, straight through, and then I stand up and walk over to the window, and read it again, very slowly indeed.

A sky and the red stains of a sunset, and behind you, the window open and green hop vines trailing across it, your shadow moving over the floor in a square of Winter light. You reach out your hand and say your name. I take your fingers in my own and they are cold, and this close, you smell of wheat and the leather of the bridle over your shoulder, and your face dips toward me, smiling, and you lay the bridle over the high-backed chair by the stove and press the palms of your hands together. The air in the kitchen is still, and behind you the sun is sinking below the velvet rim of the water. You take a cup of broth from your mother's hands and begin to drink, begin to talk of your trip to Prince George, and suddenly your face is a shield with the sun on it, burnished, indistinct, and I can no longer see you, although all through supper I look for you, and the spell of your voice I cannot fathom.

There's no way, surely, that Lucy Pritchard wrote this. The tone is so markedly different from the tone of her letters to Evans – and the cadence, and the content. I look towards the door, wondering if Marie is skulking outside on the landing, chuckling to herself, relishing her moment of mischief. Surely that's all this is: a moment of mischief, a forged diary, a joke slipped under my pillow. Lucy Pritchard couldn't have written the words I just read. Nothing in all of her published writing is as sensual or as vivid or as human as this.

I turn the page fast, to the second entry.

Dark across the ice with the moon, and me slipping my arm around you, pressing my head down onto your shoulder, and the buggy moving on and the horse's breath lifting like mist, and drifting. My shadow dancing at the wedding when I close my eyes, spinning free across the shore, and the buggy swaying over a creek shimmering with reflected stars. You ask if I am cold, your voice strangely sleepy, and I answer yes, and you take my hand, slip it into the pocket of your coat, and ask again, and I say no, and your fingers on the reins move a fraction and the horse slows. Down the long shadowy turn of Woodford Hill, yellow moonlight gleaming on a farmhouse, and your hand moves to circle my waist, a warm close pressure. I lift my head, my lips touching your face. I tell you I can taste the sea spray on your skin, and you turn, and our lips meet. And I go down helplessly before it.

I read this entry again and again, not making sense of it, but then I remember that I've brought Mo's copy of *My Dear Mr. Evans* with me, and I go and fetch it from my bag. At least Lucy's letters to Evans might provide some kind of context, a frame of reference.

I flick quickly through, and yes, there in Lucy's first letter from Carradine is a reference to a wedding, and a clam-bake down by the shore, and a buggy ride *back across the ice in the dark*. I slap my hand down flat on the open pages of the diary, delighted, because there it is, in black and white – irrefutable. I glance towards the door again, and then I stand up and venture out onto the landing, looking left and right along the corridor, wondering which room is Marie's, but then I catch hold of a sound from downstairs – a door opening and closing, footsteps – Elise.

"Honey, I'm home," she calls, a laugh in her voice, and then she hesitates. "Are you upstairs, Abby?"

"Yes. I'm just coming down, though. Won't be a minute."

I dart back into Gen's room, slipping the diary back under the pillow, and then I pull on yesterday's black fleece over my T-shirt top, and head for the door.

Elise is halfway up the stairs.

"You sure you want to go for this walk?" she asks when she sees me. "The weather's turning."

"Doesn't bother me. I'm English, remember." My voice is high and hectic. "The weather's always bloody turning where I come from."

"Ah, yes," she says, smiling. "My mistake." And then she holds out her hands to me – reaches out her hands to me, very slowly, and I take them. "The beach, then?" Her eyebrows are raised.

"Anywhere."

It comes out of my mouth as nothing but breath, but I can't help it, because she's there, on the stairs, looking up at me, and somehow language is sucked clean away, and there is only the feel of my ribs rising inside my chest, and my diaphragm falling. It's all I can do to breathe, with Lucy's words still moving thin and black and remarkable across my vision. I try to blink them away, but Elise asks, "Are you all right, Abby?"

I want to tell her. I want to run back into Gen's room, fetch the diary and brandish it at her, exultant, but I don't, because my thinking is fragmenting suddenly, confused, and I can't quite catch hold of what all of this means. I need to speak to Marie. I need to find out if this diary of Lucy's is authentic, and if it *is*, then...

"Abby?" Elise is looking up into my face.

"I'm fine. Just a bit of a headache." I touch my fingers to my forehead for a moment. "The sea air will do me good."

"Aren't you bringing your sketchpad with you?"

"Not this time. I'd just like to walk." I take a breath, pulling myself up as straight as I can, and then I smile at her. "Lead on, Macduff!"

And she does.

By the time we reach the beach, the sky has begun to darken, crowded with cloud. Even the seagulls are turning for shore, the wind riffling through their feathers, buffeting them about like tossed litter.

Their cries are sharp and surprised.

"Do you want to go back?" Elise's face is slick with sea-light when she turns. "You must be cold."

"I'm not cold."

"You sure?"

I nod, and she takes my hand then, holds it tight as we walk, trudging us on across the sand as if we have somewhere to get to. We don't, and I take pleasure in it – this motiveless walking to nowhere and back. I take pleasure in the feel of Elise's fingers tangled around my own. I take pleasure in the crash of the waves and the sting of salt on my cheeks. The wind feathers my hair away from my neck, lifts it high, lets it fall, and suddenly, out of nowhere it seems, it's raining, really hard, and there's a grumble of thunder way out to sea, and then a roar that seems to shoulder its way up from the bed of the ocean.

Elise starts to run, still holding onto my hand.

"The lighthouse," she shouts back to me, her voice whipped sharply away, but she's pointing ahead now, and yes, I can see, misty in the distance, a small white lighthouse with a dome of red, and a pale yellow light winking us a welcome.

We have to clamber up the dunes to reach it, our feet slipping away beneath us, the rain falling in sheets across the open mouth of the water, but we're laughing all the time, and so out of breath we can't speak. Even when we get to the lighthouse and tumble headlong in through the door, we just stand there, leaning towards each other, breathing hard.

"Isn't anywhere in this town *locked*?" I manage to ask at last, shaking rainwater from my hands and from my hair, watching the wooden floorboards grow damp and shadowy beneath my feet.

"Nah." Elise takes off her jacket and flaps it hard. "There's nothing to steal."

"And no one lives here? There isn't a lighthouse keeper?"

"Not any more. It's maintained by the port authority, but it's pretty derelict really."

I look around me, at the bare grey walls, peeling paintwork. There are still a few scraps of curtain, thin as mosquito net, stuck to the windows, and there's a low table with some empty beer cans toppled on it, but that's all.

"It's a bit tragic this, isn't it?"

Elise tilts her head. "Tragic?"

"Well, I mean, this was someone's home. Someone lived here. A lighthouse keeper lived here." I press my palm to the wall. "I always quite fancied being a lighthouse keeper, actually."

"Why?"

"Aaah, the deep and potent solitude of it of course." I pause. "Or maybe because of that book, *The Lighthouse Keeper's Lunch.*"

Elise grins at me. "You mean the kid's one, where the keeper's wife sends his sandwiches across to him on a clothesline every day?"

"That's it. I like the idea of my dinner coming zipping towards me across the water." I smile at Elise then, from beneath my eyebrows, inviting play. "It was a favourite of mine, that book – a formative work of fiction."

"A classic, no less!" she says.

"Better than any of the Little Hector stories, don't you think?"

I wait for an answer, a reaction, but Elise just nods and flaps her jacket dry again. The rain is still knocking hard at the windows and every now and then there's a flash of white – a spine of lightning fizzing sharp into the sea. It's twilight inside the lighthouse, but I can see the sheen of water on Elise's skin, and the dappled wet indigo of her hair. I take a breath, holding myself in, pulling myself back from the edge of her.

She looks into my face, smiling, half-smiling, and then she moves towards me.

"There's a good view from the top," she says, gesturing towards the stairs. "You can see right the way across the bay." She lifts her hand and touches her fingers to my face, slips a strand of hair back behind my ear. "It's not much of a climb."

"Okay, then."

It's a whisper when I say it, but Elise nods and moves ahead of me, up the spiral staircase. We don't speak. There's only the rasp and creak of our footsteps on the old wood, and the swoop of the rain, and the resolute boom of the sea. Even our breath is lost in so much sound, although we're both breathing hard by the time we reach the top.

We step into a small, circular chamber, its windows criss-crossed with thin bars of black – the moving light at the centre of the room cupped in a cradle of steel. A bloom of yellow throws us into sharp relief suddenly, so that we're standing for a second, lit up, exposed, shielding our eyes against each other, and then the light goes out and we are shadow.

"It's too bright," I say to Elise, blinking.

"It's meant to be. Here." She reaches out her hands to me. "Keep your back to it. Look outward."

I turn with her, towards the window, but the light comes again then, so that all I can see is our reflection in the glass – the two of us standing side by side, hand in hand.

"There's Carradine," says Elise, pointing along the cost to a cluster of lights and a black thatch of trees. "And over *that* way" – she points in the opposite direction – "is Delmont." Another cluster of lights, but snaking further down the coast, looping back inland. "And ahead of us" – she cups her hands over a space of glass – "is Woodford Hill."

I swallow hard, remembering Lucy's diary – *Down the long shadowy turn of Woodford Hill, yellow moonlight gleaming on a farmhouse.* And what was the next line? I know I know it. I can feel the inky nib of Lucy's pen scratching at my heart. I swallow again, blinking my eyes closed. *I lift my head, my lips touching your face. I tell you I can taste the sea spray on your skin, and you turn, and our lips meet...*

When I open my eyes, Elise is looking at me.

"You're shaking, Abby," she says, concerned. "We should go home."

"No." I squeeze her hand. I turn her hand over in mine and then

I bring it to my mouth, brushing my lips over her knuckles. "I want to stay."

"I think we should go."

"I don't want to go."

"Abby." Her voice is a sigh.

"But I can taste the sea spray on your skin, Elise." I say it very, very softly, and the eye of light opens on us again, lays us bare.

I turn away from the glare. I look outward, like Elise has said to do, but I can still feel the heat of it at my back, going deep, and I can feel Elise's hands moving on my body now, suddenly. I arch myself into her touch. I let all of myself – past, present, future – fall into shadow. I turn... *and our lips meet... and I go down helplessly before it.*

Elise spreads her jacket out flat on the floor and I don't care that it's damp. I lie down on it, anyway. She pulls her shirt off over her head, and then she lies down with me, her body covering *my* body. I run my hands across the smooth skin of her back, taking in the delicate swell of her shoulder blades, the muscles that tense and then relax at my touch, and then I let my fingers move down over her breasts, so that I can feel the beat of her heart against the palm of my hand, making her real, flesh and blood – and all the while she watches me, keeps her eyes on me, her left hand flat on the floor, her forearm taut, taking her weight – her right hand threading soft across my breasts. She flicks open the buttons of my jeans and slides her fingers down flat over my belly, pushes further, slipping just the tips of her fingers inside me, angling her wrist so that I can feel her *deeper* inside me. She breathes out against my cheek.

"God, you're so wet." And her voice breaks over the words, so that I turn my head fast and look for her mouth with mine, but her kiss this time is hot and anxious, and my body is moving on its own to the rhythm of her hand – twisting itself, coiling itself back and then arching toward her again. I want to say her name. I want to let the sounds crashing against my heart lift and shine and splash out of my mouth like water from a fountain, but everything in me is stopped dead in this moment, held in some kind of astonished abeyance.

She slides her palms underneath me then, clawing at me. She pushes my jeans down over my hips, tangles my top up over my head, crushing her mouth against my breasts. I sit up, struggling against her, flailing into her, and we tear at each other's clothes, as fast as we can, because the air is barbed with cold, and the swooping light above us is a searchlight now: icy, seeking us out. I tangle my fingers tight into Elise's hair, and she crawls up my body, slamming her fingers into me hard, over and over, circling my clitoris fast with the pad of her thumb, pressing hard, and I come quickly, more quickly than I ever have, and sharply, painfully, taken by surprise. Elise's name falls out of my mouth, an expelled breath.

I try to speak, but there's something felled and fallen at the centre of my body, something liquid that won't gather itself into a shape anymore, so we just lie there like that, with her fingers wet and hot inside me – the rain splintering at the glass, a swell of tears lifting thick into my throat.

After a moment, Elise tries to lift her head.

"Shit," she says, very quietly, and then, "shit," again, but her voice is water.

I lift both my hands into her hair and stroke gently, but she shakes her head, shaking me away, and then she pulls her fingers out of me and scrambles up onto her knees. She won't look at me. I watch her pull up her jeans, fumbling with the buttons, and she still won't look at me. She stands up.

"Elise." I'm lying where she has left me, but I lift myself onto my elbows.

"I'm sorry." She says it to the floor, and then she leans down and picks up my top and hands it to me. "The rain's easing," she says, and her eyes flicker over my body. "We should get back."

"Elise." I stand up unevenly, easing my jeans over my hips. "It's all right." I try to touch her, but she backs away.

"Don't," she says.

"Don't what?"

"Don't try to make me feel better."

"But it's all right. There's nothing to feel bad about." I tug my top on over my head.

"Yeah, right," she says, her face granite.

"Really. There *isn't*." This time when I reach out to touch her, she lets me. I close my fingers around her wrist. "It was what I wanted."

"There's no way you wanted *that*, Abby." She stares down at where we were on the floor, and then she leans down and picks up her jacket, but she doesn't put it on. She just holds it against her chest.

"I've never..." She shakes her head hard. "Christ! It's never been like that, with anyone."

"It was okay."

"It was awful."

I move my body into hers a little, but she tenses.

"Sex doesn't always have to be about time and tenderness and everything in slow motion. Sometimes, it's just heat, you know?"

But she frowns at me. "No."

"Elise..."

"Look. Let's just go. I can't stay here."

And she turns fast and hurries ahead of me down the spiral staircase and out into the stark afternoon. She was right about the rain easing. The air is damp and chilly, but the sea is quiet now, hushed, and the sky is breaking eggshell blue at the edges.

Elise stalks ahead of me down the beach. I don't try to catch up with her. I trawl along in her wake with my head bowed, and when we get back to the house I go straight upstairs without saying anything to her, and I curl myself up in a ball on Gen's bed.

I must have fallen asleep. Sleep must have swallowed me, because I wake to the sound of the shower. I lie with my eyes wide open for a moment, but the air is thin and empty. I turn myself over onto my back and stare hard at the ceiling – just texture, a vacancy. I badly need *something* on which to focus, otherwise all I can see is Gayle's face blooming towards me out of the black, her mouth easing into a smile, shaping my name. I swallow back a surge of tears, time and again, like I'm swallowing air, but still it sits implacable behind my breastbone. I try to think about Elise, and the lighthouse. I try to let my body remember what she felt like, inside me, but my thoughts skate clear away from me across the ice every time – smooth themselves away from me, and disappear.

I cross my wrists loosely over my eyes and breathe out, as slowly as I can, but sit up fast when someone taps at the door. It's Marie.

"Are you well, Abby?" she asks, once she's inside, her hair speckled with light from the landing. "Elise said you were sleeping."

"I was sleeping, but I'm okay. I'm well." I swing my legs down onto the floor and lean forward. "Is Elise... well?"

Marie closes the door, inclines her head. "She's..." She thinks for a moment, crinkling her nose like she can smell something toxic, corrupting the air. "She's quiet, very... held-in, I would say, today." She folds her arms tight under her breasts then, looking down at them pensively. "She's been in the shower for half an hour."

"We got caught in the rain."

"I see."

She stares down at me, the little muscles in her jaw twitching with something to say.

"You found the diary?"

"Yes."

"Did you read it?"

"I read the start of it." I rub the heels of my hands into my eyes. "Is it real?"

I watch Marie's hackles rise. "Real? Well, of *course* it's real. What? You suspect I wrote it perhaps *myself*, hmm?"

I shrug.

"*Mon Dieu*! Abigail! Why? Why would I? You think me so duplicitous, then?"

"No." I shake my head. "I don't know. I don't know *you*, do I, and

104

I don't know what your motives are in showing it to me."

She takes a step towards me. "Read it. Read it all and then we will speak of it again, and you will see how much of a great disservice you do me to suggest these bad things." She snaps herself up straight. "I am a decent woman, with a decent heart." She touches her fingers to her breast, flutters them there. "You would do well to look to your own motives here, my dear, and not to be questioning mine I think, no?"

I've opened my mouth to apologise to her, but she has spun around on her heels and is heading out onto the landing. I stand up and push the door closed behind her, and then I go back to the bed.

Lucy's diary. Real or not, it will at least be something on which to concentrate, something instead of Gayle's face circling at the edges of my vision, something instead of the sound of the shower, still running, flooding my thinking.

I slip my fingers under the pillow, and then I lift the pillow into the air, but the diary isn't there.

Eleven

By the time I get out onto the landing, Marie has disappeared. The corridor is all closed doors again, and I don't know which of them is hers, but suddenly a door ahead of me opens and Ruth steps out towards me, frowning.

"Abby," she says fast. "Can I help you with something?"

She's wearing her outdoor coat, buttoned up to the chin, and she has a sheaf of papers in her hand.

"No."

She raises her eyebrows at me, just as another door opens revealing Marie struggling herself into a cardigan, and coming out onto the landing to join us, and then, farcically, yet *another* door opens directly opposite, and Elise appears, wearing nothing but a white towel, looped snug around her breasts. Her shoulders are streaked wet, and her body smells of sandalwood. Suddenly, the landing shimmers with clean heat. I swallow hard.

For a second, all four of us stand there, looking at each other, and then Ruth purses her lips and pushes past me down the stairs. Marie shakes herself straight inside her cardigan, smiling benignly, and starts to move towards the stairs too, but I catch hold of her arm.

"Marie. Sorry. Could I just have a word with you?"

She glances at Elise, but Elise is looking at *me*. I can feel her eyes on me. I don't meet her gaze. I keep my eyes on Marie. She nods, almost imperceptibly, and follows me back inside Gen's room. I shut the door behind us.

"The diary's gone." I take a step towards the bed. "I left it under the pillow." I lift it so she can see. "But when I got back from the beach, it was gone."

Marie presses her fingers to her lips, breathes out against them.

"Ruth," she says at last. "Ruth must have taken it." She narrows her eyes. "I told you she wanted it kept secret."

"But how would she have known it was under the pillow, and why does she want it kept secret anyway?"

"I could tell you why, if you would like, but I wanted you to find out for yourself. The first time I read it, I..." She looks down at her hands. "I would not believe, but I *learned* to believe..." And she lifts her eyes then, very slowly. "I made, at last, my peace with the truth, but Ruth..." She waves the name away. "She is stubborn and she is proud, and she is afraid. The truth confounds her."

"Marie." I sink down onto the bed. "I don't *get* any of this. I mean, I read the first couple of entries, and it looked like maybe Lucy had a crush on someone in the house, but there's no great scandal in that. It was acceptable, even back then surely, for people to *fancy* each other?"

"*Fancy*." Marie huffs a little laugh into the air. "Ahh, *chérie*." She pats my hand. "If only that were all."

At that, there's a knock at the door, and Marie stiffens.

"Well, yes, we eat at seven," she says, very loudly indeed, "when Ruth gets back from the store, you see?"

She clears her throat in an exaggerated manner, and Elise's face appears. Her smile looks like somebody's taken a brush and painted it on. They haven't done it very well.

"Vivienne's here, Gran," she says quietly, drumming her fingers on the doorframe. "She's in the living room."

"Splendid." Marie moves past her. "My arch nemesis, no less." And she throws me a smile over her shoulder, and leaves the room humming to herself, very fast.

"Her bridge partner," explains Elise, after she's gone. "They cook up a storm every Friday night at the Baptist Union, with their demon card-playing skills." Her voice is small, and the painted-on smile has begun to smudge. "Do you play cards, Abby?"

"Only strip poker, Elise."

She sighs then, closes her eyes, takes a step towards me.

"Don't laugh at me," she says.

"I'm not laughing at you. I just can't bear you being so fucking *gracious* with me, so distant."

She is close enough to touch, but when I try she shakes her head and moves away, towards the window.

"I don't know *what* to be with you, Abby. I don't know what to be, now."

She stares out at the sea, her hands dug deep into the pockets of her jeans. I want to slip my arms around her waist and sink my heat into hers. I want to press my hips into her hard, and let her feel, in the way our bodies fathom and fit each other, that all she needs to be with me, simply, is *her*. Elise.

I must say her name out loud, and I must say it in the tone in which I'm thinking it, because she turns to face me, and then she reaches out her hands to me and I go to her, and she hugs me into her body until my lungs are squeezed empty, and all I can taste is the sting of sandalwood on her skin. I savour it – honey from the rock. I take it onto my tongue, and melt it there, but Elise eases me away from her then, looks into my face.

"It was like *you* weren't even there," she says. "It was like I was underwater, like I was drowning, and the only way I could get to breathe was to fight my way out, or fight my way *in*. Inside you was where the air was, but it wasn't *about* you. *This* you." She grips my arms hard, lets her eyes snake down my body and up again. "It was only about me." She shakes her head. "All my noble talk about selfless choices, Abby, and the first chance I get, I'm fucking you on the floor of a derelict building."

"Elise." I bump my head forward onto her shoulder. "It was what I wanted. You haven't done anything wrong."

"Yes, I have."

"No."

"We both have, and we both *know* we have. That's why we're feeling so bad."

She says it flat and harsh and, when I look into her face, she looks away from me and doesn't look back.

"I'll borrow a car and drive you back to Port Hove in the morning," she says, and she untangles my hands from her body and heads for the door.

"Elise." My voice folds in on itself. "Don't send me away. Don't make me *feel* like you're sending me away."

"But I am." Her fingers are on the door handle. "I have to, Abby." She half turns then, her shadow bending out of shape against the wall. "Don't you see? I can't live with feeling like this. This isn't who I am." She opens the door, says more quietly, "This isn't who I want to be, and this isn't who *you* want me to be, not really. You'd hate me for being like this, and you'd hate yourself, in the end."

"But I'm not interested in the end, remember?" I shake my head fast. "I don't want the end. I want the *now*. And so do you."

"No," she says. "That's not what I want." And with that she steps out onto the landing and pulls the door closed behind her.

I turn to look out at the sea, its grey waves drizzled with white, like spilt milk. The distant horizon is a straight line, levelled at me, thin and austere. A long way beyond that straight line, there's Gayle, sleeping, her face nuzzled into the pillow, scenting feathers, her arms thrown high above her head like she's dancing. Her dreams will be slow and humdrum, because they always are. Sometimes, at breakfast, she tells me her dreams, and they'll have been full of walking or driving or accounting. Sometimes, she's been putting bookcases together in her sleep, or folding clothes, or climbing stairs. Once, she worked out the square root of one hundred and twenty-seven, without waking up. She wrote that dream down, to keep it for posterity. How will I go back and sit across the breakfast table from her now? How will I keep my face open and smiling while she tells me her dreams? How will I tell her *mine*, when they will be bathed in sealight, tasting of sandalwood – replete with Elise?

I let my head drop, heavy with tears, but it is then that I catch sight of something on the floor next to the bed. I reach to pick it up and, when I bring it into the light, I realise that I'm holding Lucy's diary in my hands. So, Ruth didn't take it, after all. I must simply have knocked it out from under the pillow while I was sleeping. I wonder about going downstairs and telling Marie that I've found it, but instead I sit down on the bed, open the book to the third entry and begin to read.

Mountains silhouetted, soft hills crumpled up like children sleeping. I concentrate my gaze beyond you, through a misty square of window; a vague space of water, a curve of sky. I move my leg against yours beneath the table, and all the while the others are singing, Pensie's fingers ringing across the keys of the piano, and I lean toward you, your face moving close to fill my view. "Will you come upstairs with me awhile," I ask, reaching my fingers soft across the board, sliding my queen forward, and you say yes, your eyes say yes to me, and suddenly I cannot see for the glare of the lamp, which you lift from the bureau, and we climb the stairs into a diffusing brightness, and my hands move on your body as we climb. Ochre inside my room, I turn down the lamp to a candle glow, and reach for you, bring you to your knees, draw your face to mine, and beneath us still the sound of singing. Pensie's voice ringing, and our hands moving in the half-light, and our clothes falling like leaves in the half-light.

I remember Lucy telling Thomas Evans about her Christmas with the Robichauds, how they sat down to *"a succulent roast goose dinner"*, and how, after dinner, Pensie played the piano and sang, and Lucy was challenged to a game of chess, a game that had to be completed *"in the semi-gloom of my gable room"*. But who challenged her to the game, and whose body is this that her hands are touching; whose clothes are *"falling like leaves in the half-light"*, along with her own?

I find Mo's copy of *My Dear Mr. Evans* in my bag and I flick through to the relevant passage, but Lucy gives no names there. She only refers to *"my opponent"*. It must be Henri. In her first letter from Carradine, she praises him, says he's *"a handsome young man"*, and then later, she's all excited about their imminent trip to the Dougray Hotel for cousin Stella's engagement party. She's in attendance, with the family, and they are staying overnight.

I turn the pages of the diary back, to that *"buggy ride... across the ice in the dark"*, and I start to picture Henri slipping Lucy's hand into his pocket, because he knows how cold she must be, with the moonlight slicing the night to shreds around them, ice breathing blue and white beneath the horse's hooves. I picture her leaning in, her lips touching his face. I hear her say, *"I can taste the sea spray on your skin"*, and I have to lean forward, my arms hugging my knees into my body, because I'm back in the lighthouse, and Elise's fingers are pushing down over my belly, and the air is bright yellow with a swooping shine, a searchlight, invasive – seeking us out.

A sound comes out of my body, a new sound – guttural, desolate. I choke it back. I cover my mouth with my both my hands and rock myself softly back and forth on the bed. I don't want anyone to hear me. I don't want anyone coming, knocking at my door. Instead, I lift Lucy's diary up in front of my face, unsteadily, her words tangling together like roots under stones, and I start to read again.

Fingers in my hair and your breath against my cheek, warm with wine. I turn my head away, to the window, where a winter dusk breathes, a full moon rippling through the trees, but the room is strangely still, save for the flickering lamplight and our starfish bodies moving like the night moves, our limbs loud with love and the sound of Pensie singing. I am drowning in a radiance. I am struggling to the surface of the water to breathe. For a long time, your head against my shoulder, your breath slow. I ask, "Have you fallen

*asleep?" but you stir, saying, "No", look into my face, saying, "I
could lie here forever without talking", and I draw you to me again,
and suddenly it seems that all I have ever loved to look upon, or
listen to, or touch with my hands, is gone, and there is only your
body and the lamplight and the winter beat of always in my heart.*

I read this passage over and over, sinking myself into the sheer
physical opulence of it. They were in this room, this *very* room,
making love, while the family were downstairs, Pensie playing the
piano, singing – so innocent, all of them so appallingly innocent to
what was going on above their heads. How could they not have
known? When Lucy and Henri came back downstairs, their
chessboard folded safe away, how did the family not look and see
what had happened between them? How will people not look and see
what has happened between Elise and myself? It feels so visible, like
the surface of my skin has contracted, until I'm all bone.

I read on.

*Walking with Ethan and the light falling grey across the water. His
complaints like needle pricks and the taunting sound of his voice,
and the way his hip bones move when he walks, swinging the frail
cage of his body to the side and back, to the side and back,
bothersome, making me long only for you, for the lean and free feel
of you walking beside me. He talks of our future, mine and his, and
the church we will take in Summerskill, and my married life as his
wife, soothing him with spiced tea when his sermons come slow, and
how I will be his right hand and a pearl of great price, and inside my
heart is railing NO, and my fingers are reaching for the smooth-as-
fruit feel of your skin and the way the breeze turns your hair into
fern, and I'm longing to be back in Carradine, in the gable room, the
moon, you.*

*

I have to stop reading, because someone is knocking at my door, *again*. I close the diary and slip it back under the pillow, then change my mind and push it down inside my bag instead, and whoever's out there on the landing knocks once more, louder.

"Just a minute." I make my voice sing-song and cordial. "I'm just coming." Then I lunge across the room and pull the door open quickly. Ruth is standing outside it, in her outdoor coat, still buttoned up to the chin. Her hair is askew and her eyebrows are furrowed low.

"Where is it?" she asks, as soon as she sees me.

"Where's what?"

She blows a little laugh down her nose. "Don't you be playing the innocent with me."

"I'm sorry, I don't know what you m–"

"Just give it to me." She holds out her hand. It's trembling.

"It?"

"The diary."

"Oh."

"Yes, *'Oh'*." She wags her head from side to side. "Marie told me she'd given it to you, and that you'd thought *I'd* taken it, et cetera." She looks impatient. "But it wasn't hers to give. I want it back."

I try to pull myself up to my full height, but even then, I'm still a good deal shorter than she is, and the withering nature of her gaze has taken my blood temperature down by a degree or two. Even so, I lift my chin, and try to keep my voice steady.

"Look, Ruth, Marie's an old lady and I'm just humouring her, okay? I'm pretending I'm interested in what she's got to say." I try a small smile, conspiratorial. "It seems important to her, but I haven't even looked at the diary to be honest. I really couldn't give a monkey's, but if I keep hold of it, just for tonight, then she'll think I've read it and that'll satisfy her that somebody's taking her seriously. I'll be gone in the morning, and she'll be none the wiser that you and me are in on this... deal."

I make the last word a question, trying to draw Ruth in, but she folds her arms across her chest and stares at me, says flatly, "Just how gullible do you think I am, Abby?"

"What d'you mean?"

She smiles then, slowly, like her face has to think really hard about which muscles to use.

"You take me for a fool."

"No, I don't."

She holds out her hand again, says, very carefully, "Give me the diary."

I take a deep breath, deep as I can.

"No."

It is at that point that Elise's voice filters up from downstairs.

"Mom? D'you want me to make a start on supper?"

Ruth keeps her eyes on me, blazing. If this were a Greek myth, I'd be turning to stone just about now, and staying that way. But this isn't a Greek myth, and Ruth can do nothing but turn her face to the stairs.

"No," she calls. "I'll do it, Elise. You go on and see about that car." And she turns her face to me again, adds, more loudly, "To take Abby *home* in." She lowers her voice then, leaning in. "You think this is a game, you stupid, *stupid* girl, but this isn't a game, and that diary is my property, and what's in it is my property. Do you understand?"

"Not really."

She winces. "You owe me a debt of respect, since you're in this house as my guest."

"But I'll be gone in the morning."

"Until then, you *will* abide by what I say." She closes her hand over my forearm. "Give – me – the – diary."

"Mom?" Elise is at the top of the stairs. "You okay?"

"I'm fine, love." Her voice curls lightly away. "Just talking to Abby."

"That's kind of what *I* wanted to do, actually." She dips her head a little, vaguely shamed. "Would you... excuse us, please?"

Ruth can't believe it. Her mouth opens and closes like a fish on a

115

line. At last she says, crisply, "Don't be long. I need you to chop the vegetables."

"Fine."

She moves past her daughter, her feet bearing heavy on the stairs, not looking back, and Elise approaches me, sheepish, her face turned to the side.

"We need to talk."

"I'm done with talking to you, Elise."

"What?"

I shrug. "Oh, come on. What's the point? You want me gone, and I understand that, but let's not talk the whole thing to death." I fold my arms hard, defiant. "I'm involved with someone, committed, *taken*, right? Claimed. And I'm also in... love" – I swallow on the word – "with you, but that's not your responsibility, or your fault. It's mine. It's all mine. You're a good person, and I'm making you do a bad thing. I *get* that, so I'll go and I won't come back. Okay? We don't need to discuss it, do we? It's already decided."

"What are you talking about?"

Her face is lifted towards me – innocent and tender. I take a breath.

"You *know* what I'm talking about."

"Do I?"

"Elise..."

She moves towards me fast, too fast for me to close the door, and she presses me back into the room. She uses her body to press me back into the room, until we are standing close in the darkness. She kicks the door closed with her heel.

"You're *in love* with me?" Her breath is hot in my face. I can taste her. "Is that what you're saying?"

"I don't know what I'm saying."

She touches my cheek with her fingers, traces my cheekbone. "I thought this was just... play, for you. I thought you didn't mean it."

"Why would you think that?"

"Because you're *kind of married* to someone else, remember?"

"Yes." I let my head drop. "And I love her. I do. I've been with her for nearly five years. As an out lesbian woman, she's all I've known, Gayle is *all* I've known, and I feel responsible for her happiness. I *am* responsible for her happiness, but suddenly, now, it's almost as if she doesn't even exist for me. That's a terrible thing to say, I know, *unforgivable*, but..." I look up into Elise's face, but the dark has fragmented her. "I can't help what I feel for you, Elise. If I could choose *not* to feel it, I would, but I can't. I never thought this kind of thing could happen to me, but it has, and there's no help for it, no escape from it, except to deny it, and go."

"But I didn't think you cared, not like this."

"Why? Why didn't you think I cared?"

"Because you said you were only interested in the *now*. Remember? That's what you said." She closes her hands over my shoulders. "I thought you just wanted..."

"What? A holiday romance?"

She nods. I feel the air move softly between us as she nods.

"And that wasn't what *I* wanted, Abby," she says. "Right from the very first, that wasn't what I wanted."

"I thought it would make it easier, if we put a seal on it, gave it a shape."

"No."

"No."

She treads her fingertips over my breasts, cups my breasts in her hands.

"What are we going to do?" she asks.

"You're going to drive me back to Port Hove in the morning."

"Am I?"

I lift my chin, just a little, touching my lips to the blade of her jaw, and she turns her head, so that our lips meet, very gently – a whisper of a kiss. I hold myself back from it. I drag myself back from it, like I'm dragging myself out of deep sleep.

"I do want to be a good person." I catch the cadence of tears in my voice.

"So do I." Her mouth is moving against my hair. "I want to be a good person too."

She eases me away, looks into my face, but all I can see are the whites of her eyes, pale as moonlight. "But it turns out that I want you *more* than I want to be a good person, and I don't know what to do about that."

"We'll go to hell for it, Elise?"

I hear her smile. "Maybe."

And this time, when she kisses me, I don't hold anything back from her. I meet her kiss, and my body opens to her, wide. My breasts are pressed hard against hers, and her hands on my body are brisk and impatient, but it's what I want. Oh my *God*! How much I want it. Such a long time since anyone has touched me like this, like their life *depended* on touching me. Gayle's lovemaking has always been so technical and measured, and serene, but *this* – Elise's hands, clumsy with desire, her mouth, like she'll die of thirst if she doesn't taste me...

She buckles my feet out from under me, and we fall back onto the bed, hauling ourselves up onto the bed. Her body is soft, all curves – shapes and silences to sink into. We are breath, nothing more, but someone is calling: Ruth is calling, and her voice breaks the spell, cracks the mirror clean across. We stop moving.

"You should go." I say it quietly, resignedly. I don't want her to go. I want her to stay – her body covering mine, her mouth moving on mine, but already the colour is draining from the moment, and she is lifting herself away from me.

"I'll come back," she says, and I watch her walk quickly to the door and open it. For a moment the room sickens with light from the landing and Elise hesitates.

"We'll find a way to make this all right," she says, and she turns her face to me. "I promise we'll find a way to make this all right."

But, after she's gone, and the dark has claimed me, I know that we won't ever find a way to make this all right. I lie there, very still, drowning in the ravelled refrain of the sea, trying to think a way through, trying to see a path that we could take, but *every* way through, and every path, lead me straight back to the same point – Gayle.

Twelve

I lie for a long time, waiting for Elise to come back, but she doesn't, so I switch on the lamp by the bed and take Lucy's diary out of my bag. If the entries in this book are to be believed, then Lucy came to Carradine and fell in love, with Henri, and then she left, went home, married someone else. Why didn't she stay? Why didn't she and Henri find a way to be together? She wasn't married. She was, perhaps, promised in some way to the Ethan MacKay, with his bad hips and his dreary sermons, but, if she was as deeply involved as the diary suggests, with Carradine and the man she loved, then why leave and never speak of them again? I start to read.

Delmont shimmering like a handful of jewels on black cloth, and the window open, bringing the sea inside. Your hands in my hair, your cheek pressed to mine, and we are listening for the sound of footsteps: your parents coming up from the ballroom, the dancing done. Their tread on the stair will close our love shut. We press ourselves on, into each other, and you say, again and again, "This must end. This must end", but, again and again, I draw you down to me, and Stella's voice in the daytime light chides me still. "When will it be your time to marry, Miss Pritchard?" Her engagement ring, a glare of white, her mouth twisting to despise me: country schoolmarm spinster miss, and you standing close, and us with our secret burning bright but dark, and your hand touches mine beneath the wedding table, and I smile at Stella and answer, "I am happy with my present independence, Miss Robichaud" – and your fingers are smooth and white as porcelain around your punch glass, and trembling, as are mine.

*

Stella Robichaud's engagement party at the Dougray Hotel, in Delmont, and Lucy and Henri must have slipped away to make love while the family were downstairs, dancing. The risks they took to be together were remarkable. Would Elise and I have made love just now, with her mother downstairs, and her grandmother at large somewhere in the house? I'm not sure that we would, but here are Lucy and Henri, a hundred years ago, so addicted to each other, and so frantic in their need to touch and taste each other, that they cared for nothing else. Their recklessness astounds me, shames me. Is this how it's supposed to be, then? Are we supposed to give ourselves up, utterly, to our desires, like they did, and not look to the consequences? Lucy's diary seems to pivot on the belief that life is too short, and love too precious to waste, even for a second.

I read the passage over again, savouring it, and it is then that something strikes me. Lucy describes Henri's fingers as *"smooth and white as porcelain"*, which seems a little odd. He was a farmer's son, a labourer. His fingers would have been tanned brown by the wind surely, roughened by work and the brash lash of the sea. The first time she meets him, she says he smells of wheat and leather. He must have been out in the fields that day, and every day. How could he have kept his fingers *"smooth and white as porcelain"*? This diary entry is dated March 10th – early spring; no ploughing or harvesting to be done then of course, so maybe Henri had been taking it easy, warming his hands by the fire, bathing them in lavender water to soothe away his calluses. Maybe Lucy had been bathing them *for* him. I close my eyes, thinking of Henri's smooth hands on Lucy's body, thinking of Elise's hands on *mine*, and, as if she has caught hold of the glow of my imagining her, she calls to me. She calls my name.

I close the diary and slip it back into my bag, and then I hurry to the door and open it.

"Abby," she calls again, and she's halfway up the stairs. She smiles when she sees me. "Supper's ready, if you're hungry."

I join her where she's standing, closing my hand over hers on the banister, and then I say, salaciously, close to her ear, "Only hungry for you, lover."

She turns her head, so that she's looking into my eyes, and she holds my gaze then, her smile growing wider.

"Come back upstairs with me for a minute, Elise."

I try to take her hand, but she closes it tighter on the banister.

"We can't," she whispers. "Mom and Gran are waiting."

"So?"

"But they're sitting at the table, *waiting* for us. We have to go down."

"I'd like to, go down" – and I push my fingers forward quickly and start to undo the buttons on her jeans – "on *you*."

"Jesus, Abby!" She flails my hands away, starting to laugh, her eyes flashing at me. "What's got into you?"

"Lucy."

"What?"

"Lucy's got into me."

She glances down towards the kitchen, distracted.

"What are you talking about?"

"The diary. Marie gave me Lucy's diary to read, and it's amazing."

Elise stares hard into my face. "Lucy's diary?"

"Uh huh. Did you know she'd had this big affair with your great-grandfather? They had loads of sex, and I mean drop-down-dead fan-fucking-*tastic* sex, right under this roof, and all over the place, and the family never knew a thing about it. And I was thinking, God, you know, here *we* are, you and me, tying ourselves in knots over what we feel for each other, when really maybe all we need to do is take a leaf out of Lucy and Henri's book, and just shag each other's brains out and worry about the rest... of... it..."

But Elise has taken hold of my arm, very tightly, and is pushing me ahead of her, back up the stairs. She bundles me inside Gen's room and closes the door, and then she switches on the light. I blink into the sudden brightness, looking up into her face. Her mouth is set hard.

"What's wrong?" I place both my hands on her arms. "God, Elise, what's the matter?"

She seems about to say something, but changes her mind, takes a deep breath, holds it.

"Look," I squeeze her arm, "I'm sorry about what I said, on the stairs. I was just joking, you know. It's just that this whole thing has got so intense, so quickly. I was trying to lighten the bloody mood, that's all."

"Stop talking." Her voice is soft, but very deliberate. She walks me to the bed and sits me down on it, and then she sits down by my side. "Where's Lucy's diary now?"

"It's in my bag." I point. "Why?"

"I need you to give it to me."

"Why?"

She reaches across me, making a snatch for my bag, but I get there first and hold it out of her way.

"What's going on, Elise? Why are you and your mum so *intent* on me not reading this diary?"

Her face opens up in surprise. "Mom knows you've got it?"

"Yes. She was up here before, wanting it back."

She sighs then. "I bet she was."

"What the hell's in it that's so bad? I've read some of it already, and there's nothing terrible so far. So, Lucy had a fling with Henri before she got married. Big deal."

Elise just looks at me, and her eyes are black and uneasy.

"Gran shouldn't have given it to you," she says. "She doesn't know what she's doing."

"She *seemed* to know exactly what she was doing."

"No. I need you to give it to me, *now*, Abby." And she holds out her hand. "I need you to trust me."

"I'm not sure I do."

"What?" Her face is incredulous. "How can you say one minute that you love me and the next minute that you don't trust me?"

"But they don't come as part of a package, those two things. They're separate." I try to take hold of her hand, but she pulls it clear of my touch. "I *want* to trust you, but how can I, if you won't be straight with me? Trust *me* first, Elise."

She lowers her hand into her lap, clenches it into a fist, unclenches it, thinking, and then she stands up.

"All right," she says, very quiet. "Go ahead and read it. I can't stop you, can I?"

"Why do you want to stop me?"

"You'll see, Abby, and when you do, when you read it and find... out... then you must come and talk to me; before you do anything about it, you must come to me first."

"*Do* anything? Why would I, and about *what*, for Christ's sake?"

She turns her face away from me and I watch the muscles in her jaw ripple and grow taut.

"You'll see," she says, very flat, and then she walks to the door and opens it. She pauses for a second, and without turning, says, "I'll tell Mom you're not feeling well."

I stand up. "You want me to read it now?"

"No time like the present." Her tone has lifted a little, but when she glances back, her face is weighted down and wary. She won't make eye contact with me.

"I'll come back after supper," she says, and is gone.

I do as she asks. I open Lucy's diary and I start to read, as fast as I can, but the next set of entries aren't really very different from the first. She and Henri are still slipping away to make their oh-so-sweet love at every available opportunity. There's one entry where they run down to the beach and undress each other in the sand dunes, but are nearly discovered by a man out walking his Irish wolfhound. Lucy uses the startled phrase "*the dog's snout almost finds us out*", which makes me laugh out loud, softly. I can't help it. After that incident, she and Henri are more careful. They confine their sessions to the farm: in the house mostly, a couple of times in the barn, occasionally

125

in the fields, and, one chilly and inventive time, in the outdoor lavatory!

The diary meanders on, full of sex, but, a few pages short of the end, the mood changes, and the tone changes, suddenly. Something is about to go wrong.

The room is twilight and your head rests in my lap, the good weight of you upon me. I read to you, Tennyson, "The Lady of Shalott", and you lift your dear, sweet head now and then and look into my face, and your smile breaks onto my heart like sunlight. "The mirror cracked from side to side, the curse is come upon me cried the Lady of Shalott." *You stir then, and rise, and walk to the bureau. You come back to me with papers in your hands.* "My stories", *you say.* "My poems", *and I look and read and see that they are good. You stand over me, your hands touching my face, my bare shoulders where my chemise has fallen away, and I read and something burns hot in my bowels, burns crimson across my sight. All my hard-worked stories, stained and ash, when set against* these, *and you my inferior in every way that counts. How can this be? You are without intellect or imagination. How could your common hand have conjured this magic?*

There's a long gap then, between entries. Lucy doesn't pick up her diary again for two months and, when she does, her pen drips with bitterness, and cunning. She is getting ready to leave Carradine.

You come and stand by my side while I pack, and your eyes are filled with tears. You try to rest your head on my shoulder, and I permit it, but I keep my hands working. You try to kiss me, and I permit it, but my heart is a hard thing. "Don't leave me", *you say.* "Don't go from this place without me. Take me with you." *But I smile and tell you not to be so sentimental. I tell you that we knew this day would come and how can it be otherwise, with you, a labourer's child only, not*

befitting my social class. "You knew", I say. "We have had some jolly
times", I tell you, "but now they are done", and you turn away,
weeping, and even then my heart is stone. How have you shamed me
into this? You leave me alone in the room. I fill my carpetbag and my
cases with clothes. I open the bureau and take down your stories,
your poems. I read their names, "Little Hector of the Creek", "Little
Hector Wins the Prize", "Little Hector's Happy Days", "Little Hector
at Home", and I slip them into my bag, because why should they be
yours, when they could be mine? They should *be mine.*

Oh my God! I stand up, sit down, stand up again, and then I run to
the door and out onto the landing, clattering down the stairs with the
diary still in my hands.

"She stole them!" I start to say it before I reach the kitchen, and I
say it louder as soon as I'm inside. "She stole them. She stole the
stories!"

Ruth is at the sink, washing up, and Elise is sitting at the table
reading a newspaper. They both look at me, their mouths open, and
then they look at each other, holding each other's gaze. Ruth breathes
out, nodding, and Elise sits back carefully in her chair.

"God!" I go toward her, shaking my head. I can feel my cheeks
burning hot, and my voice is rumpled and high. "Her own writing was
shit, so she stole Henri's stories, the *Hector* stories, and passed them off
as her own?"

I slide the diary onto the table and sit down, and Elise leans
towards me.

"The *Hector* stories," she says slowly. "Yes."

"How did she get away with it?"

She shrugs. "I don't know."

Ruth is standing with her back to us, her palms pressed either side
of the sink, but she turns now, wiping her fingers dry on a towel.

"Henri never told anybody he'd written those stories," she
explains. "He protected Lucy, even when she became famous. He

could have gone public then, but he didn't."

"He still loved her."

"Yes."

"What happened to him?"

"He died of typhoid, when he was thirty-three."

"God, only a few years after Lucy left, then."

Ruth hesitates. "Yes."

"We only found the diary last summer," says Elise. "We were converting the loft space and had to open up loads of old boxes, clear them out. It was right at the bottom of one of those boxes. Gran found it. We nearly missed it, though."

"It was lost among Henri's things," interrupts Ruth.

"I see." I touch the diary with the tips of my fingers. "But why didn't Lucy take it with her when she left? Talk about leaving incriminating evidence behind. Blimey."

Elise nods. "Yeah, but in the last entry, you see, she says..."

"Elise." Ruth moves quickly to the table, smiling, and scoops up the diary in her hand, slips it into the pocket of her apron. "Why don't you make Abby some tea?"

Elise looks up into her mother's face. "Sure. Yeah."

"Er... I haven't quite –" I point to Ruth's apron pocket – "– finished reading that, actually."

"Yes, you have," she says, and her smile disappears like somebody's snapped their fingers to make it happen. She softens. "The secret's out, and now I think you'll maybe understand why we didn't want the diary being pawed over by every Tom, Dick and Harry." She closes her eyes for a second. "No offence intended."

"None taken."

"It's our private family business. Henri married a local girl and had a family after Lucy left, *this* family, and we are a private family, Abby. Some of his other descendants still live on the island too, and we didn't want them getting mixed up in this, after all these years. Also, of course, there's Lucy's family to think about, and then there's the whole industry that's built up around her. Prince William Island relies on its tourists, people who come here solely because it's the birthplace of the woman who wrote the *Hector* books." Elise slides a mug of tea onto the table in front of me. I lift it to my lips. "We get a lot of visitors, at the schoolhouse, in the summer months. They pay us good money to see where Lucy taught. We'd lose that. We'd lose a lot. The island would lose a lot if it ever came to light that Lucy Pritchard was a fraud." She stares down at me, and her eyes are tiny shards of light, penetrating. "Do you see? These are the reasons you mustn't tell anyone about the diary, mustn't tell anyone, ever."

"But don't you want Henri recognised as the true author of those books?" I'm shaking my head, perplexed. "There would be money in it for you, surely."

"No. This isn't about money. This is about our business staying our business. We are entitled to confidentiality. We are entitled to expect that from you, I think?"

I nod up at her. "Of course. I won't say anything. It makes perfect sense now, why you were so keen for me not to read it. I'm sorry I've been so... insistent. I can appreciate your reticence. I mean, I was a stranger, and I was also involved with a biography of Lucy. I could have... Oh, of *course*." I put my mug back down on the table. "That explains why Mo wasn't interested in the diary."

"Mo?" Ruth stiffens. "Mo Laker?"

"Yes. Marie showed it to her too, showed her the diary that day she came here, doing her research, but she said she wasn't interested in it."

Ruth and Elise exchange glances again, and then Ruth sits down heavily at the table, and pushes her hair back from her face. She looks very weary, strained.

"Marie showed the diary to Mo Laker?" She asks it slowly, and laboured, like she's trying to make sense of it.

"Yes, but Mo thought it was a fake."

"Well," Ruth sighs. "That's something, I guess."

"She would *have* to think it was a fake, though, wouldn't she?"

"What do you mean?"

"If she admitted to herself that it was real and started thinking that it might get out, go public, then all her hard work on the book would be for nothing. Nobody's going to want to read a critical biography of a writer who turns out to be a... charlatan."

I've never used that word before, but I like the sound of it, and I like the sound of my voice unravelling the mystery of all of this. I feel clever and powerful, vaguely god-like in how insightful I've become.

"No wonder she didn't want me coming back to Carradine." There's a little laugh curled up snug inside my words, but Ruth frowns at it.

"This isn't a joke," she says, very sharply. "You think this is a joke?"

"No. Not at all."

She stands up. "Mo Laker knows you're here, in Carradine?"

"No. She told me not to come back, but I did, anyway."

"Why?"

I glance at Elise. She is standing at her mother's elbow, nibbling at her fingernails.

"To draw the schoolhouse."

I say it knowing that it's only half of the truth, knowing that my real reason for coming back to Carradine was Elise, but Ruth just nods, her eyebrows furrowing low like there's gravity behind them.

"Will she be in Port Hove when you get back there?"

"She's in Vancouver until Friday."

"You won't tell her what's in the diary?"

"She already knows." I feel confused. "I mean, she read it, so she knows."

Ruth is cross with me. "Yes, *yes*," she says, impatient. "But she thinks it's a fake. What I mean is, you won't tell her that what's in it is actually true?" Her face changes, grows suddenly tender. She places her fingers on my shoulder and squeezes. "You'll keep our secret, Abby? We can trust you to keep our secret?"

I nod fast. "Of *course*."

"Which secret?"

All three of us turn to see Marie standing in the doorway with an empty glass in her hand. Ruth moves towards her with the speed of a racing greyhound, and stands with her body blocking Marie's view of the kitchen. She whispers something quick and sharp into Marie's face and then they both leave the room.

Elise sits down with me at the table.

"Well," she says. "I'm glad that's over." She places her hands over mine on the table. "I wanted to tell you, but..."

"You didn't trust me."

"It was private."

"I'd have kept it that way."

She inclines her head. "I know you would. And look, I *did* trust you, in the end. I said you should read the diary, didn't I?"

"Yes." I breathe out. "But only under duress. I mean, what did you think I was going to do exactly? Shout it from the rooftops? Let your family's cat out of the bag and not give a shit about the consequences? Is that how I come across to you – like someone who doesn't care about consequences?" I pull my hands clear of hers. "You *know* I care about consequences, otherwise I wouldn't be leaving here tomorrow, leaving you. If I didn't care about consequences, I'd just be saying fuck it, and staying, wouldn't I?"

She nods. "Yes. I'm sorry." And she sits back in her chair, her face shamed and perplexed. "I made a mistake, all right? I should have trusted you. Next time, I will. I won't lie again."

"What did Lucy say in her last diary entry?" I ask it quickly, so there's no way out for her, so the whole-trusting-me-next-time thing is still on her tongue, but she shakes her head.

"What d'you mean?"

"You were talking before, about how Lucy came to leave her diary behind, and you said she says something in the last entry about it, about leaving the diary."

"Abby." Elise sighs loud, shuts her eyes, and I start to feel bad about having cornered her. "Can't we talk about something else? Don't you think we've got more important things to talk about than something that happened last *century*?"

I just look into her eyes, keeping my gaze steady, waiting.

"I thought you were going to trust me, Elise."

"Jesus. You're like a dog with a bone." She blows a breath into the air. "She says she's leaving the diary with Henri so that he will always be able to look at it and know that she *did* truly love him, and she asks his forgiveness for stealing the stories. She tells him she's weak and vain, and that even though she's seen as his superior in the world, he will always be a better man, a finer person than she'll ever be, and she tells him that the happiest times she has ever known have been in his arms. And then she tells him goodbye."

I can feel my eyes filling with tears. "Oh." I look away from Elise. "That's…" I have to wipe them on the back of my hand. "That's lovely."

"Yes." She touches my arm. "It *is* lovely."

"I thought she renounced it, when she left. I mean, I thought it had all been a lie, maybe."

"I don't think it was a lie."

I look into her face. "No."

"And *this* isn't a lie, is it, Abby – you and me? This isn't a lie?"

"No." I lean toward her across the table, lifting myself a little, so that I can bring our faces close. "The happiest times I've ever known have been in your arms, Elise." I say it looking into her eyes, meaning it, and she slips her arms around me then, and kisses me, tastes the truth on my tongue.

Thirteen

I read a story once, a fairy tale, about a king who was determined that his daughter should marry the most intelligent man in the kingdom. Lots of sharp suitors came to court with their gifts and their tricks, but none of them convinced the king that they were *quite* good enough for his princess. At last, a common man, a labourer, arrived at the gates of the castle and requested an audience with the monarch. It was granted, and this is what the man had to say.

"Sire. Give me one year, and in that year, I will teach your horse, your favourite stallion, to talk. If I succeed, then you will grant me the hand of the princess in marriage. If I fail, then you may have me executed."

The king laughed.

"You seriously believe that you can teach my horse to talk? You are a madman then, for you will surely fail."

"Sire," said the man, "give me one year. That's all I ask. Much can happen in a year. You might die. *I* might die. I might indeed fail, and you will have me executed. But then again" – and the man smiled – "the horse might talk."

I'm thinking about that story as Elise and I drive across the island in the morning light. The sky above us is azure, thumb-printed white, here and there, with high cloud. No sign now of yesterday's rain. The air is warm, and it smells green – choked with leaves. We are driving inland, back along Highway Three, and I'm thinking about that story, about the horse talking, about how anything can happen, and I'm thinking how, for Elise and me, it already has.

I didn't see Ruth this morning. She'd already left for the store. I wrote her a note saying thank you and wishing her well, but I don't think she'll be mortally offended that I didn't say goodbye in person. Somehow, I think she'll be muttering a good-riddance-to-bad-rubbish mantra for the foreseeable future. I was sorry not have seen Marie, though. Elise insisted that we leave early because she has to return this borrowed car to its owner by tonight but, even so, I'd like to have spoken to Marie. I feel I owe her an apology. She wanted something from me, in showing me Lucy's diary, and I didn't deliver. I read it, discussed it with Ruth and Elise, instead of discussing it with her, and now I've sloped away home without even saying goodbye.

I sink down slightly in my seat, watching the trees glide past like they're on casters, and then I look at Elise's hands on the steering wheel.

"Will you make sure to say goodbye to your Gran for me?"

She nods. "Yes."

"I feel bad that I didn't see her."

"Don't worry about it. She'll understand."

She glances at me. She's wearing dark glasses against the glare of the road and the sky, but I can see her eyes when she's in profile, blinking into the light.

"What are we going to do, Elise?"

Her grip on the steering wheel tightens a little, her knuckles standing out white beneath the brown sheen of her skin.

"I'm not sure."

"We need to think."

"Yes." She clears her throat, says again, "Yes," and then she dips her head a touch, looking at a sign by the side of the road.

"Lapshadow," she says.

"Lapshadow?"

"It's a lake. It's the only lake on the island. I used to go fishing there, with my dad, when I was small." She slows the car. "Shall we stop?"

"If you'd like to."

She smiles at me. "I would." And then she takes a turn onto a narrower side road, bumpy with rutted earth, wet with old rain. "It's the stillest place there is, because it's so deep in the valley. You can't hear the sea, not even distantly, just stillness. There's just stillness."

"I could use some of that about now."

She smiles again, slips her hand onto my thigh and keeps it there, and the pulse of my blood under her touch skips and stutters.

"You'll like it," she says. "There are loons."

"Loons?"

"Uh huh. Dad used to say that the sound the loons made was actually them calling my name, across the water."

"Were they inviting you in for a swim?"

"Don't think so." She laces her fingers up around mine, squeezes. "Just saying hello, that's all."

"Because they *do* that, yeah? Loons. They greet people by name."

Elise makes a face of mock affront.

"Not *people*," she says. "Only me."

We park on a gravel slope and walk down to the lake with the sun stippling our footsteps. Elise's hand nestles in the small of my back as we walk, her fingers curling into a fist and then uncurling.

"We used to come fishing every Sunday, for a while," she says, and her voice is brisk and pleased. "We used to walk all the way round." She points to the opposite bank, violet-coloured in the shadow of the mountains. "And then we'd just sit, and fish."

"I've never quite *got* fishing."

I don't realise I've said it out loud, until Elise stops walking and turns to look at me. She takes off her glasses.

"What d'you mean?"

"It's just always seemed so dull, to me."

"Dull?" Her voice is aghast. "God. It's not dull. It's amazing. It's a real challenge, profound, pitting your intellect against the intellect of a fish."

I incline my head. "And of course we all know what intellectual creatures fish *are*!"

Elise puts her glasses back on.

"Philistine," she whispers, but her mouth is smiling, and it keeps smiling even when I loop my arms around her waist and kiss her. I can feel her smiling into my kiss, and it's a slow kiss, like that first one in the kitchen. It goes on for a long time. I'd be okay if it went on forever, but eventually Elise eases me away from her, keeping her hands on my arms.

"Let's sit, Abby," she says, and we do, side by side on the sweet-smelling grass, looking out across the lake.

"This is like Lake Ullswater at home," I tell her, shielding my eyes. "I wouldn't be surprised if good old Uncle Wordsworth came round that corner right now, brandishing a big bunch of daffodils, and sucking pensively on a quim."

Elise peers at me. "I think you mean *quill*."

"Do I?"

I'm feeling unreasonably cheerful, with the sun on my shoulders and the blue water of the lake inking my veins, but Elise looks away from me.

"I don't think quills were still in use in Wordsworth's day."

"Quims were, though." I nudge my shoulder against her, grinning. "And still are."

She takes her glasses off again. "Yes," she says, but she doesn't look like she's in the mood for play. Her eyes are dark and distracted.

"We need to decide," she says suddenly, "exactly what we're going to do, and we need to stand by what we decide."

"I thought we *had* decided? I thought you were taking me back to Port Hove and leaving me there."

"Is that what you want?"

"No. Is that what *you* want?"

She shakes her head. "It's what I *should* want." She looks into my face, pensive, says again, "We need to decide."

I swallow as hard as I can. "I know we do. I know it's coming, and we're going to have to live with it, either way, but can't we just sit for a while, like this" – I take her hand in mine and bring it to my lips – "with the stillness, and the loons..." I point out across the lake. "Look!"

Two grey and white birds, tall in the water, are pirouetting their way towards us, very slow, very graceful – their heads tilted like they're waiting for applause, and then one of them calls to us across the water, and the sound arches and falls, refracting through the air – a short hoot, high and sharp, and then a longer sound tumbling low, over and over, and I'll be darned if it isn't Elise's name, or something uncannily close to it, that reaches us. She dips her head, says gently, "Told you."

I look into her face and I know, with absolute certainty, absolute clarity, that I don't want to have to unlearn what she looks like, or what she feels like, because it's just like people say: it's as if, all my life, I've been asking a question, and now the answer has come, the *right* answer and, even though I should be feeling hopeless and guilty and lost that this answer means the end of my relationship with Gayle, I don't feel any of those things. I don't feel lost at all. I feel gloriously *found*.

"D'you know what I've always wanted to do?"

Elise glances at me, smiles with one side of her mouth. "What?"

"I've always wanted to hire a campervan, an old VW Combie maybe, and drive it all the way across Canada, from coast to coast." I look out at the water. "It would take about six months I reckon, if we did it properly."

She is silent for a moment, and then she says, "Would we tour the Rockies, because we'd need something sturdier than an old Combie. We'd need something with shit-hot suspension, for a trip like that."

"And something comfortable."

"For sure. If we were going to sleep in it every night, it would need to be comfortable, and spacious, and it would need to have a built-in TV."

"And a mini-bar."

"And a waterbed."

I nod fast. "Oh, yes. No drive across Canada in a motor vehicle would be complete without a waterbed."

We both look out at the water then, concentrating hard. The loons have come close and are staring at us. I can hear Elise breathing.

"So, that's settled, then?"

"Yes," I close my eyes, "everything except the shit-hot suspension, and the comfort, and the space, and the TV, and the mini-bar, and the waterbed."

"Just the VW Combie?" She turns her body so that she's facing me, and she takes both my hands and holds onto them very tightly. "And you and me, driving across Canada. Right?"

"It would take about six months," I say again, my mouth a desert suddenly, "if we did it properly."

"Yes."

But the word seems to choke her. She shakes her head like she's shaking something away. I place my hands on her cheeks and hold her face so that she's looking into my eyes.

"We could really do this, you know, Elise. We just have to choose it."

"I know."

"This is what I want, but only if it's what you want too."

She nods. "It is. Of course it is, but are you sure you don't just want the *now*, like you said before? Are sure you want the *end*? Because that's what this is, or that's what this will become at least."

"I know. I know it is, and yes. The answer's yes. Maybe it is going to be the most self-interested thing I do in my life – choose you over Gayle – but, God help me, I'm still going to do it!"

"Even though this has all happened to us *so* fast?"

"But love's got nothing to do with timing, really, has it? True love, I mean."

"True love. Are you sure that's what this is?"

"Yes. I'm sure. I'm sure it's what I've been looking for – someone who would be my true love, my true north. I feel like I've been headed to this moment all of my life."

"But what about everything we said, back in Carradine, about doing the right thing..."

I press my finger to her lips. "Shhh" – bumping my forehead soft against hers – "my love." I close my eyes. "Can't you see? This *is* the right thing."

She nods, very slowly, and then she starts to stand up, starts talking really fast suddenly.

"I've got some money saved. We'll be okay. And I can **get** a sabbatical from school. They offered me one last year, so I could do my Master's, but I turned it down." She glances away from me, thinking. "I'll just tell them I've changed my mind."

"Okay."

"But what about you?" She looks down at me, the sun behind her, so that she's just a star shape, spilling words. "What will *you* do?"

I stand up too and I lean my body into hers.

"I don't know yet, but I know what I *won't* do." And I lift my head so that our faces are close, her breath misting into mine. "I won't live the rest of my life without you. I just won't do it, Elise." And, as if they've heard it spoken, the loons out on the lake start to echo her name back to us, over and over, like a celebration, a homecoming, an invitation to come in and swim. We take them up on it, impulsively. Our bodies are all breath and laughter suddenly, and it's lovely – this liberation. It's like carrying lots of heavy bags up the hill from the supermarket, in the rain, and then being able put them down. It's that moment of putting them down.

We tear off our clothes, all of them, and then we run into the water, and it blazes up sharp, spearing our skin with ice, punching the air clear out of our lungs.

"Holy Moley!" My voice is a shriek. "It's freeeeeezing!"

Elise swims around me, sleek as a shark. She's laughing. Her arms circle my waist and she lifts my body out of the water for a second, sinks me back down so that I'm pressed against her. I can feel her along the length of my body, my breasts crushed against hers, the water spilling blue and grey between us. She moves her mouth against my ear, says very softly, so that I almost fail to catch it, "I really *missed* you before I knew you, Abby."

I turn my face and our lips meet, and her arms around my waist tighten, taking me under the surface of the water. I feel the water close over my head, numbly, and there are only the murky sounds of the lake for a moment, and our bodies tangling like reeds. When we surface again, the air is liquid and bright white, but there's a shadow moving through it. I wipe the water from my eyes fast and look towards the bank. A man is standing next to our clothes. He has a fishing rod in one hand and a dog lead in the other, at the end of which is an Irish wolfhound, sniffing at my underwear.

"Oh, shit," says Elise, very quietly, and then, more loudly, in the direction of the bank, "Good morning."

The man with the hound just stares at us, blank as a board, and then he tugs on the dog's lead, says gruffly, "Hector! *Come!*"

We stay treading water until the two of them are out of sight, and then we creep to the bank and dry each other off with our clothes, laughing because we can't help it and, even if we *could*, we'd probably go on laughing anyway.

"Hector?" I'm trembling with the cold. "Has *everything* on this bloody island got something to do with Lucy Pritchard?"

"Pretty much. Hey, but you know, it's a municipal offence, being naked in public." She tries to look grave. "As a Canadian citizen, I should know better. I could get fined an arm and a leg."

"Awww, but I'd still love you if you were one-armed and one-legged, my lovely."

She slips her arm around me. "Well, I'd love *you* if you had *no* arms and *no* legs! I'd love you if you were just a *torso*."

I look up into her face. "What, no head?"

"Well, no, I mean a head would come in handy, of course, if that's not mixing my metaphors."

And we start laughing all over again, helplessly, all the way back to the car. It's an impossibility, surely, this happiness. It must be. I don't deserve this but, oh my *God*, how I savour it. Every time I look at her, the lilt of it croons through my blood, and suddenly I know how it must have been for Lucy and Henri. I understand the risks they took. I understand how everything else, *everything*, fell away in the face of what they felt for each other.

Just outside Port Hove, I lean across in my seat and kiss Elise on the cheek.

She smiles at me. "What was that for?"

"For showing it to me."

"It?"

"Lapshadow."

"Ah."

"I see what you mean about the stillness." I press my fingers to my heart. "I felt it, *here*."

She nods. "Me too."

"Do you still?"

She nods again. "More every moment."

There are tears in my eyes as I direct Elise off the road at St. Catherine's Point and onto the gravel driveway leading to The Old Sea Box, and I'm actually crying when we climb out of the car. I try to breathe it away, but it's a mixture of so *many* things, all at once, crowding close. I can't dispel it.

I keep my face away from her as I unlock the door, and the dank house swims up to greet us, smelling of the sea, but her hands are on my body as soon as we're inside and she's trying to turn my face towards her. I let my hair fall like a veil, and I draw her up the stairs and into my room, with its bookcases and its patterned walls. She looks around her for a moment, taking it in, but I move towards her fast and push her back against the wall with my weight, kissing her, slipping my hands down her chest, her thighs. I'm still crying, and it's getting worse, and suddenly Elise is saying, "Shhh, my love. Shhh," very, very quietly, kissing my hair, pressing her hands down my spine as if she could stop the shaking that way, but I'm drowning in my body's water, and it's all so bewildering, because I didn't even think I was sad. I'm here, with Elise, whom I love, and who loves me, and we're going to drive across Canada together; a happy ending blazing bright above our heads like a sky full of fireworks, and yet... my heart is breaking, and I know it will *go on* breaking every time I think of Gayle, and all the sweet wonder of what I feel for Elise is pinprick small when set against the ill that I'm about to do to the person I have loved and lived with for the last five years.

"I'm sorry..." The words hurt. "Elise." But her name is a sob.

"Abby, shhh." She sinks her body into mine, rocks me tight as a seashell, and suddenly there's a sound like music, an undercurrent like the swell of the sea.

"Saskatoon... Moosonee... Prince Rupert..." Elise's mouth is close to my ear, her breath filling my head with hot sound, spellbinding. "Athabasca... Edmonton... Montreal..." She's whispering a mantra of place names, mountains, stretches of water – over and over, very soft, "Fort Reliance... Baker Lake... Thunder Bay..." – and, somehow, the cadence of them begins to lull and beguile me. I am caught in the web of Elise's words, giving myself up to the song of her.

She kisses my cheeks, "Calgary..." – my mouth, "Revelstoke..." – my neck, "Kelowna..." – pushing me back toward the bed, pulling my top up over my head, stroking her fingers over my breasts, but I can feel her trying to slow herself down. Her breath is held in now, like she's counting, calculating, holding herself back. I don't want her to hold herself back. I want to give myself up to her crashing and fighting. I want her to slam into me hard and sharp, like she did last time, and smash to pieces Gayle's face, Gayle's smile, Gayle's eyes – smoky grey and filled with tears. But it's no good. Elise is intent on tenderness. Every time I reach for her, she eases away, whispering kisses over my skin, undressing me like I'm breakable, like my bones are brittle enough to shatter if she presses too hard.

In the end, I sink myself into it. She seduces me into the slowness of it, the languor; traces her tongue down my breastbone, across my breasts, and then she lifts herself over me, lifts my hands above my head and closes her fingers over my wrists, so that they are pinned flat to the mattress. She looks into my eyes, and she keeps looking into my eyes, and then she slides down my body, in one fluid movement; slides her tongue down the centre of my body until her mouth is between my legs. I open them for her wide, wider, and she pushes her tongue inside me, circles it up over my clitoris, biting at my clitoris softly with the tips of her teeth.

I can feel tears burning in my throat again, springing into my eyes, even though I'm fighting them away. It's too much. Unbearable. I want to tell Elise that it's too much. I want to tell her to stop what she's doing. I try to adjust my position, but she has me held fast, her hands closed over my hipbones. My body is trembling hard beneath her, and there's a tidal wave gathering at the edges of my vision. I can feel the dark of it approaching, a giant surge of water leaping white into blue, a thousand rivers fallen from the mountains, churning into sprays of foam. If I turn my head, I will see it lifting at the window, swooping over us, crashing down on us, but I *don't* turn my head. I breathe deeply, as deeply as I can, and I lift my body to Elise's touch, letting her taste me, slow and easy, letting her take her time, and then suddenly, in a second, the tidal wave dissolves, sinks to one still point, one sharp, still point, when I come, with Elise's breath burning hot and dark inside me.

My eyes won't focus for a moment. The tears are gone, but everything is smudged at the edges. Elise lifts herself over me, climbs up my body, bumps her forehead forward softly into mine. She's breathing hard, her features beginning to sharpen. She's smiling. She's opening her mouth to speak, but it isn't *her* voice that I hear.

"*Un*believable."

Elise and I both turn our heads towards the door, to see Mo, standing with her arms folded. Her sunglasses are pushed up into her hair, and her face is dark as death.

She shakes her head, her mouth set in a straight line. "What the fuck d'you think you're *doing*?"

And, even though I would imagine that the answer is blatantly obvious, I actually find myself thinking how to explain, how to phrase it so it won't sound so bad. I don't get the chance, though, because Mo turns on her heels and thuds down the stairs.

Fourteen

Elise rolls off me, lies by my side. "I thought you said she wasn't back until tomorrow."

"She wasn't."

"Except she *is*."

I gather the sheet together and wrap it around me. "I'll go and talk to her. Give me a couple of minutes, okay?"

She reaches out of bed for her clothes. "I think you're gonna need longer than that, sweetheart."

I take a breath and head down the stairs, with my toga-sheet trailing behind me like an impromptu bridal veil. Mo is standing in the kitchen, looking out at the sea. She's smoking, really fast, drawing deeply on her cigarette and then blowing the smoke straight out of her mouth without a taste.

"Mo." She doesn't turn around to look at me. I try again. "Mo?"

And this time, she *does* turn around, and I really wish she hadn't, because the look on her face shrivels my insides to dust and ash.

"Look, what you saw, upstairs... I'm really sorry..."

"Are you?"

"Yes."

"Sorry it happened, or sorry I saw it?"

I draw myself up to my full height, clutching the sheet tight around my breasts. I clear my throat.

"Both. Sorry you saw it. Sorry it happened in your house. Sorry..."

"... I caught you fucking a stranger, cheating on your girlfriend, cheating on your *wife*, perhaps?"

I look down at the rug beneath my feet, and I'm shamed and speechless, and so unutterably sad suddenly that any words I *might* have said, any defiance I *might* have managed, have liquefied and disappeared.

Mo comes quickly towards me and takes hold of my wrist, very tight.

"I thought I told you not to go back to Carradine."

"You did, but... I wanted to draw the schoolhouse."

"Oh, *really*? That's what you wanted, is it?"

I nod. "I wanted to do a good job on the book, for you."

"For *me*?" She hisses the word. "Don't fuck with me, Abby. Your going back to Carradine had nothing to do with me, or the book. It had everything to do with you wanting to screw the tour guide."

"No."

She pushes her tongue into the side of her mouth, narrows her eyes. "No?"

"Well, yes, I suppose, but not *screw*. Jesus, Mo. I didn't go back with the express intention of... *this*." I look down at myself, wrapped in a sheet, and then I look to the stairs, where Elise has appeared, descending sheepishly, raking her fingers back through her hair.

Mo makes a contemptuous sound at the back of her throat, starts smoking again, frantically, turning away to the sea.

"I should go." Elise's voice spirals small. "I'm really sorry about this," she offers, to Mo's back, but Mo doesn't respond. Elise shrugs, takes a step towards me, and then a step back.

I incline my head, sighing out loud, even though I don't mean to, even though it sounds melodramatic, and morose. It's just that there are *so* many things that I need to say to her, in this moment, and I can't say any of them. I follow her to the door.

"Elise. God, this wasn't supposed to happen."

"Well, no." She smiles, touches her fingers to my arm. "It's okay though. It'll be okay, won't it?"

I nod fast. "Yes." I clear my throat, stiffen my tone to sound certain. "I'll talk to Mo. She's cool, really. She'll be cool about it."

She leans in to kiss me, but I shake my head, backing away.

"I'm sorry..."

"It's all right. I understand."

"Do you? Christ. *How?*"

She glances away from me, smiling, but it's a vague smile – a house of cards. The afternoon is wide and white behind her.

"I'm picking up the starter motor for your car, Mo's car, tomorrow. I'll drive it over to you, in the afternoon, and then we'll go – you and me, like we said. Yes?"

"Yes."

She takes a big breath. I watch it happen, and then she says, "Are you *sure?*"

I say again, "*Yes.*"

Elise smiles. "Okay, then. It's a deal." And then she lifts her eyebrows, says very quietly, "A week ago, if someone had told me this was going to happen, I'd have staked my life on their being wrong. The idea that I could meet a woman, randomly, and be willing to alter the course of my future for her, after a matter of *days*... It's just..." She lifts her hands, pushes at the air, "... unfathomable."

"But we've fathomed it."

She nods. "Oh, yes. I don't know *how* we have, but we have."

I lean against the doorframe for a moment, my limbs feeling slick and heavy.

"Lucy should have stayed." I say it softly, looking into Elise's face. "You only get a chance like this once in a lifetime. She squandered hers, with Henri. I'm not going to squander mine, with you. I'm not going to make her mistake." And I do lean forward then and kiss her, as tenderly as I can, touching her face. When I move away from her, she looks quickly down at her feet and then she glances towards her car. For a second, she won't look at me.

"I should go," she says, but she doesn't.

"Elise." I touch her arm. "Everything *is* all right, isn't it? *You're* all right?"

"I will be, tomorrow, when we're on the road." And her face

brightens. "You need to decide where you'd like to go first."

"Winnipeg."

"Why Winnipeg?"

"Because I remember it from when I was small. I had two old aunties, one called Winnie and one called Peggy, and when I first heard the name Winnipeg I thought it was somewhere they'd visited together and that it had been named after them."

Elise smiles at me, shaking her head, narrowing her eyes against the sunshine.

"Winnipeg it is, then. I have some family there, actually. We could see them."

"Okay."

She takes her car keys out of her pocket and looks at them. "Tomorrow, then?"

"Tomorrow."

She nods her head, just the once, and then she turns away and climbs into her car. She doesn't look back. I watch until she turns onto the road at the end of the driveway, and for a minute or two I keep watching, because I don't want to have to turn around and face Mo. Facing Mo will mean, ultimately, facing Gayle, and the thought of that is like a razor in my throat.

"I want you out of here tonight, Abby." Mo's voice is shiny and hard and, when I *do* turn to look at her, I see that her face is the same. "I'll call you a cab and you can find a hotel in town."

"If that's what you want."

She sighs, stubs her cigarette out. "It's *not* what I want, but..." She takes another cigarette from the pack on the table, and lights it, her eyes growing cloudy behind a blue bloom of smoke, "... you can't stay here." She pushes past me and sits down heavily on the old sofa. "You do see why I can't let you stay?"

"Yes."

She sits smoking, looking at me, and then her brow furrows and she sits up straight.

"Where's my car?"

"In Carradine. The starter motor went. Elise's getting a new one for you." I turn away from her, because I can't take how she's looking at me any more. I clear my throat. "She's driving the car back here tomorrow."

Mo doesn't say anything else, but I can feel her watching me as I climb the stairs. Near to the top, my feet get tangled up in the sheet and I stumble, and Mo is there, at the bottom of the stairs suddenly.

"Are you okay?"

I nod without looking at her, and I hear her sigh – a long breath, full of moths.

"Look," she says, slow and weary. "Get some clothes on and come back down and we'll just... talk, for a bit, okay?" She sighs again. "And, believe me, that's the exact *opposite* of what I would normally say to a good-looking girl wearing nothing but a sheet."

I glance down at her then, and she manages a wisp of a smile.

"Thanks, Mo."

She nods, draws deeply on her cigarette again. "Christ knows how you got yourself into this situation, but we'll do our best to get you out of it." And, with that, she moves out of sight, adding in a low and placatory tone, "I'll open us some wine."

I clean myself up in the bathroom, and then I choose some fresh clothes from my rucksack: a faded pair of Levis and an old check shirt – my comfort clothes. I feel in need of some comfort just about now. I look at myself in the mirror, and the face that looks back is flushed, and thinner than I remembered it, but it also has a kind of incandescence to it that I've never seen before – a candour. It takes me by surprise.

I tidy my hair. I even put on a little make-up, although I'm not sure why. Maybe I'm trying to get back in touch, physically, with the self who got off that plane last weekend. Maybe, if I can make myself *look* like her, then I'll start thinking like her again, but is that what I want?

By the time I get back downstairs, Mo is already halfway through a bottle of Chianti. She splashes some of it into a big glass for me, and gestures to the seat next to hers on the sofa.

"Abby Martin," she sighs, shaking her head, "you were only supposed to come here to draw, sweetie. There was to *be* no shagging."

"I know." I take a big gulp of wine, and then another. "I don't know how it happened."

"I do."

"Oh?"

"You're bored as a stick with dear old Gayle. It's not hard to see. She just doesn't do it for you any more, does she? So you were keeping a lookout, subconsciously or not, for someone who *could*, and, lo and behold, along comes Mademoiselle Robichaud, with her Celtic good looks and her sensitive soul." She sips at her wine, narrowing her eyes over the rim of her glass. "A *coup de foudre*."

"A what?"

"Love at first sight, roughly translated."

"Ah."

I lean my head back and Mo leans hers back too, looking at me.

"So, what now?"

I take a deep breath. "Elise is coming back tomorrow, like I said, with your car, and then she and I are going away together. We're going to drive across Canada together."

Mo starts to laugh. She has to sit up and steady her glass on the coffee table because she's laughing so hard.

"It's not funny." I start to stand up, indignant. "It's not a joke, Mo."

"Isn't it?" She takes hold of my hand and tugs me gently back down onto the sofa, choking her laughter back the best she can. "I'm sorry, but you can't seriously be considering this as an option." She lifts her glass and drains all of what's left in it. "You met this woman five days ago. *Five days*. You barely know anything about her."

"I know enough."

"Really?"

"I've learned more about Elise in those five days than I've learned about Gayle in five years!"

"Oh, don't be such a bloody drama queen."

"I'm not."

But Mo just shakes her head. "Look, leave Gayle if you have to. When you get back, if it's really *so* bad with her, so unbearable, then yes, leave her, end it, for its own bad sake, but don't end it *because* of what's happened here. Don't throw a long-term relationship, a *marriage*, away for some ridiculous ideal that doesn't exist."

"Elise is not a ridiculous ideal. She's more real to me than Gayle's ever been."

"There you go again." Mo's grinning, but she doesn't mean it.

"What?"

"Talking Harlequin romance bloody heroine at me."

"Mo." This time I stand up and I stay standing up. "You have *no* idea what my life with Gayle is like, and you have no idea about me and Elise." My hands are on my hips. I let them fall to my sides. "This has happened. This miraculous thing has happened to me, and I'm not sorry. I am in love with Elise, and I trust her, implicitly. Five days' worth of love and trust, yes, okay – not much, but enough *to make me sure*, and that's the point." I dip my head towards her. "Things like this just come looking for us, even if we're not looking for *them*. Love comes looking, sometimes. Don't you think?" She's watching me, her face held steady. "Don't you believe in love any more, Mo? Don't you believe in true love?"

"I did once," she says, and she tips the wine bottle high. Only a few red drops trickle into her waiting glass, so she hauls herself up off the sofa and stalks to the kitchen, with me following. She takes another bottle of Chianti from the wine rack and opens it, but then she just stands looking down at it and, when she lifts her eyes to mine again, she's crying.

I take a step towards her, but she shakes her head.

"Five days' worth of flirting and fucking *isn't* love." She wipes her eyes on her sleeve. "Five years' worth of a relationship *is*. What I felt for my ex *was*." She slips herself into a seat at the table then, staring at the bottle in her hand like it's a grenade with the pin pulled out. "We'd been together since college. Eight years. Eight years of living together, building a home, consolidating. We even talked about having children." She looks up into my face. "And then she up and left me for a woman she met at a festival – a *weekend* festival. She went on the Friday, in love with me, and she came back on the Sunday in love with someone else."

"I'm sorry." I sit down opposite her at the table.

"Me too." She lifts the bottle to her lips and drinks from it. "So, no, I don't believe in true love any more. I'd like to, but it's a lie, as far as I can see. It used to be my *raison d'être*, as your Elise might say. It used to be my holy fucking *grail*, but now..." She hunches her shoulders. "It's shit. I'm not of the faith. I don't believe in true love. I believe in working at relationships, getting on and getting by, doing the best you can with what you've been given. That's what love's about, for me, *and* for you. You've just forgotten that's what it's about, that's all."

"What happened about your vacation, Mo, with your new girlfriend? Why are you back early?"

She shrugs. "Didn't work out. I'm not bothered."

But I can tell by her face that she *is*. I take a deep breath in, looking at her.

"You told me, when I arrived, that you believe in holding onto the good stuff, savouring it, however fleeting it turns out to be. D'you remember saying that to me?"

She nods. "Yeah, I remember, but I'm full of shit. Haven't you realised that by now?"

She offers me the bottle of Chianti and I take a quick slug, but some of the wine misses my mouth, dribbles down my chin. Mo reaches across and wipes it away with her fingertips, very soft suddenly. She cups my cheek in her hand.

"Abby," her voice is despairing, "you just *can't* leave Gayle for Elise. It isn't right."

"It feels right."

She shakes her head. "You're making a mistake."

"*Not* leaving Gayle for Elise would be a mistake. It would be the mistake Lucy made, and I'm not going to let it happen."

Mo sits back in her chair, looking puzzled.

"Lucy?"

"She never should have married Ethan MacKay. She should have stayed in Carradine with the man she loved."

Mo raises one eyebrow, arches it.

"So," she says slowly, "the old lady showed you the diary too."

"Yes."

"It's a hoot, isn't it?"

Suddenly, I remember my promise to Ruth, my promise not to tell, and I hoist it up and hold it in front of my face like a fan.

"A lot of it's crap, I reckon, wishful thinking, but the stuff about her being in love *could* be true, maybe, and even if it's not, well..." I lift the bottle to my lips again, playing for time. "I'm going to take it as a sign."

"A sign?"

"Yes. Maybe, somehow, Lucy's trying to tell me what choice to make. Maybe she's trying to tell me to make the choice she *didn't* make."

Mo smiles at me indulgently.

"Of course," she says, "she could just as easily be telling you to make the choice she *did* make."

"I don't think so."

"No." She moistens her lips with the tip of her tongue. "Somehow, I didn't think you would."

We are silent for a moment, looking at each other, and then Mo asks, "Does Elise know you've read the diary?"

"Yes. We've talked about it."

"Really?"

"Ruth knows too."

She looks interested then. "How did she take it?"

"What d'you mean?"

"How did she take you *knowing*?"

"She was okay about it." I say it guardedly, but Mo is leaning in.

"God. She's managed to keep it all under wraps for so long, I figured she'd be spitting feathers when she found out two outsiders were in on the secret."

I shrug my shoulders. "It's probably fake though, anyway, yeah?"

"Shit, *no!*"

"What?"

"It's not a fake. I've had the handwriting analysed. It's definitely Lucy's."

"But…" I look around me, bewildered. "Marie told me she'd shown it to you and you weren't interested, because you thought it was a fake."

"Well, of course, I had to *say* that, otherwise they'd have been onto me in a second."

"Onto you?"

"They'd have tried to stop me using it, in the biography."

I feel my face flush hot. "You're going to use it in the biography?"

"Er…" Mo looks at me like I'm thick as two short planks. "Ye-es. Of *course*."

"You can't."

"Why?"

"Because it's private family business."

"Oh, *please*." Her voice is high and incredulous. "That diary should have been made public property years ago. All of Lucy's other diaries are, and her letters, and –"

"That's not the point. The family don't *want* it made public."

"They will, when they see how much the cheque is for."

"You're going to buy them off."

Mo lifts the bottle of wine to her lips and winks at me. "Absolutely."

"And what if you can't?"

"It's going ahead, anyway. The Robichauds don't have the money to take anything through the courts, and besides, I don't understand why they don't want the real author of the *Hector* books made known. It's time the truth came to light, don't you think?"

"But it's their property. The diary *belongs* to them. What about the copyright?"

"The copyright was Lucy's, and Ethan MacKay, unworldly old duffer that he was, *sold* all the interests in Lucy's estate to her publishers after she died." Mo grins at me. "And Lucy's publishers are..."

"... your publishers too."

She goes on grinning.

"Why didn't you tell me what you were planning, Mo?"

"Because I had to talk to my editor and my publishers about it first, in confidence. It was always going to be down to them, whether the diary would feature in the biography or not." She shakes her head. "That's why I was none too keen on you going back to Carradine without me. I wanted things left alone, until I knew the parameters, but I forgot to delete the school from the list of sights I wanted you to draw, which was pretty thick of me."

I lean my elbows forward onto the table, perplexed. "But look, if you include the diary in your book, doesn't it negate the whole myth of Lucy Pritchard? If you reveal her as a fraud, won't your book become unsaleable?"

"Don't be so naïve, Abby. It's scandal. It's intrigue. It's illicit love. When have those things ever been unsaleable?"

"Oh, fuck." I let my head fall deadweight onto my folded arms.

"What are you getting so bent out of shape for, anyway? It's no big deal, is it?"

"Yes, it is."

"I don't see why." Mo wags her head at me. "This'll make us famous – me *and* you."

"I don't want to be famous for breaking my word."

"Oh, good *grief*!" She slaps her hand to her forehead. "This doesn't need to be *such* a drama, surely. It's history. It's a hundred years old. Nobody's going to be hurt by it."

"But what about the whole tourist industry here? It's *based* on Lucy Pritchard."

"No, it's not. It's based on Hector Price. It's *his* face you see plastered all over the island. It isn't Lucy's. Nothing's going to change. And what do you care, anyway? This time tomorrow, you'll be out on the open road with your one true *lurve*."

I shake my head slowly. "Elise won't leave. She won't leave when I tell her what you're going to do."

"Then don't tell her."

"I have to. She trusts me. I can't lie to her."

"I'm sure Gayle trusts you too, but that hasn't stopped you lying to *her*, has it?"

"I haven't lied to her."

"I bet you haven't told her the truth, though, either, have you?" Her eyes are sharp. "I bet you haven't even spoken to her since you arrived."

I lift the bottle of wine to my lips and take a long drink, and Mo sits back in her chair, watching me.

"Jesus, Abby," she says, "you haven't even spoken to your girlfriend of five years, your life fucking *partner*, and yet you're sitting there planting your flag in the moral high ground for a woman you *barely* know!" She shakes her head. "How the hell did you get like this?"

I stand up then and walk away from the table. I crumple down onto the bottom stair and fold my arms tight around my body. She's right. Mo's telling me the truth about myself. Of course she is, and it's intolerable to me. She comes to stand over me and, when I look up into her face, she's no longer angry, or contemptuous. She just looks unbearably saddened by me, which is even worse.

"Don't look at me like that, Mo. Please don't look at me like that."

She sighs, sits down on the stair next to me and puts her arm round my shoulder.

"We all make mistakes," she says softly. "That's all this was, with Elise – a mistake, and it's mendable."

"Is it?"

"When she comes back tomorrow with my car, just tell her you've changed your mind."

"But I haven't."

"You *will*, though, yes?"

I shake my head, emphatic. "No. I won't. I'm sorry, but I'm *meant to be* with Elise. I know I am."

"Because of Lucy? Because Lucy's diary was a *sign*." She snaps the word out sour.

"If you like."

"I don't like." She drops her chin. "I don't like at all. I think you're being ridiculous, and self-seeking and –"

"You're a fine one to be criticising *me* for being self-seeking." I shake her arm off my shoulder. "You've stolen someone's personal history and you're going to expose it publicly, without a thought, just to sell a few more copies of your book. If that's not self-seeking, I don't know what is – and Jesus, what about Lucy's family? How are they going to feel – and what about Henri's family? What about the Robichaud's? Don't you care *anything* about how they feel?"

Mo just looks at me and then she stands up. She tilts her head to one side, says quietly, "*Henri's* family?"

"Yes." I wag a finger at her. "And a lot of his other descendants are still living on the island too, you know."

She opens her mouth, seems to be tasting the air, and then she steps past me and begins to climb the stairs.

"Come up here a minute, will you, Abby?"

Her voice is very even now, very calm, but she's breathing fast, and when I join her on the landing she is down on her hands and knees, rummaging around inside her bag. She brings out a flat brown A4 envelope and opens it up.

"You didn't read the whole diary, did you?" she asks, not looking at me.

"No. I read up to the entry when Lucy steals the stories from the bureau."

"I see."

I fold my arms. "Elise told me the rest, though. She told me about the end, where Lucy leaves the diary with Henri so that he'll always know that she *did* love him really, that it hadn't been a lie."

Mo slips a single sheet out of the envelope and holds it out to me.

"Here," she says, very gently. "Take a look at this."

"What is it?"

"It's the last entry from Lucy's diary."

I take it from her, but my fingers are trembling.

"How did you *get* this?" I look down at the glossy paper, but its sheen bounces little flecks of light into my face, makes me blink.

"I have a camera. A tiny James-Bond-y looking camera that I use in my research, to photograph maps and plans, in libraries mostly, and museums. It comes in handy, at times like these." She points to the sheet. "You might want to sit down to read that."

I thrust it back at her. "I don't want to read it. It's private."

"Yes, it is."

"I don't need to read it. I know what's in it, anyway."

"No, Abby," Mo slips me a sliver of a smile, "you don't."

"Yes, I do. Elise told me. Lucy tells Henri goodbye."

Mo stands up and moves in close, her face filling the space of my vision.

"Lucy doesn't tell Henri anything."

"What?"

She places her hand over my forearm. "It wasn't Henri."

"What d'you mean?"

"Lucy's big affair, all that wild and windswept sex by the sunny seaside. It wasn't with Henri."

I look down at the sheet again, but it has begun to blur. The words are melting. My fingers are wet with them.

"If it *wasn't* Henri, then who was it?"

"Read."

"No. You tell me."

Mo shakes her head slow. "You need to do this one all by yourself, sweetheart."

I try to think, but the air is white noise suddenly, and Mo's smile seems to be sliding towards me and away, over and over. I can't hold her steady.

"I don't want to work it out. I don't need to. Elise *told* me what's in the last entry."

"Your precious Elise." Her eyes are black and scornful. "She lied through her pearly whites, my dear."

"No."

"See for yourself."

I go into my room and I sit down on the bed, and for a moment, I just look out at the sea. If Lucy wasn't in love with Henri, if he isn't the *you* in her diary, then who *is*? I wonder if it might be the father, Charles. Maybe Lucy had a thing for older men, but then I remember that she referred to her lover as the *"child of a labourer"*, so Charles wouldn't fit, and in the Dougray Hotel entry, she and her lover are upstairs, *"listening for the sound of footsteps: your parents coming up from the ballroom"*, so it really can't be Charles.

I think my way back through the early entries, and then, of course, it hits me. Didn't Lucy describe her lover as having hands that were *"as smooth and white as porcelain"*? I'd thought it a strange way to describe Henri's hands, a farmer's hands, but it wouldn't be a strange way to describe, say, a woman's hands. Emilie! Of course. Why on earth didn't I think of that before? It would explain how the two of them could spend so much time in each other's company without arousing suspicion; be alone together in their *shared* gable room, slip away from Stella's engagement party without a chaperone…

I look quickly down at the sheet in my hands and begin to read.

You stand by the buggy with your face turned toward me, and the sky behind you is as white as fury, and your face is whiter still. The family will come soon to bid me their goodbyes, but, all at once, yours is the only goodbye I can bear, and not bear. You hold me to you, my hands crushed in yours, and all the cruel and flippant words I said to you in the house come flooding back to wring my heart, burn and sear my soul. I look into your eyes, for the last time, aye, the very last, and I speak the truth to you. I tell you of my weakness and my vanity. I tell you of the stories in my bag, your stories, and you answer that they will be your gift to me. You tell me to do with them as I please, and even now, I know I could choose a different path. I know I could choose to look for all time upon the pale light of Carradine, falling like rain over the ocean. I know I could choose to stay, looking for all time, upon you, my love, my sweet, but I press my lips to your cheek and I tell you goodbye, though the word comes chokingly. I tell you that the happiest times I have known have been in your arms, and you weep into my hair, and I turn away, toward the house, and I know that we will never meet again. It is ended – for this life at least, and as I believe and hope – or fear, I cannot tell which – for all and every life to come. Never, never will you know, truly, how I have loved you, but I will leave this diary in your keeping, that you might forgive me, that if we should meet, one distant day, in the shadows of the Hereafter, you will not pass me coldly by, but draw me down beside you, for all eternity, my love, my precious love, my dear sweet Edouard.

Fifteen

I feel my heart skip like a pebble across a stream, and there isn't enough air in my body suddenly. I have to concentrate really hard on my breathing, like it's a skill I've only just learned, a language I'm not very fluent in. My hands are trembling. Mo is standing in the doorway.

"Edouard," she says, her tone gentle and a little doubtful too, as if she's looking for corroboration, as if she still can't *quite* believe it herself. She says again, more certain this time, "Edouard."

I nod slowly. "How old was he again? He wasn't very old."

"Fifteen. He was just fifteen when Lucy arrived."

"And she was?"

"Twenty-seven."

I shake my head, trying to shake it away, but it's no good, because, suddenly, everything makes absolute sense. Everything fits. All the jigsaw pieces are in place and the picture they make is appalling.

"She seduced him."

"Yes, and then she left him, and he was dead within a year."

"What did he die of?"

Mo comes and sits next to me on the bed. "The parish records say consumption, but the old lady, Marie, she says he died of a broken heart. He stopped eating, sleeping; gave up the ghost. He ended up in an asylum, last couple of months of his life. The family managed to keep it quiet though."

"God."

I let myself fall back onto the bed. "So, not only did Lucy Pritchard steal all the *Hector* stories and pass them off as her own, she also spent her whole year in Carradine having sex with a fifteen-year-old boy?"

"And sending him bonkers, by all accounts." Mo makes a little clicking sound out of the corner of her mouth, leaning back on her elbows. "Turns out Lucy Pritchard was what my mother would refer to as 'no better than she ought to be'."

"I've never understood that saying."

"Me neither."

I blow a sighing breath towards the ceiling. "What would have happened if they'd been discovered? I mean, it would have been bad enough her having a pre-marital fling with Henri, but with his little teenage brother! Geez."

"She was an adventuress."

"The Mrs Robinson of her day. Shit. Who'd have thought it?"

Mo is smiling and, somehow, I am beginning to feel lighter too, heartened. I'm not sure why. Surely, I *shouldn't*. Maybe it's because all this unravelling business has taken my mind off Elise, and Gayle, or maybe it's because someone else's dramas, even century-old dramas, have a way of putting one's own dramas into perspective.

"Can you see now why I *have to* include the diary in the biography? The record needs to be put straight."

"I guess, but you're not doing it with wholly noble intentions, are you, Ms Laker?" She just raises her eyebrows at me. "You're doing it to make a buck, no?"

"I've got to make a living, and I don't think honesty's a bad route to be taking to do that. Honesty's usually the right way to go, no?"

"Even when people stand to get hurt because of it?"

"Even then." She takes a big breath, thinking. "I wonder why Elise wasn't honest with you, about the diary." She's watching me closely. "I wonder why she lied to you."

I blink my eyes closed for a moment, feeling something damp and sheer lifting inside my chest.

"I don't know."

"I guess she doesn't trust you."

She says it softly. She isn't trying to hurt me. She's just trying to make me see what I do not want to see. I turn my face away from her, and as I do, the phone starts to ring downstairs. Mo gets up quickly and heads for the door, but I call after her, "I don't want to speak to anyone, if it's for me."

Without turning, she asks, "Not even Elise?"

I don't answer her. I lie back onto the bed and listen to her feet clattering down the stairs. She catches the phone on the fourth ring, and her voice muffles a hello through the floor beneath me. I can't hear what she's saying after that, and I'm not interested. I just lie there, breathing lightly, staring up at the mottled ceiling, but suddenly Mo is calling up the stairs to me, calling my name. When I step out onto the landing, I find her standing at the foot of the stairs, the telephone receiver pressed to her chest. She looks up at me.

"It's Gayle," she says quietly. "I think you need to speak to her."

I shake my head fast. "I can't."

But she holds the receiver up towards me then, a small white slippery gift, undesired, and she says again, louder, "It's Gayle."

I mouth at her, *"Please, don't make me."* But she starts climbing the stairs, with the receiver still held out to me, and I realise there's no avoiding it. She'll chase me all over the house with it if she has to.

My hands are trembling when I take it from her. I bring it to my ear, and Gayle is already saying my name.

"Hi, Gayle." I turn my voice inside out with cordiality. It hurts. "How are you?"

"I'm okay." But she doesn't sound okay. "I was *worried* about you, though, Abs."

In that moment, the moment of her calling me by the name she always calls me, a sudden rush of light blazes inside my head – a veer of bright air, with my life at home shimmering inside it. I can see our flat in Winchester, with its narrow rooms, cornflower blue curtains, green Cathedral view, the communal stairway leading up to the front door, choked, as usual, with bikes and the tang of patchouli. I can see the library where I work, with its grey glass doors opening onto the banks of the river. I can see my friends lifting their wine glasses to me, wishing me *bon voyage* on this trip, and I can see Gayle of course – clearer, suddenly, than I've been able to see her since I arrived here.

"Abs? Jesus. I've left you a shitload of messages, and I've been mailing you as well. Where have you been?"

I sit down on the top stair. "I went to the other side of the island, to do some drawing, and my car broke down. I had to stay a couple of nights away."

"Why didn't you call me, then?" She's cross, but trying to reel it in. She says again, more softly, "I was worried about you."

"I'm sorry."

Mo is looking up at me, her hands on her hips. She disappears from view for a moment, and then reappears with a bottle of wine in one hand and an empty glass in the other. She starts to climb the stairs, pouring as she goes. By the time she reaches me, the glass is full. She holds it out to me.

"Thanks."

"What?" says Gayle.

"Sorry. Not you. Mo's just brought me a glass of wine."

She breathes a little laugh down the line. "She's not trying to get you drunk, is she?"

"Don't think so."

"Only, you have to watch her." Her voice is lifting. "She's never been great at keeping her hands off other people's…" She hesitates, and for a second I think she's going to say "property", but instead, she says, "… lovers."

I draw a breath into my lungs; steady it there, and then, inexplicably, I say, "But we're not just lovers, are we, Gayle? We're partners these days – wife and wife."

She laughs. She thinks I'm making a joke. It's a true laugh, and familiar. I can picture exactly what her face will be looking like, right now, laughing that laugh. I can see the crow's feet at the corners of her eyes, her lips stretching pink across her teeth. She gets a little dimple in her right cheek when she laughs like that – a pale grey dent, a tiny fingerprint.

"Mo sounds on good form, though," she says. "How's she doing?"

Mo is sitting a few stairs below me, her back against the wall. As if she senses she's being discussed, she looks up into my face, inclines her head a touch.

"She's doing okay," I tell Gayle. "She's been busy with the book. We both have."

"Yeah? Are you nearly done, then?"

"Kind of."

"When d'you reckon you're coming home?"

I take a sip of wine. "Not sure, exactly."

"You'll be back for Grandma's eightieth, though?"

"I don't know."

"Oh, Abs," her voice is a whine, "you promised."

"I know but... the book's taking longer, and it's... more complicated than I expected."

"Let me talk to Mo."

My heart flutters inside my chest – a whirl of dry leaves. "Why?"

"So I can talk her into letting you come back."

"It's not Mo's fault. I'm just taking longer with the illustrations than I should. I'm just being slack, really."

"Well, stop being slack." I can hear her wagging her head at me. "Get your finger out, get your work done, and get your sexy arse *back here*." Her voice is smiling. "I'm missing you something awful, and Grandma's gonna be heartbroken if you're not there for her party."

"Your grandma hates me. She thinks I'm a slut, remember?"

"No, she doesn't."

"She used to."

"But that was aaaaaages ago. Since you made an honest of woman of me, she *lurves* you. You're the best thing since incontinence pads, as far as she's concerned." She sighs. "Please try and make it back."

"I'll do my best." But the words are shards of glass.

"Good girl," says Gayle, as if I'm a dog who's just learned to sit on command. "Good girl."

"I'd better go, Gayle."

"Okay. Mail me, yeah?"

"Okay."

She hesitates. I hear the sound of the TV being switched on.

"Bye then," she says, already distracted by whatever's on the screen in front of her, and then, briskly, "Love you."

She hangs up before I can respond. I bring my wine glass to my lips and drink all that's left in it, and Mo holds the bottle out to me again.

"Top you up?"

I shake my head. "I don't think so."

"Ah, but that's the whole point, isn't it? Drinking's one of the few things that you're not supposed to *think* about. That's its inherent beauty. It drives thought out." Her words are blurred at the edges now. "Drinking's like dancing, and sex, Abby, one of life's freedoms. You need a drink, tonight, I *think*. You need to get drunk."

"I think you might be getting drunk enough for the both of us, Mo."

"Well, no shit, Sherlock!" She laughs, lightly, but her eyes are watery and sad. She runs her tongue along her bottom lip, looking at me.

"What are you going to do?" she asks.

"I don't know."

I stand up and step past her, make my way down the stairs and into the living room. Its blond walls look translucent in this light, viscous – like you could pass clear through them and out into the night if you tried.

"You know you can stay here as long as you want." Mo is close behind me, and when I turn to look at her, she smiles. "I know I came on all 'never darken my doorstep again' earlier, but..." She flops down onto the sofa, red wine sloshing softly from her glass into her lap. She looks down at it, puzzled. "I didn't mean it."

"Yes, you did, and you were right to mean it. I've abused your hospitality."

"What, you mean by bringing the luscious Elise home for a swift shag in my spare room?" She purses her lips. "That was hardly an abuse of hospitality. Now, if you'd let her use my chanterelle and vanilla bath salts without asking, it would have been a very different matter *indeed*, young lady!"

I sit down next to her on the sofa.

"Why are you trying to make me feel better?"

"Oh, I dunno." She closes her hand over mine in my lap. "I think you probably feel shitty enough about all of this without me heaping bitter coals on your head."

I lean my head against her shoulder then. "I deserve coals, though. I deserve to burn in the sizzling fires of hell."

But she just chuckles. "I think not. You're completely redeemable. You made a bad choice, but now you have the chance to do the right thing." And she squeezes my hand tight – three squeezes on the three words: *the, right, thing.* "It's got to feel easier now, surely, anyway? Now you know what Elise's really like. Now you know that she doesn't trust you. If she doesn't trust you, then how can she pretend to *love* you?"

But I remember what I said to Elise about love and trust being separate issues, and I hold tight to that, because I believed her when she said she loved me, and I still believe her. I'm just not sure I believe *in* her any more. Why didn't she tell me about Lucy and Edouard? Why didn't she trust me with the truth? She promised that she wouldn't lie to me. She said she'd made a mistake in not trusting me. Why would she choose to make that same mistake again?

I close my eyes, sleep circling nearby, like an unpredictable animal.

"I'm shagged, Mo."

"Well, I know." She slips her arm around my shoulder. "I was there, remember? I *saw*!"

I look up into her face.

"I'm really sorry about that you know, about you having to come home to that."

"It's okay. My sensibilities aren't exactly what you'd call delicate."

"Even so…"

But she presses a finger to my lips, says "Shhh," softly, narrowing her eyes. "Don't beat yourself up about it, okay? I'm not… affronted. I'm not even cross with you any more. I'm just a bit disappointed in you."

"I know, and I'm sorry. I'm disappointed in me too – cheating on Gayle, and in *your* house as well. Shit."

"Well, yes, there *is* that, but it wasn't quite what I meant." She takes a sip of wine from her glass, watching me over the rim. When she takes the glass away, she's smiling. Her eyes are very bright. "I'm just a bit disappointed in you for not choosing more wisely."

"What d'you mean?"

"Well, if you came here looking for an affair, my lovely, why the fuck didn't you have one with *me*?"

Sixteen

I sleep badly. My dreams are complex and dark and full of sound. I keep waking up out of breath. In the end, I wrap a blanket around myself, go downstairs and make some coffee, and then I sit at the kitchen table, looking out over the mist of the ocean. It is nearing dawn now. The air is pale and very still.

In a few hours, Elise will come for me, and we'll leave together, and my life will change forever. All the routines upon which I've relied, all these years, will fall away. Nothing will be the same as it was. Not even *I* will be the same, and the thought is both terrifying and exhilarating to me.

I can't drink any more coffee, because I'm nauseous suddenly, very nauseous in fact. I have to stand up fast and lurch across the kitchen to the sink, where I retch last night's red wine onto the white enamel. It splashes dark as blood. I stand for a minute or two with my hands closed around the cool metal taps, steadying myself, and then I sit down at the table again and rest my head forward onto my arms. The blanket around my shoulders smells of mothballs and lavender. It reminds me of my grandma. I curl myself around the cosy thought of her and close my eyes, and then I must fall asleep, because it's the sound of the telephone that wakes me.

My voice sounds drugged when I say hello into the receiver.

"Abby? Is that you?"

It's a woman's voice, but I don't recognise whose. She's whispering.

"Yes." I clear my throat, try again. "Yes, it is. Who's this?"

"It's me. Marie."

I sit down on the sofa.

"Marie? Are you all right? How did you get this number?"

"I looked the Laker woman up in the book, but..." Her voice veers away, circles back with a hiss. "Shhh," she says, although I'm not saying anything. "I have to be quick."

"Okay."

But she's silent.

"Marie?"

"Yes."

"Why are you calling? Are you okay?"

"Yes, but I wanted to speak to you."

"What about?"

"You left before I had a chance to talk to you about the diary."

I lean my head back into the cushions, another wave of nausea pulling my muscles in tight. My stomach seems to be at sea without the rest of me. I swallow hard.

"Yes. I'm sorry about that, but we needed to get an early start."

She sighs. "But you left before I could tell you the rest."

"It's okay. I know the rest. I know about Edouard."

"No, no." Her voice is urgent. "Not Edouard. I didn't want to talk to you about Edouard. Well, not exactly about Edouard. I wanted to talk to you about the letter. I wanted you to read the letter."

I blink my eyes closed. "What letter, Marie?"

"Lucy's letter. The one I found inside the diary. You need to know the whole –"

But suddenly, someone else's voice prickles like static down the line – a blur of words, intrusive, and Marie hangs up

I sit with the receiver in my lap, and then I have to rush to the kitchen and be sick in the sink a second time. My head feels hot, on the inside. I barely register the sound of someone knocking at the door but, when I go to answer it, I find Elise standing on the doorstep.

"You look awful," she says as soon as she sees me. She reaches out her hand and presses her palm to my forehead. "Are you ill?"

"Just a hangover, I think." I look down at myself, wrapped in my mothbally old blanket, and then I look at Elise. "Not a very glamorous reception for you. Sorry."

She shakes her head. "Don't be. I like the consumptive look."

"That's handy. Just call me Camille, then, yeah?" I beckon her inside, yawning. "What time is it, anyway? I wasn't expecting you until later."

"It's 10.15."

"God, is it? Time flies when you're... asleep."

I gesture to the sofa and she sits down on it, leans forward, looking at the riot of empty bottles in Mo's hearth.

"Good party, was it?"

"Not so much of a party as an inquisition, to be honest." I fold myself down onto the floor at her feet. "It was intense."

"I'm sorry."

"Don't be." I close my hands around hers. "I invited the intense..." I think for a moment, but all I can come up with is, "... *ity*."

Elise smiles, hunches herself forward to kiss me, but I ease back onto my heels.

"You might not want to do that until I'm minty fresh."

She nods. "Thanks for the warning."

We just sit looking at each other then, very softly, very easily, smiling, and I don't know whether to tell her that I know about Lucy and Edouard, and I don't know whether to tell her about Marie's call. I know that I will have to tell her about both, in time, and that there will be consequences in telling her, but, just for this moment, I want to hold her fixed and flawless. I want just a hint of finality with her, before all the confusions inside me have to be brought to light and unravelled. There are some moments in life that you recognise as unforgettable, *as you experience them.* They are once-in-a-lifetime moments, cherishable and rare. This is one of those moments, with me on my knees on Mo's wooden floor, draped in my mothbally old blanket, and Elise looking down at me, sea-light slanting sheer into her hair, her eyes dark and deliberate with love for me.

"You should get dressed," she says quietly. "We can call a cab to take us into Port Hove. There's a hire car waiting for us at the station."

"I don't think Abby's planning to go *anywhere* with you, Elise."

We both look towards the stairs, where Mo has appeared, dressed all in black. She has her arms folded tight across her chest, and her face is a tablet of stone. She looks like she could give the Grim Reaper a run for his money.

"It's all right, Mo." I haul myself to my feet and approach her. "Really. I can deal with this." I place both my hands over her arms. "It'll be okay. Trust me."

She looks into my eyes, and then she looks over my shoulder at Elise, and then she sighs, loudly enough for Elise to hear.

"I'll make some coffee," she says crisply, and stalks away into the kitchen.

Elise is looking perplexed.

"What did she mean, you're not planning to go anywhere with me?" She stands up. "What did she mean by that?"

"I'll go and get dressed, and then we'll talk, okay?"

"Talk about what?" Her fists are clenched. "There's nothing to talk about. No more talking. It's decided. *We* decided it, remember?"

"I remember."

Her face has narrowed suddenly. She is standing in shadow. She takes a step towards me.

"Look. Just sit, for a minute, okay? I'll go and get dressed."

She stays where she is, but I don't look back at her as I climb the stairs. I get dressed as quickly as I can, and then I go to the bathroom and splash some cold water onto my face, and I clean my teeth. I still feel sick, but only vaguely now. I gulp down a big glass of water and it shoots an icicle clear to my stomach, makes me feel steely and resolute.

By the time I get back downstairs, Mo and Elise are sitting opposite each other, not speaking. Both have mugs of coffee in their hands, but neither is drinking. They stand up when they see me.

"Would you like me to go?"

Mo offers it as a question, very polite, but if I said yes, I'm sure she'd reply, well, I'm not bloody going to, so I just shake my head.

"No, it's okay. *We'll* go."

"What?" Mo looks startled.

"We'll go for a walk. We'll go down to the beach. You stay and drink your coffee."

But she looks down into her mug dubiously. I suspect that her hangover is even worse than mine.

Elise and I leave quickly then but, once we're outside, I find that my steps are laboured, and the sunlight streaking in off the sea makes my eyes hurt. I borrow Elise's sunglasses, and they help a little, as we snake a slow route down the grassy steps and over the dunes. Soon, we are kicking up puffs of white sand, and walking along the water's edge letting our feet get wet.

Elise is talking fast about her plans for us. We can pick the hire car up at the station, she says, and then drive to Woodmill and catch the lunchtime ferry across to the mainland. From there we can drive north, towards Prince Rupert. She knows a place there where we can hire a campervan, a decent one, with a proper bed, instead of a pull-down mattress, and a refrigerator, and a stove and a...

"Elise."

I have to stop her, because her words are a roller coaster of eager sound, and I'm having trouble keeping up.

She stops walking and turns to look at me, and a bristly white wave slaps up over her feet. Her shoes hiss with water.

"Look." I reach forward and take hold of her hand. "I need you to slow down."

"Why?"

"Because there are some... *issues*..." I glance away on the word, not liking the shady look of it, "... that we need to talk about."

She eases her hand free of mine, very slow, says guardedly,

"What issues?"

I take a breath, but it's prickly with salt, and it catches in my throat. I have to swallow.

"Abby?" Elise is looking at me hard. "Have you changed your mind?"

"No."

"Then what?"

"Mo showed me the last entry in Lucy's diary."

"How?" She looks cornered. "I mean, how *can* she have? She hasn't got the diary."

"She photographed the whole thing, page by page, and she's planning to use it in her biography. I tried to talk her out of it, but..."

Elise is looking out to sea.

"It had to happen eventually," she says, very quietly, turning to look at me. "It's a relief, in a way."

"Why didn't you tell me?"

"About Edouard?"

I nod. "You didn't trust me."

"I did. I do. I wanted to tell you, but Mom was adamant that I shouldn't."

"So you let me think it was Henri?"

"I'm sorry."

"You promised you wouldn't lie to me again."

"I had no choice."

"Yes, you did."

"No. You don't understand. I had to think about my family. The Robichauds have never been accepted in Carradine. We've always been outsiders. When Dad left, we became a kind of curiosity as well, people to point at. If the diary gets out, then we'll become..." She sighs then, squinting towards the horizon. "Christ *knows* what we'll become, Abby; a laughing stock? Mom wouldn't be able to bear it, if she heard people talking in the store, saying that 'only shit-for-brains trash like the Robichauds would allow one of their own children to carry on a cheap affair under their own roof and not know about it'.

She wouldn't be able to bear that, not on top of everything else, not now she's on her own."

"But it wasn't Edouard's fault, what happened with Lucy, and it wasn't his parents' fault. The Robichauds aren't to blame for anything, as far as I can see, and it was all so long ago. It can't still mean this *much*. You can't care about it so deeply, surely?"

"Yes, I can. It's still family. Don't you get that?"

I take off the sunglasses and press my fingers to the bridge of my nose. Something is pumping hard inside my head, black as a Nazi fist, obdurate.

"I guess I don't, get it, no. I don't get how something that took place over a hundred years ago can still have such a hold over you, and over your family. I mean, don't you want the record set straight? Don't you want Edouard recognised as the true author of the *Hector* books?"

But Elise has edged away from me and has stopped listening.

"She's going to use it in the biography? Mo's going to use the whole diary: the affair, and Lucy taking the stories? Everything?"

"I think so – even Edouard ending up in the asylum. I think she's using all of it."

She starts walking back towards the dunes, very fast. "I need to talk to her."

"She won't listen to you."

"Then I need to go back to Carradine," she says, without turning to look at me.

"D'you want me to come with you?"

My voice is whipped away by a sudden gusty breeze. I don't think she's heard me, but after a few steps, she turns around. The white sand flurries around her ankles like new snow.

"Yes," she says, very clear. "I do. I want you to come, and after we've been to Carradine, after I've talked to Mom, then we'll go, like we said. We'll drive to Prince Rupert."

She holds out her hands then, and I walk towards her.

"Nothing's changed," she says, drawing me into her arms.

"Nothing's changed for me, about us."

She whispers it into my hair, touching my hair with her fingers, and I want to hold onto her tight, and kiss her, and tell her that nothing's changed for me either, but somehow, I don't. Instead, I follow her back to the house and she uses Mo's phone to call a cab. Mo isn't at home. Her car is missing from the drive, which seems a bit odd, but I'm relieved. Her absence means I can pack my rucksack, and leave with Elise, without having to contend with Mo's derision, or her wearisome truth-telling.

Elise is very quiet. We barely speak while we wait for the cab to arrive. She sits on Mo's sofa, staring into the hearth, and I keep on the move, pacing to the kitchen and back, because I'm still feeling nauseous, and each time I sit down the room starts to tilt slightly at the edges of my vision. I wonder if this might be a virus or something, and not a hangover after all. I really didn't drink enough last night to feel as bad as this.

When the cab arrives, Elise takes my rucksack and her own bags out to it, while I write Mo a note. It's the least I can do. I don't just want to run out on her. I keep it brief and friendly, thanking her for her letting me stay in her house, and apologising for "the way things have turned out". I can't think of another way to phrase what's happened. I tell her that Elise and I have gone to Carradine to warn Ruth about the biography, so she'll know what to expect if there are any repercussions, and then I tell her goodbye. I leave my sketchpad – all the drawings inside it clearly labelled and dated – on her desk, but I take the proofs of the biography with me. I assume she must have reworked the whole book, to accommodate the Carradine revelations, so these old proofs will be redundant. I want them as a keepsake. I'm not sure why. Maybe just to remind myself that I *did* come here with a purpose, a professional purpose. I didn't come here looking for an escape from my relationship with Gayle, and I didn't come here looking for Elise. I came here to work. My motives started out as noble, even if they haven't ended up that way.

I lock the door to The Old Sea Box, and drop Mo's keys through the letterbox, and the cab takes Elise and me into Port Hove, to the station, where our hire car sits looking sleek and new and full of promise. On the way out of town, I see a sign saying WOODMILL FERRY TERMINAL, 2KM, and I think suddenly that if I hadn't told Elise about Mo's plans, then she and I would be headed for that ferry terminal right now. Our six-month drive across Canada would have begun, our future together – a magic carpet unfurling – but I *had* to tell her. I had to do the right thing. For once, I had to.

I must have slept for some of the journey, slumped against the window, because I wake up with a hot ache in my neck, and a passing view of tall sage maples and green fields, fuzzy with sheep.

"What time is it?"

Elise looks at her watch. "Nearly three."

"How much further?"

"Not long. Half an hour, maybe." She glances at me. "You don't look so good, love."

"I'm okay. Just can't take my liquor these days, that's all."

"Lightweight." She winks at me.

"Is this going to be all right, d'you think?"

"This?"

"Your mum."

She shakes her head slow. "Don't know. She'll have to cope with it, I guess. She's not gonna like it, but…" She shrugs. "Sometimes you don't get to choose how things work out, do you? Sometimes the choice gets made *for* you."

"Yes."

I look out of the window, watching for the blue gleam of the sea, waiting for the distant whisper of it to come close, but there are only meadows and fences for now, and tiny towns with dogs and scattered clapboard houses.

I must have fallen asleep again, because next time I open my eyes, we are in Carradine, and Elise is pulling up outside the general store.

I feel befuddled for a moment, my head still musty with sleep, but Elise has switched off the engine already and is opening her door.

"You stay here," she says. "This won't take long. I'll talk to her and then we'll go. Okay?"

I nod, shuffling myself upright in the seat.

"You don't want me to come in with you?"

"No."

She climbs out of the car and closes the door, and I watch her step up onto the wooden verandah and peer through the store window. She tries the door handle, cups her hand over the glass, but then she turns to me, puzzled, shaking her head.

"Nobody there," she says, once she's back in the car. "That's weird. She never closes up in the afternoon usually."

"Maybe she's not well."

"Maybe."

We drive on to the house then, and when we get there Elise hurries inside, while I climb out of car and just stand for a couple of minutes, feeling the pale air slide like silk into my throat. The sea seems to be breathing for me – a hush in my mouth, the scarlet linings of my lungs smoothed and cooled by sea spray misting the air. I'm still standing there, leaning against the car, when Marie finds me.

"I knew you'd come back," she declares, closing her fingers around my arm. "I have it for you, *chérie*. I have it here." She reaches into the pocket of her cardigan, brings out a frail-looking envelope. It was probably blue once, powder blue, but now it's grey as dust. A harsh touch would flutter it into pieces. Marie hands it to me.

"The final piece of the jigsaw," she whispers, "or almost the final piece." But then she jerks her head towards the house and leans in close. "Best you don't read it here, though. Walk with me" – and she tugs at my arm like a child – "walk with me down to the beach, out of harm's way."

"But I'm waiting for Elise."

"She will find you." She starts to lead me forward. "Come."

I haven't the strength to argue with her, and, of course, I can't deny that I'm intrigued by the contents of the envelope in my hand. I hold it carefully, with just my fingertips. I can feel how thin and sheer the paper is. It's almost as if I were not holding anything at all.

We take a steep path down through a swatch of trees, their leaves standing out black and shiny against the pallid air and, when we reach the beach, Marie sits down very carefully on a patch of sand and pats at the ground by her side for me to sit too. When I do, she smiles.

"The Laker woman is going to tell the truth after all, isn't she?"

She looks delighted and, when I nod, she claps her hands together.

"At last," she says, and her eyes are brimming with tears. "I heard Elise telling Ruth, in the kitchen, just now. Ah, Ruth is so *full* of rage." She shakes her head. "But this is no cause for rage. This is a cause for celebration, that Edouard will be realised as the author of those books, that the *truth* will come to light, after all these many years. This is good news, no?"

"I'm not sure Elise sees it that way."

She waves it away, inconsequential.

"Elise will be fine. She fights her mother's corner, nothing more."

"I think it's the scandal, more than anything, that Ruth and Elise are worried about."

"The scandal will be old news in no time. Memories are short." She looks at the envelope in my hand. "I didn't show the letter to the Laker woman."

"Why are you showing it to me?"

"Because you love Elise."

I look into her face. "I do, yes, but why does my loving Elise mean I get to see the letter? I don't understand."

"Read," she says softly, "and you will understand."

So, I open the flimsy envelope, while Marie watches, and I take out the single sheet inside it. It's as thin as tissue paper, thinner, and the writing on it, although recognisably Lucy's, is scrawled and hard to read, as if it's been written in a hurry. I bring it closer to my face.

The Manse,
Summerskill,
P.W.I.

March 20th, 1900.

My Dear Edouard,

I feel certain that you will have heard by now the news, that my husband Ethan and I have been blessed with a baby daughter. She was born a week ago last Tuesday, a tiny white lady, and the delight of my life. I have named her Rosalie. Ethan put a notice in the Island papers, announcing the birth, and since I know that your family takes the Tribune, *I must assume that you are already aware of what has happened. You will not be aware however, since none but myself is aware, that the child is yours. Ethan and my family believe the birth to have been premature, but it was not. I knew I was with child when I left Carradine last summer*

I can only ask that you search your heart and forgive the ill that I have done you, and I ask also that you will keep my secret, since it is our *secret, just as surely as Rosalie is ours. She is a bonny child, dark like you. When I look at her, I see you. You gifted her to me, Edouard. Be assured that I will love her and cherish her, just as I do the sweet memory of our times together, always.*

   Lucy

I look up from the paper, and Marie is staring at me, her eyes wide.

"Well?" she says. "What do you think?"

"I think she should have told Ethan the truth."

"Really? You don't think she was entitled to keep Rosalie secret - secret from everyone but Edouard?"

I feel cold suddenly, the breeze churning chill at my neck.

"I don't know." I fold the paper carefully and slip it back into the envelope. There are tiny particles of dust frosting my fingertips. "I don't know what she should have done really, or what she shouldn't, but she couldn't ever have been happy, surely, without Edouard. She couldn't have been happy being married to one person while she was in love with another, and she couldn't have been happy with her child being a lie."

Marie nods sadly. "She made a mistake in leaving Carradine, I think. She should have stayed. It would have been hard, very hard, but at least she and Edouard would have lived it through together, toiled it together. As it was, she made the best of her marriage. She made the best of her life, but it was a mistaken life, no?" She dips her chin towards me. "It was a wrong choice."

I look out to sea, seagulls riding currents of air, their feathers ruffling in the wind.

"Yes," I say at last. "It was a wrong choice."

"And you will choose differently."

She doesn't say it as a question and, when I look at her, she isn't looking at me anymore. She is shielding her eyes against the gleam of the ocean.

"What do you mean, Marie?"

"I mean, of course, that you will choose Elise." She *does* turn to look at me then, and her black gaze is poised and steady. "You will not go back to England, to your lover, to your mistaken life. No. You will stay, and you and Elise will live here with us, in Carradine."

"You seem very sure of what I should do."

"As should *you* be. Certainty comes with want. You just have to *want* something enough in order to make it happen." She smiles at me then, says, very softly, "*Nouvelle vie,*" and then, a little louder, "a new life."

She tilts her head a little, looking away from me. "You know, Abigail, I used not to have a great deal of respect for the truth. I used to think it was something I could manipulate, to my own ends." She glances at me out of the corner of her eye. "We all try to order the world to our own desires, yes?"

"Yes."

"Yes." She nods slowly. "When we found Lucy's diary last summer, and this letter…" She reaches forward and touches it with the tips of her fingers, "… I realised my mistake. The truth isn't ours to do with as we please, Abigail. It is in charge of *us*, not the other way around, and, sooner or later, we have no choice but to give ourselves up to it. Do you see?"

"Yes. I do."

She smiles, lifting her closed palms to her lips and breathing out against her fingers. "I need to tell someone the truth now."

"The truth? About Lucy?"

"No." She shakes her head slow. "*My* truth. I need to tell someone my truth." She looks into my eyes. "I need to tell *you*."

"Why? I mean, why me?"

"As I have said, because you love Elise." She looks at me impatiently. "You don't understand what that means, do you?"

"I understand what it means to *me*."

She clicks her tongue against the roof of her mouth. "But it has a meaning for others too. Love has a meaning for others too. It is… clarifying, you know?"

I can feel my eyebrows furrowing. I open my mouth to speak, but Marie lifts her hand to silence me.

"Elise's father was called Laurent," she says quickly. "And *his* father was called Patrice. Patrice was my husband. He was some years older me, but a good man and a kind man." She looks at me closely. "I want you to understand, that he was a good man and a kind man."

I nod. "Okay."

Marie takes a deep breath, her black eyes cloudy with the prelude to tears. I pretend not to notice how sad she has become. I look away.

"When Lucy Pritchard's eldest daughter, Rosalie, was thirty-five years old, Lucy Pritchard took it upon herself to tell Rosalie that Ethan MacKay was not her natural father. She told her about Carradine, and about Edouard, and, as a result, Rosalie came here looking for her family. She found them. She found *us*, but, of course, she also found her father long dead."

"Why did Lucy tell her, after all those years?"

Marie shrugs. "No one knows. Not even Rosalie knew."

"There must have been a reason though."

"Perhaps, like me, she was growing old. Perhaps she wanted to leave this world at peace with herself, and at peace with the truth. I don't know, but whatever the reason, she came here – Dr Rosalie MacKay came here." Marie pronounces the name very precisely, looking out to sea, her eyes narrowing.

"I was one year married at that time – an innocent. My husband was an impressionable man. A good man, as I have said, but impressionable, and restless. I see now that he was thwarted. He didn't want the farm. He didn't want the monotony of it. He wanted something more, and in Rosalie he found it..." She falters. "And, like her mother before her, Rosalie saw something *she* desired also, and she took it."

"They were lovers?" I say it too quickly, want to catch it back, but can't. "Marie..."

"Yes. They were lovers, although I knew nothing of it at the time. In fact, their *relationship*..." The word seems to hang cobwebbed in the air for a moment, waiting for one of us to tangle our fingers inside it, waft it into dust, "... their... *liaison*..." Marie shakes her head, confounded, "... only came to light some months later, when Rosalie returned to Carradine, with her child."

I swallow hard. "Her child?"

"Her baby." Marie clears her throat. "Two months old. A boy. She was a professor by then, Rosalie, a career woman, very successful, well respected. She had thought to keep the child herself, of course, but soon realised her mistake. There was no loving or attentive space in a life like hers, to accommodate a child." She looks into my eyes. "My husband's child."

"God. Marie..." I press my fingers to her arm.

"So, we kept him. We kept Laurent, and I brought him up as my own blood. Assuredly, I *loved* him as my own. He knew no mother but me. He was my child."

"You never looked at him and saw *her*? You never resented him?"

"No. I never did, nor ever would have *thought* to. None of the blame was his, and besides, he was a gift, to me." She presses her palm closed over my fingers. "I was never to be blessed with babies of my own, you see – babies born from my own body, but I was blessed with Laurent."

"And you forgave Patrice even?"

"I did. In time, I did." She smiles, wryly. "I saw what drew him to her, and I couldn't compete, and I couldn't rail against it, *because* I saw and understood it. She was refined and accomplished and intelligent and gracious. She was everything I was not." She shrugs. "He was a simple man, and he was flattered by her." And she squeezes my hand in hers. "And he was sorry. *Mon Dieu*! Was he *sorry*!"

"Did Laurent know? Did you ever tell him the truth?"

She lowers her head. "I wanted to. For a long time, I wanted to, but Patrice wouldn't permit it."

"Why?"

"He wanted things kept simple and orderly. He abhorred..." She thinks for a moment, "... fuss. He abhorred fuss."

"So Laurent never knew, about Rosalie?"

"He knew, eventually, because I told him, eventually."

"After his father was dead?"

She nods. "A year ago. When we found the diary, and I found Lucy Pritchard's letter. That's when I told him."

"And that's when he left."

She nods again, turns to look out at the straight line of the horizon. "He hated the farm, as much as his father had ever hated it, if not more. When I told him, about Rosalie, it suddenly seemed to make sense to him *why* he hated it. He wasn't a farmer, you see. He was the son of a doctor, the grandson of a famous writer."

"But he'd been brought up as a farmer?"

"Detesting every moment of it."

"But he knew nothing else?"

"He *wanted* to know something else. He was hungry for something else. So, he went looking for it. Why would he *not*?"

"But what about Ruth, and Elise and Gen? He just upped and left them, as easily as that? And he left you, as easily as that?"

"I don't know how it easy it was for him to do, in the end, but yes, he did it. He left us."

I move towards her, as softly as I can, and slip my arm around her shoulder. "I'm so sorry, Marie."

She smiles at me. "No need, *chérie*. We follow our destinies, each of us, and to leave us was Laurent's destiny, eventually."

"Have you heard from him since?"

"Once or twice."

"Where is he?"

"With his family. Lucy Pritchard's children, and grandchildren and great-grandchildren; most of them live in Seattle now. That's where my son is, I believe – with his family."

I shake my head hard. "But *you* are his family."

"Maybe one day he will see it that way also, but not yet; not *this* day, *chérie*." She inclines her head a little, seems to be thinking. "I wonder now, if I'd told him the truth a long time ago, whether he would have dealt differently with me and with his life here." She turns to look at me. "Maybe he would have forgiven me, and stayed. Do you think he would?"

"I don't know. Maybe."

She nods slowly. "Maybe. Yes. When Rosalie had done with us here and her visit was over, all those years ago, she went back to Lucy Pritchard. *She* forgave her mother." She flutters her fingers to her chest for a moment. "That gives me some hope that

Laurent will forgive too, in his own time."

"Yes."

"I still believe I was in the right to tell him." She sounds like she's trying to convince herself. "When one is as old as I am, life sinks down to specifics – all the excess dissolves, and then there are just the real things left to look at, the lasting things: love and compassion and truth. Most of all, truth."

"Yes." I sit back on my heels. "Does Elise know the truth?"

"No. Ruth knows, but Elise and Gen..." She shakes her head, "*Non.*"

"Elise needs to know, though. She deserves to know."

"And you will be the one to tell her." Marie grips my arm suddenly, very tight. "The work is yours now. Elise's happiness is yours now. Her future is yours, your responsibility, and only yours." She lets go of my arm. "*Nouvelle vie*, remember, *chérie*?" Her eyes are hard and very dark. "New life..."

Seventeen

"No." I shake my head. "I mean, I *don't* know." And it's sudden and bright inside me, and unexpected, this blaze of doubt. It burns hot.

I clamber to my feet, Lucy's letter crumpled in my fist. Is my life at home the mistaken life, or is this life going to turn out to be that? Is Elise's future mine? Is her happiness *my* happiness? Am I to be responsible for her now? All this talk of truth has cut something loose inside me. My heart is adrift. I think back over the last few days and I start to think what if Elise is a liar after all? What if she will continue to keep secrets from me – bigger secrets? Everything here in Carradine seems to be so layered and convoluted. What if our life together here is soured by mistrust? I think back to her promise not to lie to me again, after misleading me about the diary, and then I think about her face, blatant, telling me Lucy's lover was Henri and not Edouard, an untruth, and something begins to break down inside me, and disperse. I try to breathe it back into shape, but I can't do it.

I feel afraid suddenly, but Gayle's face edges in at the periphery of my vision then, smiling, her eyes full of candour and tenderness, and I remember what she used to say to me when we first met, how, when we looked into each other's eyes, we could see each other's soul, and all at once our life together at home no longer feels like a mistaken life. It feels safe and certain and simple, and unutterably *proven*.

I start to walk then, fast, with Marie calling after me, stumbling back up the path through the trees. I disturb a pheasant in the undergrowth, and it flaps up wildly over my head, panic-stricken. I watch it go. I gulp at the air, trying to suck the sky into my body, trying to take the cool white shine of it inside me, but there's no room for the sky suddenly, because my heart is filling my chest, and tears are filling my throat.

I start to run then, up and up and up, desperate to get clear of the trees, blinded by the thick black of their leaves, blinded by tears, but, as I come stumbling out into the clearing, I can see that someone is coming toward me, calling my name. For a second, I can't make out who it is, but then I hear a voice that I recognise.

"Abby." Mo is reaching out to me. "What the hell's wrong? Sweetheart. God, what's *wrong*?"

I run straight into her arms, almost knocking her to the ground, but she holds onto me tight, smoothing her hands over my hair, saying my name, over and over, very softly.

"What *is* it, love?" She eases me away from her at last, looking into my eyes, pushing back the hair back from my face. "You can tell me." Her tone is gentle. "Come on. Is it Elise? Have you told her it's over?"

I shake my head.

"Well, what, then?"

Suddenly, there is a noise behind us, a rustling, and Marie steps out of the trees. Her face is flushed and she's out of breath, but she says straightaway, firmly, "Tell her."

"Tell me what?" Mo looks from Marie, to me, and back again. Her face is puzzled. "Abby?" She purses her lips. "Tell me what?"

I just shake my head, and go on shaking it, and Mo closes her hands around my wrists tightly, trying to make me keep eye contact with her, but it's no good. I can't do it, and I can't say the words. In the end, as I knew she would, Marie says them for me.

"She's staying here, in Carradine. She is finished with the old." Marie is grinning. She lifts her palms to the air. "She is *embracing* the new."

That's all she says, nothing more, and then she moves past us, keeps walking, doesn't look back. I watch her go, all the way to the house and in through the front door. I can't look at Mo, but I can hear the sharp rasp of her breath, and when at last I *do* make myself look at her, she says quickly, "She's got it wrong, the old lady. Tell me she's got it wrong."

"I don't know." The words stutter out of my body.

"What d'you mean, you don't know? How can you not know?"

"I just *don't*."

"I thought you were going to tell Elise that you'd made a mistake?"

"I never said that was what I was going to do."

I shake my head, and Mo takes a step back, presses her palm to her forehead, shrieks at me, "Why are you being so obtuse?"

But the tears are lifting inside me again, spilling out of my body, hot as lava. I try to swallow them back, but it's no good, because there's something with sharp edges pressing against my breastbone. It makes me lean forward, folding myself in half, and then it makes me go down on my hands and knees in the grass. I retch, over and over again, my diaphragm stretching taut, retracting. In the end, I just hunch myself forward and start to rock, as softly as I can, back and forth, and suddenly Mo is on her knees with me, and she has her arms around me.

"I'm sorry." Her voice is low and anxious. "I'm *sorry* I shouted. Shit. It's just…" She squeezes me tighter. "Oh, Abby." She turns me so that I'm facing her. "Look. This is getting ridiculous. You have *got* to decide, once and for fucking *all*." She huffs a sigh into the air, really quick. "You can't go on like this."

My head is a blur, everything inside me fragmenting, reassembling, but I try hard to focus, to think.

"I thought I had decided. I really did, but now… I just feel so scared, Mo."

She leaps to her feet then, dragging me up with her. "I think I have something that will seal it for you."

She takes hold of my hand, like I am her child, and starts to walk.

"What d'you mean?" But she doesn't seem to hear me. I pull back. "Mo? What are you talking about?"

She spins around then, and her face is a beam of light. "It's time this was all done and dusted."

I shake my head. "Done and dusted?"

She grins. "She's here."

"Who?"

"Gayle."

I breathe out, very slowly, trying to concentrate on what she's saying, because her words are garbled surely, and absurd.

"She's not here." I press my fingers to my temples. "Gayle's not here."

"Yes, she is. She's here on the island. She and I planned the whole thing, weeks ago, for her to come out and surprise you."

"What?"

"Oh, yes." She nods. "It's your fifth anniversary, tomorrow, although that fact seems to have slipped your mind. Can't think why." She clears her throat. "Gayle flew out last night. I picked her up at the airport less than" – and she glances at her watch – "three hours ago."

"Tell me you're joking, Mo."

"Nope. When we got back to The Old Sea Box, I found your note. I told Gayle you'd had to come back to Carradine to finish some drawings, but that you'd be back by tonight. She said she'd sleep off her jet lag." She folds her arms across her chest, looking me straight in the eye, unwavering. "And then I drove like a bat out of hell to get here before you and Elise left."

I can't help it. I sit down on the grass and bury my face in my hands.

"Why didn't you tell me?"

"I'm telling you now."

"Why didn't you tell me yesterday?"

"Because it was supposed to be a surprise. I tried my best to stop you from leaving, didn't I? It was supposed to be a fucking *surprise*."

"Well, it's certainly *that*."

She sighs. "Look, don't you see? It'll be okay now. We go back to my house, you and Gayle have a nice romantic meal, a big old smoochy reunion, and you'll remember all the reasons you want to be with her. Don't you see?" She's looking pleased with herself, self-satisfied, but her face changes suddenly, darkens. "It's a blessing, Abby" – she says it quietly – "Gayle being here. It's going to save you from yourself. You're committed to Gayle, and you love her. Deep down, you *do*. You don't want to lose her for the sake of some stupid holiday romance, do you? *I* can't let you lose her for the sake of a five-day fling."

I think of Lucy's letter earlier. I think of what Marie said about Lucy's "mistaken life". I think of what she said about the truth, about how we must give ourselves up to it, because, in the end, it's all that will be left to us, and something catches like a fish hook in my throat. I blink my eyes closed, feeling the cool air breathing over my eyelids. I hear a door close, footsteps approaching.

"Abby."

Elise's voice smokes out soft onto the air. I can taste it. I open my eyes.

"Abby," she says again, dropping down onto her haunches by my side. She takes my hand in hers looks into my face. "What's going on?"

We go to The Merchantman's Pub, Elise and I, while Mo waits crossly in her car, and when we get to the pub, there's nobody in there, except the winking landlord from the other night, and an old man, sitting alone at a table in the window. He's playing clock patience.

Elise goes to the bar to order our drinks and, when she comes back to the table where I'm sitting, I gesture to the old man and his cards.

"Did you ever play that game when you were small?"

She glances over. "Clock patience? Yeah, all the time. I think I managed to get right to the end once maybe, in my whole childhood."

"Don't think I *ever* got to the end." I take a sip of the mineral water that Elise has bought for me. It bristles bright with bubbles. "I didn't know it was possible really, to get to the end."

"It's just a matter of luck, though, where the kings are in the deck."

"It never felt like luck. It felt like those kings *positioned* themselves on purpose."

Elise shakes her head, smiling at me.

"You really think the universe is out to get you, don't you? Whatever *can* go wrong *will* go wrong, right?"

Beneath the table, I press my palm to my belly, and hold it there. "Something like that."

Elise reaches across and takes my other hand in hers. "Things can just easily go *right*, though, if you let them. You have a bad habit of programming your disappointments in advance. D'you know that?"

I shrug, looking again at the man playing patience. He is rapt, absorbed – turning over each card with supreme delicacy, and very slowly, almost as if he can catch the kings out, keep them at bay with his watchfulness. I find that I'm holding my breath.

"It was always the king of clubs."

Elise lifts her bottle of beer to her lips, takes a long drink. "What was?"

"The king that turned up last every time. The king that beat me at clock patience every bloody time." I let my head drop a little, remembering. "The king of clubs."

"Evil incarnate."

"Yes." She dips her head towards me. "Trust you to let things be governed by such a negative symbol."

"What d'you mean?"

"Oh, come on. You can't get a much meaner or moodier motif for life than the king of clubs." She tries to smile, but it's shaky at the edges. "Why couldn't you pick something cheery to live by: the bluebird of fucking *happiness*, for instance?"

"I don't believe in the bluebird of happiness." I try to smile too. "Now, the ostrich of unspeakable sorrow – *him* I believe in."

Elise lifts her eyes to the ceiling.

"Now, *why* doesn't that surprise me?" She shakes her head slowly. "Well, I guess I'll just have to believe in the bluebird enough for the both of us, then, huh?"

I look into her face then and I know, suddenly, what I have to say to her and what I have to do, even though my heart wants to say and do neither.

"Abby." Her voice is wary. "Just tell me, baby."

"I don't know how."

She leans forward. "Whatever it is, we can deal with it, you know."

"I don't think we can, not this time."

"Don't sell *us* short, Abby. We're strong, together. We are. Already, we are. You know it." She sounds so convincing. "Whatever the problem is, it's solvable."

"Gayle's here."

"What?"

I lean my elbows forward onto the table. "She and Mo planned all along for her to come out, to the island, for our anniversary."

"And you knew nothing about it?"

"It was supposed to be a surprise."

Elise's face is sealed tight.

"I hate surprises," she says, and she lifts her bottle again and drinks all of what's left inside it. When she sets it down on the table, I reach across and lace my fingers around hers, stroking across the back of her hand with my thumb. She watches me doing it, keeps her eyes lowered.

"What are you going to do?" she asks at last.

"I don't know."

She looks up then. "But you know what you're *not* going to do. You're not going to drive with me across Canada, are you?"

I slide my hand free of hers, say, as quietly as I can, "I don't think I can."

"You're making a mistake."

"Maybe."

She takes a breath. "Then why *make* it?"

"Because she's here, don't you see? While I could think of her distantly, keep her as a fact, a set of circumstances, it was okay, or, at least, not okay, but I could live with it, somehow. But now..." I sit back in my seat, "... she's here. She's less than three hours away, and somehow she's brought my life at home *with her*. It all feels real again." I shrug, helpless. "*She* feels real again."

"She was always real. Nothing's changed except proximity, and that alone can't be *enough* to make you change your mind about us."

"I haven't changed my mind about us."

"Then don't go back to Port Hove. Come with me."

"I can't." I let my head drop heavy. "It's too hard. I just feel so... confused, and torn. I feel completely *torn*."

"I never wanted you to feel that way."

"Well, I do."

"I'm sorry."

"It's not your fault, Elise. It's mine."

She takes a big breath. "Look. I'll wait. You go and talk to her. Maybe things will feel clearer after you've talked to her. I'll wait here, or, better still, I'll come with you. We'll talk to her together."

The air is slanting grey across the table. I lean into it, looking for shadow, but the space inside my head is pure white, an aching glare.

"I don't know."

Elise sits up straight. "Well, not knowing is better than *no*."

The old man in the window sighs loudly then, shaking his head. He scoops the cards up off the table and starts to shuffle them, and the barman calls to him,

"No luck for you today, then, John?"

The old man makes a little clicking sound out of the corner of his mouth.

"No. And I was down to my last three cards, too."

I turn in my seat, ask him quietly, "Which was the last king?"

He fingers quickly through the pack in his hands, pulls out the card and holds it up for me to see. I nod, thanking him, and then I turn back to Elise. She is trying to smile at me.

"Your nemesis."

"I told you."

She nods. "Just when the game looks won, disaster turns up."

"Yes."

"Gayle, I mean."

"Gayle isn't the king of clubs here, though, Elise."

She looks doubtful. "No?"

"No. My conscience is, and so is yours."

Eighteen

Mo is waiting for us when we get back to the house of course. She's sitting inside her car, glaring through the windscreen, but she climbs out as soon as she spots us, and comes towards us quickly. She's looking at Elise, her mouth set solid in a frown.

"Take Abby's bags out of your car and put them in mine, please." She folds her arms across her chest. "We need to go."

Elise doesn't answer her, but she *does* open the boot of the hire car and lift my rucksack out, handing it across to her. Behind her, I can see Ruth and Marie hovering in the doorway to the house. Marie is smiling at me. Ruth isn't.

"Is this what you want?" Elise has taken a couple of steps towards me. "You want to go?"

I nod slowly. "I think I have to."

"You don't have to do anything you don't want to do."

"I have to do this. I *want* to do this."

She touches my face, strokes her fingers across my cheekbone. There are tears in her eyes, and something inside me fractures, cracks clean across when I see them.

"I just want you to be happy." Her voice is very quiet. "I love you, Abby, and your happiness is what I care about. If you tell me that going back to Gayle will make you happy, then I'll believe you, and I'll let you go."

Mo is clearing her throat, kicking the heel of her boot lightly into the dust, over and over again, like an impatient child. I turn to look at her and she makes eye contact with me and holds it, and in the seconds that pass between us, her face slips from purpose and resolution, to perplexity, to sadness. She is sad for me, suddenly, helplessly. It's there in her face. She turns away.

"Abby."

Elise's voice calls me back, but from a long way it seems, and when

197

I turn to look at her, she has grown indistinct, like I'm looking at her through mist, through a fog of water.

"I *have* to go."

I push myself forward into her arms, lurch myself into her arms, and she holds me for a moment, very soft and shadowy, her mouth pressed to my hair. I can feel her breath against my forehead.

"I meant it all, Elise. Don't ever doubt it. I *did* mean it."

She breathes out slowly. "I know you did. I meant it too."

"I have to do the right thing. I have to make the right choice, otherwise I won't know myself any more."

"I understand."

I press my cheek against hers. "What will you do now?"

"I'll go, like we planned. I'll go anyway."

"Alone?"

"I can't stay here. My bags are packed. I'm on sabbatical. I'll go, alone, unless you change your mind. I'll go alone."

But I drag myself away from her then. I have to. I turn away without looking at her, and Mo is there by my side, her arm around my waist, steering me towards her car. I hear someone calling my name, and when I look towards the house, I see Marie tottering out toward me. Her face is ashen. She is lifting her hand into the air. But it's no good. Mo folds me down into the passenger seat and closes the door fast. I lean forward, wrapping my arms around my body, staring down at my feet, and Mo is already in the driver's seat beside me, saying, "Shit! Shit!" – over and over again.

She jams her keys into the ignition and starts to drive, the gravel beneath her tyres crunching like bone. I try to make myself look up. I try to make myself look for Elise, but I can't do it. I keep my head down until we are back on the main road and out of Carradine, and even then, even when we're safe out on Highway Three, I still can't bear to lift my eyes. The afternoon is thick and leaden, and something dark is slouching itself clear of the horizon, seeping towards me like blood.

Mo keeps her hand on my leg as she drives, and every now and then she says quietly, sighing, "It's going to be okay. Everything's going to be okay" – but her voice is vague, and there are tears in it. I can hear them.

A couple of times her concentration must falter, because she has to brake really hard, throwing us forward in our seats, and I think, suddenly, that maybe it would be best if that's how the story ended, with a crash – a clean, clear tragedy, a point from which there is no moving on. Maybe that would be best for me, not to move on. Suddenly, I don't want to move on.

I wind down the window and breathe deeply, and there is green on my tongue suddenly, feathers of fern leafing my gums, and I can smell the sea again, thick with salt. I focus all of my thinking, and all of my feeling, on how the world tastes. I open my mouth to the air, fluting it into my throat, and, for a moment or two, I am steadied by textures, but then the road ahead begins to grow familiar and signs for Port Hove start to snap by, counting down the kilometres that are left between myself and Gayle.

By the time we reach The Old Sea Box, I am so nauseous, I have to make Mo drop me off at the end of the drive, so that I can walk the rest of the way, trying to even out my breathing, trying to stop myself turning around and heading straight back to Carradine. I take as long as I can to walk the hundred metres or so to the house, and when I get there, Mo is standing just inside the front door.

"Gayle's still asleep," she whispers. "We have some time. We'll have a drink, take it easy for a bit, and then you can go and wake her."

"I don't want to."

"Yes, you do. Gayle's your girlfriend, your partner. She's your future, remember?"

"But what about Elise?"

"She isn't anybody's future but her own."

I shake my head, a sudden panic, black and murky in my stomach.

"But what if I *want* her to be my future? What if she's worth the risk, and coming back to Gayle is a terrible mistake?"

Mo purses her lips. The skin around her mouth puckers and pinches.

"We've already *been* through this," she says flatly. "You've made your choice, and it's the right choice. It's the right thing to do, and you want to do the right thing, don't you? You want to be a *good person*, Abby?"

I wince against her words, trying to fight them, but there's a languor sinking into my bones, weighing me down, and suddenly I don't care. I don't care about any of it. I don't care what happens now. I just want it all to stop. I just want oblivion, for a moment. If I can't have Elise, if I can't reconcile myself to the possibility of having her, then I don't want anything. I shut my eyes, feeling myself swaying into the wall, but Mo's hands catch me, straighten me.

"Go and freshen up," she says quietly. "Then come downstairs and have a drink with me, relax for a while. There's no hurry. Slow and easy, okay?"

I do as she says. I go and freshen up, and then I sit with her at the kitchen table, looking out at the sea. I drink what she gives me. I relax, and then I climb the stairs and wake Gayle, just as Mo has said to do. She looks bemused for a moment, Gayle, and a little worried, like someone waking up in a hospital bed, but then her eyes focus on me, softly, and she smiles.

"Hey, you," she says, and she reaches out for me, pulls me into her body.

I sink her back into the pillows, pressing my lips to her cheek.

"Am I a dark horse, or what?" Her voice is smiling. "You had no idea I was coming, did you?"

"No."

She rocks me from side to side, kissing at my hair, playful as a puppy.

"And you say I'm never spontaneous!"

"This wasn't spontaneous, though, was it? You and Mo must have planned this ages ago."

"Abs." She nuzzles me away from her, keeping her hands on my arms. "Go with the flow, yeah?" Her face is a pale disc in the grey of the room. "Aren't you pleased to see me?"

I take a breath. "Of course I am."

"Well, fucking well *show* me then?" And she pulls me down onto her chest, her hands moving over my breasts.

"I was dreaming, just then, when you woke me up." Her voice is tight and concentrated. She kisses me, whispering her lips against mine. "It was one of those really *vivid* dreams, you know? Like it was actually happening, present tense."

I kiss her back, trying to make it real and candid, but I know what her dream will have been – folding clothes, counting numbers, climbing stairs...

"I was high up, at the summit of a mountain," she says, "and there was an old lady, knitting, like one of those women who used to knit at the foot of the guillotine. What were they called, those women? They had a name I think."

"I don't know."

She shakes her head. "Anyway, she called me over to speak to her, smiling and everything, winking at me, and then she told me that there was a promise to be kept. That's what she said, 'There's a promise to be kept,' and she pointed to this little stone cairn, and when I went to look inside it, there was this fuck-off big diamond, glinting in the sunlight, but when I tried to pick it up, it burnt my fingers." She looks into my eyes. "And then you were there, suddenly," she says. "And you picked up the diamond without burning your fingers, and you gave it to me, and you giving it to me somehow meant that it *didn't* burn my fingers. It was really heavy, but cool and smooth and full of colours. You told me it was mine to keep." She swallows. "It was the nicest thing anyone had ever given to me, and it was mine to keep, you said, but somehow I didn't think it was. I thought I'd have to give it back. Still, it was a lovely thing for you to say, Abs, that it was mine to keep, even for a little bit, you know?"

I touch her face with my fingers, a sudden rush of tenderness springing tears into my eyes. She looks sad, for a moment, and tired, and I just want to gather her up in my arms like a child. I want to be her solace, a safe place for her to lay her head. I want to keep her world steady and peaceful and loved. None of what has happened between Elise and me is Gayle's fault. She is the innocent in this. Of *course*, it's her needs I should be looking to, and not my own, but she shuffles forward in the bed then and slips her hands up under my top, climbing my ribs with the tips of her fingers. She's grinning.

"D'you think it was a metaphor?" She thumbs at my breasts. "The diamond? D'you think it was a metaphor?"

"A metaphor for what?"

"A shag, perchance." She starts to tug my top up over my head, and I let her. "An anniversary shag?" She makes a little whooping sound, chuckling to herself, her breath coming quickly. "It's good to see you, Abs. Shit. It's good to see you." And she turns me with her hands, flails me down onto my back, climbs over me.

I think about the diamond. I close my eyes tight shut, thinking about the "promise to be kept", and I let Gayle's hands, my lover's hands, undress me, so familiar in how they move, in how they feel. I let her touch take me back to the person I was before I met Elise, and I can still see that person clearly. She was a good person, open and honest, and wanting the best for the people she loved. Except that she was stone inside, of course. She was desert dust, and now, suddenly now, she isn't, and all things are new. I remember that old Bible story, about the Israelites in the desert, dying of thirst, and how God told Moses to tap his staff against a rock, and when he did, water came flowing out of it – clean, clear water, a lustre of water, limitless. I know how that feels, for everything that was hard and calcified, to suddenly melt and become fluid again. I know how that feels because that is what Elise has done to me, and now I'm about to deny it all and turn my face from her, forever? No.

I sit up straight suddenly, nearly knocking Gayle to the floor. She looks at me, bewildered.

"What's wrong?"

"Nothing."

I swing my legs down onto the carpet and start reaching for my clothes, but Gayle catches hold of my arm.

"Abby?" Her face is all curves. "What's wrong? Come on." She slips her palm onto my shoulder and squeezes. "You can tell me."

"I can't."

"Of course you can."

And there's nothing I can do about it, because a sob comes spilling out my mouth, an animal sound, visceral, and Gayle sits back with a start.

"God. Abby. What the fuck?"

"I'm sorry. I'm so sorry."

I cover my mouth with both my hands, trying to draw my tears back in again, but I can't do it.

"*Tell* me, Abs." She is shaking her head. "Just tell me."

"It's too hard."

"It can't be."

"You don't understand."

"And I *won't* be able to, unless you tell me."

I hunch myself forward on the bed, not looking at her. I can't bear to look at her, or to have her look at me. I could slip away from this if I wanted to. I could make something up, cover my tracks, convince her otherwise. I could stick to the plan that Mo devised for us, and take it to its logical conclusion: Gayle and I, back in Winchester, picking up where we left off, except I would still be in love with Elise, and my relationship with Gayle would be a lie. It would be a mistake, forever – Lucy's mistake, *forever*.

I take a breath. "I've done something, Gayle."

"Oh?" Her voice is wary.

"I love you. I do, and I don't want to hurt you. God knows I don't, but this thing I've done, it *is* going to hurt you."

She leans back against the wall and folds her arms across her chest. "What have you done?"

I look away from her, out of the window, but all I can see is sky, vacuous and white, nothing on which to focus.

"I met someone, in Carradine, while I was drawing for Mo."

"Someone?"

"A woman."

She hesitates. "And you had sex with her?"

"Yes."

"How many times?"

"Twice."

And with that, she suddenly flings back the bedclothes and starts to get dressed.

"Gayle?" I try to catch hold of her hand, but she wrenches it away from me. "We have to talk about this. Don't you want to talk about this?"

"There's nothing to say about it." Her voice is crystalline. "*I* have nothing to say about it."

"But…" I stand up. "I'm telling you because I'm sorry, and I didn't want to lie to you."

"I don't care."

"What?"

"I don't care that you're sorry."

"Don't you want to talk about it?"

She glares at me. "There's no talking to be done. It ends here. All of it. Don't you see that?"

"But I *do* love you. This isn't about me not loving you."

"If you loved me, you wouldn't have felt the need to have sex with a stranger, within a *week* of being away from me."

I let my head drop. "I'm sorry."

"You keep saying that, but it makes no difference to me. You can tell me you're sorry. You can tell me it was a mistake, but why would I want to be with someone who could *make* that kind of mistake? Why would I want to be with someone who could forget me so easily?"

"But I didn't forget you. You were there. All the time, you were there."

"Even while she was fucking you?"

I don't know what to say to her. All the words I *thought* I had, all the words that were supposed to mend and heal, are shattered now, and there is just Gayle's rage filling the room, black as pitch. I sit down on the edge of the bed, naked, watching her getting dressed, watching her picking up her bag, watching her leaving the room, and I don't move to stop her, *can't* move to stop her. My body feels deadweight, dead.

In the doorway, she pauses and turns to look at me.

"If I hadn't come out here, to surprise you, would you ever have told me?"

"Yes."

"I don't think you would." She sneers at me. "I think you'd have come home and pretended nothing had happened. I think you'd have lied forever."

I swallow hard. "No."

"Doesn't matter now, anyway. I'm done with you."

"But where are you going?"

"Home. Where else?"

"But you've only just got here." My voice is despairing. "You can't go."

"I can't stay." She narrows her eyes. "When I get back, I'll pack your stuff up and take it to your mum's."

"And that's it? It's as easy as that for you, for our relationship to be finished?"

"No. It was as easy as that for *you*, sweetheart. You're the one who finished it."

"But we can't finish it like this. Shit, Gayle." I can hear my heart pounding hard in my chest. "I feel like my head's gonna explode."

She shrugs. "I don't give a fuck how you feel."

"Gayle..."

"Don't."

She grits her teeth, shifts her bag from one hand to the other, lifts her eyes to mine one last time, and then she leaves, just like that. I listen to her feet hammering down the stairs. I listen to the sound of her and Mo talking, and then to the sound of someone climbing the stairs. I pull the duvet up around me, and Mo comes breathless into the room.

"You told her," she says, and she doesn't sound cross with me like I thought she would. She just sounds taken by surprise. "You told her, Abby?"

"Yes."

"Why?"

"Because I love Elise, I just *do*, and I couldn't lie about it. If I'd lied now, then I'd have had to go on lying, forever, and I couldn't."

"But what will you do?"

"I don't know." I let my head drop heavy. "I don't care."

Mo takes a couple of steps towards me and presses her hand against my shoulder, and then she moves in close so that my head is resting against her belly.

"This is all wrong, though," she whispers, but her voice is tender, and uncertain.

She runs her fingers over my hair, and I look up into her face.

"I just can't spend the rest of my life with one person, when I'm completely in love with another. Don't you see that?"

She inclines her head, taking a deep breath in. "Yes," she says at last, grudgingly. "I see that."

Gayle is calling her name from downstairs. She turns towards the door.

"I'll get back as soon as I can," she says quietly, and she leaves the room, heads down the stairs.

I listen to the front door opening and closing, and then to the sound of her car starting up, driving away.

As soon as there is quiet, I climb into bed and pull the covers up over my head. Now, all I can hear is the rasp of my own breathing, and the rumble of the sea. I concentrate on those sounds, sinking into them, like sinking into quicksand, and the afternoon seems to shrink me to something small, inconsequential, utterly meaningless. I think, If I can just stay here, under the covers, then everything will be all right. If I can just claim this soft space for myself and keep it, forever, then everything will be all right. But this soft space smells of Gayle, and I know I don't belong in it. I don't belong here, in Mo's house, and I no longer belong at home and, if I belonged with Elise, then the fact of that is too late in coming. She'll be on the mainland by now. I close my eyes, looking for tears, looking for something to *feel*, but there isn't anything. There's just the dry heap of my bones and my skin and my hair, and the wearying thud of my heart.

I fall asleep, and I must have slept for a long time, deeply, because the light in the room is a murky purple when I wake. Twilight. I climb out of bed and get dressed slowly, and then I make my way down the stairs, holding onto the banister as I go. It is cool and very smooth beneath my fingers, reassuringly solid, and that's what I need: something unyielding, something constant. The air is spiralling around me, everything in flux, and I seem to be out of breath after just a few steps. I have to sit down on the bottom stair to recover. There's still no sign of Mo.

After a few minutes, I stand up and falter to the kitchen, switching on the lamps as I go. They cast little puffs of yellow into the air, like blooms of old smoke. The house turns to cloud. I find a bottle of Jack Daniel's in one of the cupboards, and I take it with me, out of the front door and down the grassy steps, over the dunes, to the beach. The air is spiked with cold and salt, and the dark is coming on fast, but I don't mind. I want the dark. I want its wet mouth to swallow me whole.

I walk right the way down to the water's edge, and sit, with my legs folded beneath me, the bottle of Jack Daniel's dug into the sand beside me. And, for a long time, I just look out at the horizon, watching it shimmer to grey, watching the stars flowering into the sky, one by one, very tender and slow.

I think about Lucy. I wonder how she ever reconciled herself to a mistaken life, because that's what it was, surely. She was never in love with Ethan MacKay. She says so in her journals. He was never the man for whom she was meant – her true love, her true north. It was never him. The last section of Mo's biography details Lucy's decline into old age and senility, describes the last months of her life spent in a sanatorium on the mainland – how she would roam the corridors in the dead of night, a frail old lady in a nightdress, and if the staff found her and asked her where she was going, she'd tell them, "Home, I'm going home", and she'd start to talk then about the sea – pale light falling like rain over the ocean, an azure sky, the dear, sweet boy she'd left behind. Everyone thought she was referring to one of her sons, of course, but no. She was referring to Edouard.

I don't know what makes me look back along the beach, but *something* does and, when I do, I see two figures approaching me. They're some way off yet, but coming closer. One is a woman, in a long black dress, and the other is a man, and their tread is even and measured and purposeful. They are looking at each other, talking to each other as they walk. Their bodies are smiling. I blink my eyes closed, open them again, trying to focus, because Lucy and Edouard are walking down the beach towards me, and that can't *be*, surely. I turn my body so that I'm facing them, watching them stepping every moment closer. Lucy, in her long black dress, and Edouard, his dark hair catching a handful of moonlight, gifting it back to the gloomy air. I close my eyes again, the night sifting into my bones, but this time when I open my eyes, Lucy is no longer approaching me. Mo is. She's wearing a long black coat, hunched inside it against the cold. And the person walking beside her isn't Edouard. It's Elise.

I try to stand up, but my body has forgotten how it's done, so I stay sitting, helplessly, and the water laps up over my shoes, and Elise starts to run towards me then, fast, the sand splashing up thick and black beneath her feet.

Suddenly, Mo lifts her hand high into the air, and calls out to me, "True love." And she is laughing. I can hear laughter in her voice. "Turns out I'm a believer after all, Abby! Who'd have thought it, my lovely, eh?"

She has stopped walking. She just stands for a moment, with her hand held high in the air like that, a salute, and then she turns and starts to make her way back up the beach, toward The Old Sea Box.

When Elise reaches me, she drops to her knees in the sand and takes my face in her hands, looking into my eyes. Her skin sheens silver.

"I thought you'd gone." My voice breaks. "I thought you'd be on the mainland by now."

"No," she says softly, kissing my cheeks. Her lips are warm. "I was waiting for you." She folds herself down by my side, taking my hands in hers. "I've always been waiting for you. Don't you know that?"

My heart swells inside my chest, something hot and crimson carolling through my veins.

"Mo told you – what happened with Gayle?"

"Yes. She called the house, told me to come. She said she'd looked in on you, while you were sleeping, after Gayle left you, and that your sadness had broken her heart into pieces, that's what she said, and that there was nothing she could do about it, except *this*." She glances away from me. "I'm sorry, though, about Gayle."

"So am I. I just wanted to be a good person, you know? I just wanted to do the right thing."

Elise brings my palm to her lips. "But *this* is the right thing. You said so yourself, remember? This has always been the right thing. It was a promise to us before we ever knew about it. Don't you feel that?"

I nod. "Yes, I do." And I lean in against her. "A promise to be kept."

She lifts the bottle of Jack Daniel's out of the sand and unscrews the cap. "So, what now?"

"We follow our hearts."

"Are you afraid?"

"Little bit."

She smiles. "Me too."

"It's a risk we're taking, on each other."

"Yes."

She lifts the bottle of JD to her lips and takes a sip, and her face tightens as she swallows. She dips her chin, looking down at the sand.

"Hey, look at this." She reaches her fingers forward, and lifts something into the meagre light. "It's a moon shell, I think." She inspects it closely. "Yep. It's a Hebrew Moon."

She dusts it clear of sand then, and hands it to me. It's as cold as pearl, a bubble of ice – its blue eye startled by dry land.

Elise is smiling. "You usually only find moon shells in Western Europe, the Aegean, mostly."

"It's pretty."

Even in this light, the shell is all colours and sheen. Its creamy whorls are threaded with strands of lilac and pink and silver, and its columella is as smooth as porcelain. I bring it to my lips, slip the tip of my tongue inside, tasting tides and sunlight.

"It doesn't start out looking like that."

"What d'you mean?"

"It starts out brown."

"How can it start out one colour and end up another?"

Elise smiles. "The sea does it. The more a moon shell gets turned by the tides, mixed up with shingle and sand, the more its underlying colours come through. The brown gets worn away, until, eventually, you end up with one like this." She points to the shell in my palm. "It's a long way from home, though, this one, and it's seen some action en route, I reckon." She makes a little clicking noise out of the corner of her mouth. "It's probably had to brave storms and sharks and all sorts of shit to end up as beautiful as it is now, and to end up here, in your hand."

I make to give the shell back to her, but she waves it away.

"You keep it."

So, I close my palm around it, keeping it, feeling the colour of cool against my skin. I hold onto it tight, and Elise says, "D'you think this is our happy ending, then?"

"Not yet."

"But we'll *get* one of those, right?"

"Hope so."

"We only have to want it enough. That's what Grandma always says. You only have to want something hard enough, and with all of yourself, and you can make it happen."

"I like that idea."

"Me too." But then she frowns, just a little. "We don't know each other very well though, do we?"

"No."

"What if we find stuff out about each other that we don't like?"

"Occupational hazard, I guess."

She nods, resignedly. "Yes." And then says quietly, but like she means it, "We'll be okay, though, because in *here*," and she presses her fingers to her own heart and then to mine, "we're as safe as houses, aren't we? We're loved."

"Yes."

She smiles then. "Gran told me, about Rosalie MacKay."

"I kind of figured she might. How d'you feel about it?"

She shrugs. "Better for knowing the truth."

"You don't feel unsettled, or cheated or anything?"

"Nah." She sounds certain. "My family's still my family. The roots just tangle a little different is all."

"And you can understand now why your father left?"

"Yes, I can." She takes my hand in hers and holds it tight. "I wanted to talk to you about that, actually."

"About your father?"

"In a way." She looks into my eyes. "I know you had your heart set on Winnipeg as our first port of call, and I know we said Canada only, and Seattle's not this side of the border, but it's only *just* the other side, and, I was wondering if, maybe…"

I slip my hand free of hers and press my fingers to her lips. "What time are we leaving?"

She smiles against my fingers and, when I take them away, she says, very quietly and slowly, "Ahh, but there's no hurry now, is there, *chérie*? After all, we have all the time in the world."

"Yes."

"Hey." She glances up into the sky suddenly, pointing, something catching her eye. "What's that?"

I follow the line of her finger. "What?"

"That? Up there? Look! Can't you see it?"

I peer hard as I can into the mottled grey above us, but there's nothing there.

"I can't see what you're pointing at, Elise."

"I do believe," she says, her neck still angled to the stars, "that it may very well be..." She starts to smile suddenly, turning her face toward me, "... the bluebird of fucking happiness."

And I lean in against her then, pressing my lips to her neck, turning to look out at the ocean. The moon is rippling slowly towards us, carried on the waves – a column of pale air, a lilting path of gold, and, at the point where the sky meets the water, the North Star punctures the surface, reflected, blazing as bright as true love.

If you enjoyed this book, why not one of these other books from DIVA and RED HOT DIVA?

Necrologue	Helen Sandler (Ed.)	£10.99
Absent Kisses	Frances Gapper	£8.99
Groundswell	Helen Sandler (Ed.)	£8.99
Sunbathing in Siberia	Elizabeth Lewis	£8.99
Treasure	Helen Larder	£8.99
Woman In Beige	V. G. Lee	£8.99
Mush	Kathleen Kiirik Bryson	£8.95
Hearts & Minds	Jay Taverner	£8.95
Maddie & Anna's Big Picture	Jane Marlow	£8.99
The Ropemaker's Daughter	Virginia Smith	£8.99

Erotica

Starburst	Tanya Dolan	£8.99
Scarlet Thirst	Crin Claxton	£8.99
Peculiar Passions	Ruby Vise	£8.99
As You Desire Me	Fiona Cooper	£9.99
The Fox Tales	Astrid Fox	£8.99
The Escort	Kay Vale	£8.99

Please add postage and packing:
UK:	1 item - £1.95	2 or more - £3.90	TOTAL...............
Overseas:	1 item - £4.25	2 or more - £5.95	

Order By Phone:	0845 430 9113 (+44 20 77 39 46 46)
Order Online:	www.divadirect.co.uk
Order By Post:	Millivres Prowler Ltd 75B Great Eastern Street London EC2A 3HN

I enclose a cheque for £............ made payable to Millivres Prowler Ltd.
Please charge £............. to my VISA/MASTERCARD/AMEX/SWITCH:
Card No.s: ....
Exp. Date: .... Valid From: .... Issue No.s: ....

NAME ....
ADDRESS..
POSTCODE..SIGNATURE.......................................